The yellowbacks... classics of popular fiction

The yellowjackets or yellowbacks were a great series of bestselling adventure and crime thrillers that had its origins in the mid to late 19th century following on from the 'penny dreadfuls'. They virtually began the mass market revolution of the early 20th century with a clear standard format and imprint/series livery (what would today be called branding). Hodder & Stoughton published the yellowjackets in two main series with series run dates of: 1923-1939 and later 1949-1957.

As the tagline ('where thrillers really began') on the back cover implies, the imprint and series focused on thrillers that were the bestsellers of their time. This current reissue or retro revival if you will, brings back many of these masterpieces, now classics in their own way and extends it further by including key titles from that period that were either great crime or thriller or even general commercial fiction (including sub-genres of noir, horror, gothic, romance, westerns, etc.) influences of their time. There are some perennial favourites and many rarities either lost or not easily available being revived in the current series. Writers and characters ranged from adventure heroes like Bulldog Drummond, Allan Quatermain, Richard Hannay or the Saint through thriller grandmasters Edgar Wallace and E. Phillips Oppenheim, crime and mystery maestros like Patricia Wentworth, GK Chesterton, Agatha Christie and the Detection club, to western and swashbucklers like Zane Grey, Max Brand, Captain Blood and even romance or general fiction classics like Hermina Black, Denise Robins, Marie Corelli or Stella Morton. These were books that had storytelling at their heart and always entertained.

The yellowbacks had both hardback (with varying design elements) and paperback (which built the series look) versions with the latter still carrying the imprint 'yellowjacket'. The current reissues pay tribute to both and use an amalgam of elements from both editions while retaining the complete yellow (or 'mustard-plaster') livery with the author's name in blue beveled type with a 'simulated emboss' effect and a white outer 'outline', and the book title in black. These reissues retain the distinctive size of the original mass market paperback and follow the three main category variations—the thrillers (crime, westerns, mystery, adventure) had blue lettering for the author's name, while Romance and softer general fiction had red; and other categories like humour had green.

For more detail and a full list of titles visit https://www.hachetteindia.com/home/yellowbacks

THE CHRONICLES OF SOLAR PONS

THE CHRONICLES OF SOLAR PONS

August William Derleth (February 24, 1909 – July 4, 1971) was an American writer and anthologist. Though best remembered as the first book publisher of the writings of H. P. Lovecraft, and for his own contributions to the Cthulhu Mythos and the cosmic horror genre, as well as his founding of the publisher Arkham House (which did much to bring supernatural fiction into print in hardcover in the US that had only been readily available in the UK), Derleth was a leading American regional writer of his day, as well as prolific in several other genres, including historical fiction, poetry, detective fiction, science fiction, and biography. Derleth wrote more than 150 short stories and more than 100 books during his lifetime.

THE CHRONICLES OF SOLAR PONS

August Derleth

HODDER AND STOUGHTON YELLOW JACKET

hachette INDIA

The Chronicles of Solar Pons

First published in book form in 1973 by Mycroft & Moran

(Registered Name: Hachette Book Publishing India Pvt. Ltd.)
An Hachette UK Company www.hachetteindia.com

1

The texts in these editions in most cases have been reprinted as is, with minimal editorial changes and by and large no bowdlerizing for political correctness; though in some editions, a few words and phrases considered archaic, or those considered offensive now, along with archaic punctuation may have been modified in places to make the text more accessible to today's readers. The narratives, language, beliefs, social mores and/or cultural depictions, in these volumes are a reflection of their times and must be viewed as such. They may also contain certain cultural, racial and gender prejudices and stereotypes that may be outdated or clearly wrong then and wrong today; but their removal would be tantamount to claiming these prejudices never existed. The Publisher does not endorse or support those depictions or stereotypes; and these books have been made available for a discerning audience that will read it for entertainment value and a chronicle/record of popular fiction of past times.

Cover design by Priya Singh adapted from the original classic yellowjacket by Hodder & Stoughton.

Cover illustration by Ishan Trivedi.

Series note: Some of the books in the series (unless otherwise credited) may have cover or inside illustrations from the original yellowbacks or early editions, and while full restoration has been attempted, some images may be grainy or faded due to the condition of the original material. The end notes or bonus material or blurb details may have been sourced from the public domain or free use publications such as Wikipedia and attribution is hereby made also allowing similar free use reproduction from here. Sources requiring further specific attribution may write in and further detailing and/or corrections shall be made in subsequent printings/editions.

Reprint specifications may be subject to change including but not limited to finishes, paper, colour sections.

ISBN: 978-93-5731-180-9

Hachette Book Publishing India Pvt. Ltd.
4th & 5th Floors, Corporate Centre,
Plot No. 94, Sector 44, Gurugram - 122 003, India

Typeset in Electra LT STD 10/12.5 pt by Manipal Technologies Limited

Printed and bound in India by Manipal Technologies Limited

MIX
Paper from responsible sources
FSC™ C043100

CONTENTS

Foreword

The Chronicles of Solar Pons

AUGUST DERLETH
THE CHRONICLES OF SOLAR PONS
FOREWORD by ALLEN HUBIN

Foreword

NO LESSENING OF QUALITY
BY DAVID MARCUM

When *The Chronicles of Solar Pons* was published in 1973, two years after August Derleth's death, the friends of Mr. Solar Pons must have been both saddened and relieved. The sadness would have come from the belief that these were, in fact, the final Pons stories to appear. Dr. Parker's Literary Agent had died, and it was probably unlikely (then) that any new Pons stories would appear. (The first of Basil Copper's newly authorized Pons stories wouldn't be published until 1979, and this was before the first Pinnacle paperback release of *In Re: Sherlock Holmes* appeared the next year, in 1974.) But the relief must have come from having these stories collected in book form.

After Derleth had published *The Casebook of Solar Pons* (1965), he'd continued to steadily producing additional Pons adventures. He wrote some entries from Dr. Parker's notebooks that were published in the Praed Street Irregulars newsletter, *The Pontine Dossier*, (and also included in the slim volume A *Praed Street Dossier* 1968. These are included in the final volume of this authorized reissuing of the Pontine Canon, *The Apocrypha of Solar Pons.*)

"The Adventure of the Red Leech" had appeared in the October 1966 issue of *Alfred Hitchcock's Mystery Magazine*, but that was the only contemporary magazine publication of one of *The Chronicle*'s stories. Another, "The Missing Tenants", had originally appeared decades before, in *The Dragnet Magazine* in June 1929, and had amazingly never been collected and published in any of the subsequent Pons collections. (The original version of "The Missing Tenants", along with some of the other early published versions of Pons's adventures, can be found in Mark Wardecker's amazing labor of love, *The Dragnet Solar Pons et al.* 2011). This is a wonderfully atmospheric story, and one that's been in my head ever since I first read it as a teenager.

A couple of other stories in this volume also had unique first appearances. Both "The Orient Express" and "The Unique Dickensians" had initially appeared as standalone volumes, and are some of the rarest of Solar Pons treasures. "The Orient Express" was first published in 1964 as a softcover chapbook with a dust jacket. "The Unique Dickensians" was also first printed as a chapbook in 1968, the same year that *Mr. Fairlie's Final Journey* and *A Praed Street Dossier* were published.

In 1973, two years after Derleth passed away, I was eight years old. That was the year that I first discovered Solar Pons – two years before I read my first Sherlock Holmes story at age ten in 1975. I was in third grade in 1973, and told by my teacher to check out a library book. Not having any ideas, I was drawn to *The Mystery of the Green Ghost*, an adventure of *The Three Investigators*, as written by Robert Arthur. That book changed my life, making me both a voracious reader, especially of mysteries and detectives. Robert Arthur also edited a number of mystery anthologies, and one of them had a Solar Pons adventure in it, "The Grice-Paterson Curse". I read that anthology because of Robert Arthur and loved this story. (I still do – it's my favorite Pons adventure.) I credit that enjoyment for grooving the path in my brain that helped me to appreciate Holmes and Watson when I discovered them a couple of years later.

Of course, I had no idea then who August Derleth was, or that he had died two years earlier. I can only imagine the sadness that the event caused. And then, someone had the idea to gather what was then believed to be the remaining uncollected adventures of Solar Pons and publish them as one final volume. The arrival of *The Chronicles* in 1973 must have been as welcome to Pontine scholars and fans as would the discovery of a new Shakespeare play. (I know that I'd much rather have more Pons than more Shakespeare.)

The adventures in *The Chronicles* may have been assembled posthumously, but there is no lessening of quality. These aren't plugs and dottles scraped up after the fact. These Pons adventures can stand alongside any other in the Pontine Canon, and it's wonderful that they're back in print once again and easily available for a new generation.

For those meeting him for the first time, Pons is very much like Holmes. He solves crimes by using ratiocination and deduction. He plays the violin, smokes pipes, and lounges around his rooms in dressing gowns, as well as occasionally conducting chemical experiments there. His brother, Bancroft Pons, is an important fixture in the British Government, rather like Sherlock Holmes's brother, Mycroft. His landlady is Mrs. Johnson, and his closest contact at Scotland Yard is Inspector Jamison. And his friend and biographer, in the mold of Dr. John H. Watson, is Dr. Lyndon Parker.

While most of Holmes's Canonically-recorded adventures stretch from the 1870's until his retirement to Sussex in 1903, Pons operates in the post-World War I-era, with his cases extending from when he and Dr. Parker meet in 1919, after Parker has returned to England following his war service, to 1939, just before the beginning of World War II. Pons had also served in the War, in cryptography, and when the two meet, Parker is disillusioned at the England to which he has returned. However, this is quickly subsumed as the doctor's interest in his new flatmate and friend grows when he joins Pons on a series of cases that he later records.

For too long, the Solar Pons adventures have been too difficult to obtain. Fortunately, these new editions will change that. Here's how that came about.

In the late 1970's, I had been a Sherlockian for just a few years, having found Mr. Holmes in 1975. Those were the early days of the Sherlockian Golden Age that began with the publication of Nicholas Meyer's *The Seven-Per-Cent Solution* in 1974, and has continued to the present. Meyer reminded people that there were *other* manuscripts by Dr. Watson out there, still waiting to be found – hidden in attics, filed away in libraries, or suppressed by paranoid individuals for a plethora of reasons. These began to be discovered, one by one. Meyer himself subsequently published the amazing *The West End Horror* (1976), along with an explanation as to how the appearance of the first book had led to the second. Other Sherlockian adventures continued to surface – *Hellbirds* by Austin Mitchelson and Nicholas Utechin (1976), *Sherlock Holmes and the Golden Bird* by Frank Thomas (1979), and *Enter the Lion* by Sean Hodel and Michael Wright (1979), to name just a very few. The Great Sherlockian Tapestry, after consisting of mainly just sixty main fibers for so long, was about to get much heavier.

And around that time, someone with great wisdom realized that Solar Pons should be a part of that.

Pinnacle Books began reprinting the Pons adventures in late 1974, just months after the July publication date of *The Seven-Per-Cent Solution*. In the world of book publication, at least in those days when things took forever, Pinnacle certainly didn't jump on the bandwagon at the last minute to get the books immediately into print, after seeing how popular both *The Seven-Per-Cent Solution* and Sherlock Holmes were. Rather, the re-publication of the Pons books must have been planned for quite a while, and it was just their great good luck that their Pons editions appeared right around the same time as Meyer's *The Seven-Per-Cent Solution.* Planning and setup would have required a great deal of planning and effort, as would designing the distinctive "Solar Pons" logo that they would use on both their Pons books, and later on Sherlock Holmes books by Frank Thomas. And most of all, they would have needed time to solicit the wonderful cover paintings of Solar Pons and Dr. Parker.

It was these paintings that drew me into the World of Solar Pons.

Living in a small town in eastern Tennessee, finding things related to Sherlock Holmes in the latter 1970's was difficult. My hometown had both a new and used bookstore, and I regularly scoured them looking for new titles. Strangely, several of my most treasured Sherlockian books from these years were found – not in the bookstores – but on rotating paperback racks at a local drugstore. However, it was at the new bookstore, a few weeks before my fourteenth birthday, that I happened to notice seven books lined up in a row, all featuring a man wearing an Inverness and a deerstalker.

I grabbed them, thinking I'd found a Holmesian motherlode. Instead, I saw that they were about... *Solar Pons?*

I had a limited amount of Sherlockian research material then, and I don't recall if I found anything about Mr. Pons to explain why he dressed like Sherlock Holmes. (I had quite forgotten then, although it came back to me later, that I'd first read a Pons story back in 1973 – before I'd ever truly encountered Sherlock Holmes. That story, "The Grice-Paterson Curse", was contained in an Alfred Hitchcock children's mystery anthology, and I credit how much I enjoyed it then with shaping my brain to be so appreciative when I first read about Holmes a couple of years later, in 1975. That one is still my favorite Pons story to this day.)

Those seven books haunted me, and I somehow managed to hint strongly enough to my parents about it that they ended up being birthday gifts a few weeks later – along with some other cool Holmes books. And so I started reading the Pontine Canon, as it's called – the first of countless times that I've been through it. (It's strange what the brain records. I vividly remember reading and re-reading those books frequently in an Algebra class throughout that year – particularly one story on one certain day, "The Man With the Broken Face". I was lost and behind for a lot of that year in that class, and instead of trying to catch up, I'd pull out a Pons book, which felt much more comfortable. The teacher, who later went on to be beloved and award-winning for some reason that escapes me, knew what I was doing and did nothing to pull me back. Pfui on her! But I did like reading about Pons.)

As time went on, I discovered additional Pinnacle paperbacks, featuring new Pons stories by British horror author Basil Copper. It was great to have more Pons adventures, but his weren't quite the same. Around the time I started college, I discovered that Copper had edited a complete *Omnibus* of the original Pons stories, and it was the first grown-up purchase that I made with my first real paycheck. (Many thanks to Otto Penzler and The Mysterious Bookshop!) I was thrilled to see that the stories had been arranged in chronological order, which appealed to me. (That kind of thing still does.) Little did I realize then that Copper's editing had been so controversial within the Pons community.

For it turned out that Copper had taken it upon himself to make a number of unjustified changes. For instance, he altered a lot of Derleth's spellings in the *Omnibus* edition from American to British, causing some people to become rather upset. I wasn't too vexed by that, however, as I was there for the stories.

Copper continued to write new Pons stories of his own, published in various editions. I snapped those up, too, very happy to have new visits to 7B Praed Street. Over the years, I noted with some curiosity that Copper's books came to take on a certain implied and vague aspect – just a whiff, just a tinge – that Pons was *his* and not Derleth's.

Meanwhile, the Battered Silicon Dispatch Box published several "lost" Pons items, and also a new and massive set of the complete stories, *The Original Text Solar Pons* (2000), restoring Derleth's original intentions. It was in this book that I read Peter Ruber's extensive essay explaining Copper's changes in greater depth, and the reaction to them within the Ponsian community. However, Ruber didn't mention what I found to be Copper's even more egregious sin. But first a little background...

Over the years, there have been various editions of the Pons books – the originals published by Derleth's Mycroft & Moran imprint, the Pinnacle paperbacks, the Copper *Omnibus*, and the Battered Silicon Dispatch Box *Original Text Omnibus*. (There has also been an incomplete set of a few titles from British publisher Robson Books, Ltd.) Only a few thousand of the original Mycroft & Moran books were ever printed, and for decades, Pons was only known to a loyal group of Sherlockian enthusiasts by way of these very limited volumes. The Pinnacle books made Pons available to a whole generation of 1970's Sherlockians – such as me – that would have never had a chance to meet him otherwise if he'd only remained in the hard-to-find original editions.

As time has passed, however, even these Pinnacle books have become rare and quite expensive. For modern readers who have heard of Pons and are interested in learning more about him, or for those of us who are Pons enthusiasts who wish to introduce him to the larger world, it's been quite difficult, as all editions of his adventures are now quite rare and expensive, unless one is stumbled upon by accident. The Mycroft & Moran books can be purchased online, usually for a substantial investment of money, and the Copper and Battered Silicon Dispatch Box *Omnibi* were always expensive and hard to come by, and now it's only worse. Finally, with these new publications, the Solar Pons books will be available for everyone in easily found and affordable editions. With this, it's hoped that a new wave of Pons interest will spread, particularly within the Sherlockian community which will so appreciate him.

In 2014, my friend and Pons Scholar Bob Byrne floated the idea of having an issue of his online journal, *The Solar Pons Gazette*, contain new Pons stories. Having already written some Sherlock Holmes adventures, I was intrigued, and sat down and wrote a Pons tale – possibly almost as fast as Derleth had written his first Pons story in 1928. It was so much fun that I quickly wrote two more. After that, I pestered Bob for a while, saying that he should explore having the stories published in a real book. (I choose real books every time – none of those ephemeral e-blip books that can disappear in a blink for me!) When that didn't happen, I became more ambitious. Bob put me in touch with Tracy Heron of The August Derleth Society, and he in turn told me how to reach Danielle Hackett, August Derleth's granddaughter. I made my case to be allowed to write a new collection of Pons stories, as authorized by the Estate, and amazingly, I received permission. I introduced Danielle (in this modern email way of meeting people) to Derick Belanger of Belanger Books, and then set about writing some more stories, enough to make a whole book. Amazingly, the first new authorized Pons book in decades, *The Papers of Solar Pons*, was published in 2017.

But that started me thinking...

Realizing that this new books had the possibility to reawaken interest in Pons, or spread the word to those who didn't know about him, I wondered if the original volumes could be reprinted. After all, interest in Sherlock Holmes around the world is at an all-time high, getting the word out by way of the internet has never been easier, and shifts in the publishing paradigm mean that the old ways of grinding through the process for several years before a book appears no longer apply.

The Derleth Estate was very happy with the plan. Now came the hard part.

Being fully aware of the controversy surrounding Copper's *Omnibus* edition, it was evident that new editions had to be from Derleth's original Mycroft & Moran volumes – for after all, he had edited and approved of those himself. Thankfully, modern technology allows for these books to be converted to modern electronic files with only a moderate amount of pain and toil.

I had several friends, upon hearing of this project, who very graciously offered to help me to "re-type" the original books. I can assure you that, if these books had needed to be re-typed from scratch, there would have been no new editions – at least not as provided by me. Instead, I took a copy of each of the original Mycroft & Moran Pons books, of which I am a very happy and proud owner, and scanned them, converting them all into electronic files. So far so good – that only took several hours of standing at a copy machine, flipping the pages of the books one at a time, and hitting the green button. (And sometimes re-doing it if a scanned page had a gremlin or two.)

After that, I used a text conversion software to turn the scans into a Word document. That raw text then had to be converted into another, more easily fixed, Word document. Then came the actual fixing. Early on, it was decided to try and make the new editions look as much like the originals as possible. Therefore, many inconsistent things that niggled me as an editor-type remain in the finished product, because they were that way in the originals. For instance, Derleth's punctuation improved quite a bit from his early books to the latter – but it was very tempting to start fixing his punctuation in the earlier books. If you see something that looks not-quite-right, chances are it was that way in the original books.

There were times that a letter or a note, as quoted in a story, would be indented, while on other occasions it would simply be a part of the paragraph. I wanted to set up all of those letters and notes in a unified way throughout the various books, but instead I kept them as they had appeared in the original editions, no matter how much the style varied from story to story. Finally, some of the racial stereotyping from those stories would not be written that way today. However, these are historical documents of sorts, and as such, they are presented as written, with the understanding that times have changed, and hopefully we have a greater awareness now than before.

Since the early 1980's, whenever I've re-read the Pons stories – and I've done so many times – it's been by way of the Copper *Omnibus* editions. I enjoyed having them all in one place in two matching handsome and heavy books, and I was very pleased that they were rearranged for reading in chronological order. The fixing of British-versus-American spelling didn't bother me a bit. This time, as part of the process to fix up the converted-to-text files, I was reading the stories as they had originally appeared, in the order that they had been published in the original volumes. I hadn't done it that way for years. The conversion process captures everything, and that means some items do have to be corrected. For instance, when setting up for printing, original books from the old days often *split* words at the end of a line with hyphens, whereas modern computer programs *wrap* the text, allowing for hyphens to be ignored. When converting the text of the original books, the program picked up every one of those end-of-line hyphens and split words, and they all had to be found and removed. Likewise, the text-conversion program ignores words that are italicized in the original, and these each have to be relocated and re-italicized. (However, in some cases, Derleth himself was inconsistent, italicizing a word, such as a book title or the name of a ship, at one point in a story, and not at a later point. That had to be verified too.)

I have long been a chronologicist, organizing all of the thousands of traditional Sherlock Holmes stories that I've collected and read into a massive Holmes Chronology, breaking various adventures (book, story, chapter, and paragraph) down into year, month, day, and even hour to form a *complete* life of Holmes, from birth to death, covering both the Holmes Canon and traditional pastiches. It was inevitable that I would do the same with Pons. For several decades, I've had a satisfying Pons Chronology as well, based on research by various individuals, and largely on Copper's arrangement of the stories within his *Omnibus* – with a few disagreements. By re-reading the original stories in their original form, for the first time in years, I realized that, in addition to changing spelling, Copper had committed – as referred to earlier – a far bigger sin.

I discovered as I re-read the original stories for this project that a number of them weren't matching up with my long-established Pons Chronology, based a great deal upon Copper's arrangement in his *Omnibus*. Some of the stories from the originals would give a specific date that would be a whole decade different from where I had placed the story in my own chronology. A quick check against Copper's *Omnibus* revealed that he had actually changed these dates in his revisions, sometimes shifting from the 1920's to the 1930's, a whole decade, in order to place the story where he thought that it ought to go. Worse, he sometimes eliminated a whole sentence from an original story if it contradicted his placement of that story within his *Omnibus*.

As a chronologist, I was horrified and sickened. This affront wasn't mentioned in Ruber's 2000 essay explaining why Ponsians were irritated with Copper. I can't believe that this wasn't noticed before.

There has always been ample material for the chronologist with the Pons books, even without these changes. Granted, the original versions, as written, open up a lot of problems and contradictions about when various stories occur that Copper smoothed out – apparently without anyone noticing. For this reason, and many others, I'm very glad and proud that the original Solar Pons adventures, as originally published by Derleth, are being presented here in these new volumes for a new generation.

David Marcum
"The Obrisset Snuffbox", PSI
(excerpted from the Belanger edition reissues)

A SOLAR PONS FOR THE MID-TWENTIETH CENTURY
BY DERRICK BELANGER

I first read *The Chronicles of Solar Pons* as part of the Pinnacle reprints published in the 1970's. For some unknown reason, Pinnacle put *The Chronicles* as the second Solar Pons book instead of in its correct chronological sequence as the last Pons short story collection. To go from *In Re: Sherlock Holmes* to *The Chronicles* and then to *The Memoirs* was jarring to say the least.

Now that *The Chronicles of Solar Pons* has been returned to its rightful place as the final Pons story collection, I think it is a perfect fit. Most of these stories were written in the 1960's and it shows. While Derleth tried his best to stay true to the voice of Sir Arthur, he was living in a time of very different detective stories. Tales of espionage were mixed with hard-boiled detectives and *Noir* fiction. Stories were much more violent, sex and affairs were not just implied but could very well be the focus of cases, and detectives were much more flawed becoming more anti-heroes than heroes.

Throughout *The Chronicles,* Solar Pons remains The Sherlock Holmes of Praed Street. However, the modern detective story seeps into the narratives in many ways. Take for example, "The Adventure of the Missing Tenants", which has Pons solving the disappearance of a man who seems to have vanished into thin air. The last person to see him alive was his mistress who waited in bed for her lover to join her, but the man never showed. Another story (which I shall not name for I don't want to give away any surprises) deals in part with women who had been sold into sex slavery – a plot point Sir Arthur could never have penned in his day.

The excellent novelette, "The Adventure of the Orient Express", borrows from the hard-boiled detectives in both its use of violence as well as having a dangerous *femme fatale*. It also uses spies and espionage common in Cold War narratives. What makes this story delightful though is its use of literary guest stars. Do The Saint and Hercule Poirot make an appearance? You'll have to read the story to find out.

Of course, as much as Derleth delves into darker, modern detective fiction, he never ventures too far. Pons remains firmly set in the world of Sherlock Holmes. In fact, *The Chronicles* includes two of the untold tales from the Holmes canon. "The Adventure of the Red Leech" and "The Adventure of the Aluminium Crutch" will make fans of the original Holmes stories smile, as these cases finally get revealed to the public – as solved by Solar Pons.

And a true gem is the last story in the collection, "The Adventure of the Unique Dickensians", the sole Solar Pons Christmas story. It is a festive traditional adventure just as ripe for an annual yuletide reading as that of a missing Blue Carbuncle.

While I wish Derleth had written more Solar Pons stories before his passing in July of 1971, I think this is a fitting final story collection for The Sherlock Holmes of Praed Street. Solar Pons may have changed ever so slightly with the times, but he always remained true to The Master of Baker Street.

Derrick Belanger
October 2018

The Chronicles of Solar Pons

INTRODUCTION

BY ALLAN J. HUBIN

(From the 1973 Mycroft & Moran Edition)

I met August Derleth but once, during the summer of 1970, when I chanced to drive through central Wisconsin and stopped one bright Sunday afternoon at the home he had built and personalized. My first impression of him was of openness and friendliness – he had paper in his typewriter and a story to write, but he gave me several hours for talk on subjects criminous and otherwise.

My second strong impression was gained from a chronological display of his books on shelves in his office. What astonishing literary versatility it demonstrated! And so much greater thus the loss to the world of letters when August Derleth died in July of 1971.

Shortly before that visit Derleth had asked me to write the introduction to *The Chronicles of Solar Pons,* then in the writing stage. I was a bit diffident, for previous Pons books had introductions by notable luminaries in detective fiction. Derleth pressed his invitation and I accepted – but there could be little doubt who would be the more honored, me or *Chronicles*.

Now, years and August Derleth's passing having intervened, I had before me the typescript of *Chronicles*. I settled myself confidently to the pleasures I knew to be in store, and when the last page was turned I leaned back in my chair fully rewarded, rested my eyes, and contemplated the remarkable career of the consulting detective known as Solar Pons...

...It seemed I walked a country lane. A crispness in the air suggested autumn, but the sun cast clear shadows of the tall stand of timber on my left.

A few steps farther along brought into view a simple cottage, nestled against the trees on the edge of a large meadow. As I came even with the tidy structure, the figure of a man moved toward me from it on the cobblestone walk that communicated with the road I trod. I had the curious sensation of an appointment fulfilled.

The man was clearly old, but his movements were sure and his eyes bright. And I could not mistake that aquiline face. "Mr. Solar Pons!" I cried.

He seemed to know me, and led the way into the cottage.

After waving me to a chair, he first cautioned me about disclosing the whereabouts of his Sussex retirement home. Inspector Jamison, he told me, knew where he was, as well of course as Dr. Parker and his brother Bancroft. But he did not wish to be bothered with trivial matters, and largely his time was devoted to what had latterly become a rather abiding interest of his.

I raised inquisitive brows, and he nodded at a row of double white boxes visible several hundred feet away through a window.

A little hobby, he said, shared with a professional colleague not far away...

"Am I to understand that we will not have the pleasure of more of your investigations?" I asked. "The Pontine Canon must close at 68 accounts?"

He nodded, and said that while many inquiries not without trifling points of interest had gone unreported, Dr. Parker had found the services of his literary agent so felicitous that going on without him was not to be contemplated.

A regrettable but not altogether surprising state of affairs, I agreed. Perhaps, I suggested, Mr. Derleth had played an important role in maintaining the leaven of fun and good adventure throughout the more than four decades during which Dr. Parker made reports available to an insatiable public. Nowhere in the canon could I recall a sense of pure enjoyment more evident than in "The Adventure of the Orient Express" and "The Adventure of the Unique Dickensians" in *Chronicles*.

A reminiscent gleam grew in his eyes, and he leaned forward.

"Let me tell you about several even more curious and spirited affairs," he said...

And I awoke.

Allen J. Hubin
December 13, 1972

I

THE ADVENTURE OF THE RED LEECH

When I look over my notes on the riddles my friend Solar Pons explored in the course of the summer and autumn of 1931, I am struck by their diversity, ranging as they do from the curious affair of Ashness Bridge to the strange adventure of Symond's Yat, from sanguine murder to cunning theft. Yet perhaps the mystery surrounding the death of David Cosby takes precedence over them all.

We were introduced to it one August day at high noon. We had been walking that morning along the Edgware Road and Pons had been entertaining – and instructing me with the exercise of his extraordinary faculty for observation and deduction. As we turned into Number 7, a somewhat troubled landlady appeared before us.

"Oh, Mr. Pons, there's a lady waiting to see you," she said apologetically. "I showed her into your rooms. Perhaps I shouldn't have done it, but she seemed so disturbed, and she did beg so to talk with you."

Pons' eyes brightened. "We shall just see what is troubling her, Mrs. Johnson," said Pons. "We have been idle all of three days. I chafe under idleness."

Our client sat, evidently, just where she had been put by Mrs. Johnson, her gloved hands folded on a reticule in her lap. She sprang to her feet at our entrance, her dark eyes moving from one face to the other, and fixing unerringly upon my companion.

"Forgive me, Mr. Pons. I had to come!"

"Pray be seated, Miss..."

"Cosby, Mr. Pons. Agatha Cosby."

"You have had a long ride from the country to bring me something that has disturbed you," said Pons tranquilly.

She gave a satisfied little nod and sat down. She was a small, sprightly woman certainly around fifty years of age, though no hint of grey as yet showed in her ash-blonde hair. Her fingers were ringless, which was no doubt the basis for Pons' conclusion that she was unmarried, and her trim black slippers – which were sturdy footwear rather than dainty – showed dust, suggesting that she had been riding in an open carriage and had neither home nor hotel to return to, in order to wait upon Pons' return to our quarters. She was modestly dressed in an almost Victorian fashion, and in uniform black, from shoes to hat.

"You have recently suffered a bereavement, Miss Cosby."

"My brother."

"Suddenly."

"Yes. It was about his death – and the events that preceded it – that I came to see you. I seem to have become involved, sir." So saying, she took from her reticule a little cardboard box and handed it to Pons.

Pons opened it. A slight cry of surprise escaped him at sight of its contents. I crowded closer. What lay there, only crudely pinned to the bottom of the box, was a repulsive worm – a red leech.

Pons flashed dancing eyes at me. "Have you ever seen its like before, Parker?"

"Never."

Pons looked toward our client, his eyes narrowed. "Posted to you from Rye, I see."

"That is where I live – on the edge of the village. We lived, I should say, for I am the last of the family. I received this in the post early today, and in view of what happened to my brother, I thought it best to seek help. I know something of your work, Mr. Pons. and I hope you will be able to help me. I am frightened. You see, my brother died after receiving one of these worms."

"Also in the post?"

"Yes, Mr. Pons."

"From Rye?"

"No, indeed, Mr. Pons. Posted from Paris."

"Ah," said Pons. "Pray tell us about it." He lit his pipe and leaned upon the mantel, waiting.

Miss Cosby bit her lip and wrinkled her forehead. "I hardly know where to begin, Mr. Pons," she said apologetically, "but I suppose it is with the arrival of the post. It was ten days ago that the little box came for David. Because I was curious, I managed to be in the library when he opened it. Mr. Pons, I was hardly prepared for the effect of the worm on my brother. He gave a great, hoarse cry – dropped the box, and fell back, struck dumb!

"Of course, I didn't understand at once. I saw only my brother was very ill, and telephoned for Dr. Landsdown. He said my brother had had an apoplectic seizure, a 'cerebral accident' he called it. I didn't, therefore, connect the box and the worm to my brother immediately. So I destroyed them. It wasn't until after I received this that I began to suspect there must have been some connection between the worm and my brother's seizure. He lay only semi-conscious for three days – precisely where he was, in his chair, for Dr. Lansdown feared to move him. All to no avail, sir – he died at the end of the third day. And he had begun to improve, too – he was talking a little."

"Ah! What did he say?"

"I fear his mind was affected, Mr. Pons. He seemed so desperately anxious to tell me something, yet all he seemed able to say was something about our old kennels – we kept dogs at one time, Mr. Pons – and he muttered about our dog Scottie. But we had given up the kennels years ago, and Scottie has been dead four years."

"Nothing more?"

"Nothing, Mr. Pons. That was all he spoke about. It was maddening. His eyes looked so desperately toward the wall on the side of the grounds where the dogs were housed as if he were trying to summon them from the past. I listened in vain for something of meaning. There was nothing."

She fell silent. For a few moments Pons, too, was silent, drawing thoughtfully at his pipe, and seemingly unaware of our client's raising her dainty handkerchief to protect her nostrils from the reek of the abominable shag he smoked.

"I take it your brother was a retired man," said Pons then.

"Yes, Mr. Pons. He was in the importing business and had an office in Hanoi, Indo-China. He came home seven years ago. He was then fifty-three, and he was moderately wealthy. He spent his time reading and working his garden. He took pride in his delphiniums. He went out but little – except to the flower shows. You don't suppose," she ventured, looking anxiously at Pons, "that the leech had anything to do with his flowers?"

"I should be inclined to doubt it," replied Pons dryly.

"Nor was there anything in his papers to give me any clue to the meaning of the leech, Mr. Pons. Anything that is, that I could understand." She smiled diffidently, reached into her reticule, and brought forth a folded sheet of paper. "This was there. I concluded that my brother was at work on some kind of mathematical problem."

Pons glanced at the paper and handed it, without comment, to me.

It was certainly not a problem, I saw at a glance, but an arrangement of numbers that evidently held some meaning for our client's late brother.

"90.33.7 – 117.17.5 – 131.34.2 – 289.6.4 – 314.10.9 – 368.12.1 – 371.6.8 – 416.7.5 – 439.6.5 – 446.28.2 – 451.3.5."

"I would have thought nothing of it," continued our client, "but it was in an envelope and carefully put away. Can you read it, Mr. Pons?"

"I will retain it, if I may, together with the cardboard box."

"I have the wrapping here, too," said Miss Cosby, almost as an afterthought. So saying, she took another neatly folded paper from her reticule and handed it to Pons.

"Your brother must surely have had something more with which to occupy his time than gardening," ventured Pons.

"Oh, he was a great reader, Mr. Pons. For a while he used to read the papers, but in the past two years it was all books. He was in the habit of making notes on what he read, but he discontinued that, finally. My brother had an extensive library. Of course, part of it was my father's – the nucleus, you might say. So he only added to it."

"You have always lived at Rye?"

"We were born in that house, Mr. Pons."

"Someone in your family was previously in the business of importing?"

"Well, we did have a great-uncle who lived in Hanoi until he died there ten years ago. I don't particularly know what he did. My brother had been in the bank at Rye, but he disliked that work and he had some little trouble, so he left it and went into importing at Hanoi."

"Was your brother known to have had heart trouble of any kind?" asked Pons.

"He suffered from a rise in blood pressure, Mr. Pons, of some years' standing."

"Since his return from the east? Or before?"

"Since."

"And was this widely known?"

"I believe only the doctor, my brother, and myself were aware of it." Our client clasped her hands together and appealed to Pons. "Oh, Mr. Pons. Do you think I am in danger? I am so frightened!"

"Pray do not be unduly alarmed, Miss Cosby. Dr. Parker and I will be at your home before sundown tonight. We will plan to spend the night. It would not surprise me if the sender of that curious message were to call."

"Oh, do not say so!" cried our client, her eyes widening in alarm.

"Fear not, Miss Cosby. Dr. Parker and I will be on hand."

After our client had departed, Pons sat for a few minutes with the three items she had brought ranged before him on the table, regarding them thoughtfully. I watched him covertly, and observed that presently he took up a page of notepaper and began to jot down something. Looking over his shoulder, I saw that he had rearranged the numerals of the late David Cosby's mathematical jottings into three columns –

90 33 7
117 17 5
131 34 2
280 6 4
314 10 9
368 12 1
371 6 8
416 7 5
439 6 5
446 28 2
451 3 5

Pons leaned back, his eyes dancing. "What do you make of it, Parker?"

"It's a cipher of some kind."

"Elementary. Does the arrangement of the numerals suggest nothing to you?"

I looked at them long and hard. "I am no cryptologist."

"Tut, tut! One need not be." He pushed the paper aside and drew over the cardboard box. "The leech, then."

"I see that it is a red leech, no more," I said, a trifle impatiently.

"I submit there is one distinctly odd feature to be observed," said Pons with that irritating air of harboring some secret knowledge.

"I have seen dozens of leeches in my practise," I said, stiffly.

"But not, I'll wager, one like this. There are various members of the Hirudinea, which belong to the Chaetopod worms. The majority of them are aquatic, but there are parasitical land leeches common to the tropics. This leech is one such. There are leeches of a brown color, of green, black, yellow, olive. *Herpobdella atomaria – Nephelis vulgaris* – is reddishly transparent in young specimens and many have a reddish hue when fresh blood is visible through their skins. *Hemidepsis marginata* is somewhat pink in color, with strikingly red dots – an aquatic leech which particularly preys on ducks. One or two others – notably *Haemodipsis* – have red stripes. But there is no such red leech as this."

"How can you say so? It lies before us!" I protested.

"Say rather a leech of an obviously red color lies here," said Pons.

"You are playing with words."

"On the contrary. This leech is not red by nature. It would appear to be brown in hue. The red has been added."

"Painted!"

"So it would appear."

"But how then could a red leech have any significance to anyone if there is no such leech?" I cried.

"Precisely. That is the problem. Particularly such significance as to bring on a fatal seizure. I submit, however, that it was not intended to bring on such a seizure. I fancy it was meant to convey a message which perhaps only David Cosby could understand – or someone presumably privy to the knowledge that gives it meaning."

"Like his sister."

Pons nodded. "It would then have been a message Cosby never expected to receive," he went on. "Only such a message would have so startled him."

"A death threat!"

"Gently, Parker! We are not yet justified in that assumption. Let us suppose for the nonce that it was intended to convey a certain intelligence Cosby had no reason to believe he would ever receive. It may have been meant to inaugurate or foretell a chain of events which might very well have followed had Cosby survived his seizure, which, I assume from our client's description was paralytic in nature, perhaps a cerebral thrombosis."

I agreed.

"The sender was obviously approaching England from some he tropical country, the leeches being tropical in origin, though he might very well have obtained them in Paris. He mailed Cosby's from Paris, and took his time in going to Rye. Once there, he learned of Cosby's death. He learned also that his sister survived him and concluded that the business he had so dramatically announced to Cosby might be taken up with her. He does not yet know that his conclusion is in error."

"Do we?"

"I think we may safely believe that Miss Cosby is as mystified as we are at this moment – perhaps more so," he added enigmatically.

I refused to play his little game longer.

Thereupon he took up the wrapping which had covered the cardboard box and handed it to me. "What do you make of that? You know my methods."

I studied it for a few moments with care. "It is written in a strong hand with a broad pen," I said. "The writer is certainly a man." Encouraged by Pons' smile, I went on. "He wrote this in some haste, but he would seem not to be ordinarily careless, for he went to more pains with his leech than he did with this address. The paper would appear to be ordinary market paper, obtainable in any shop; the absorption of the ink makes the letters seem broader than in fact they were at the writing of them."

"Capital, Parker, capital!" cried Pons. "It cheers me to be provided with such evidence of your progress in ratiocination." I bowed to acknowledge his praise.

He got to his feet abruptly. "Now, if you will excuse me, I have one or two little inquiries to make, and then, if you can spare the time, we are off for Rye."

Our client's home stood near the foot of the knoll on which the picturesque village of Rye stands, not quite at the edge of the salt marshes, on the far side of Rye from the coast, and in the middle of grounds that covered at least four or five acres, devoted, as was apparent in the late afternoon sunlight, to lawns, trees, and gardens. A low stone wall shut it off from the lowland, and shrubbery outlined the boundaries of the property. Here and there stood statuary – all, save for two pieces, Oriental; the two were a conventional Venus and a bust of Queen Victoria over against the stone wall, as were the Queen the patroness of the gardens, for a bed of roses was arranged not far before the bust. The Oriental pieces were of just such nature as might be expected of someone who had been engaged in importing primitive art and artifacts from southeast Asia.

All this we took in as we made our leisurely approach up the cobblestone walk to the entrance.

Our client had seen us, and threw open the door as we came up to it.

"Oh, Mr. Pons!" she cried. "I am so glad you are here. I dreaded the coming of night."

"The anticipation of what one fears is always worse than what one anticipates, Miss Cosby," said Pons.

"May I show you to your rooms?"

"It is too early for that, thank you," said Pons. "I would like to see the room in which your brother received the mail on the day of his seizure."

Without a word, Miss Cosby turned and led the way down the hall to the library, the entire outer wall of which was lined with shelves from floor to ceiling, and the shelves crowded with books of all description, though I saw at a glance that our client's late brother had been much given to sets of authors.

Miss Cosby pointed to an easy chair drawn up beside a Queen Anne table and a reading lamp. "It was just there, Mr. Pons."

"The chair, I take it, was in that position?"

"Yes, Mr. Pons."

"And the kennels were off on that side of the house?" Pons gestured toward the outer wall.

"Yes. They were disused, except for Scottie, when David returned from Indo-China. The very first thing he did was to move Scottie, tear down the kennels, and put in his rose garden. I don't know who will tend it now he's gone, but I suppose it will fall to me."

Pons nodded absently. He looked from the chair to the bookshelves, and then wandered idly over to the shelves.

"Your brother seems to have been a devoted reader of our classical authors."

"Oh, he was, Mr. Pons. Some of those older sets, of course, belonged to our parents. My father, too, read books voraciously."

"Hardy," mused Pons. "A complete set. Commendable, indeed! And Conrad! What other writer in our time has so effectively portrayed the sea? Unless it were William Hodgson, who had an eye for its terrors! And here are Dickens, Scott, Thackeray, Dumas – one would expect to find them here."

He walked slowly along the shelves of books, scrutinizing their titles. Now and then he paused to take down a book and open it, and make a terse comment or two, while our client favored him with puzzled glances, looking to me for assurance that Pons was about his quest.

"Who is Dickens's peer at the creation of memorable characters?" he asked. "And who so loves the English countryside as Hardy? – Though he has an eye for the dark side of his fellowmen. – Sir Walter is currently in eclipse, but I fancy the wheel of taste will turn again."

At length he selected a book and turned to our client. "And now, if you please, Miss Cosby, to our quarters."

Our client showed us to an ample room on the floor above, and, assuring us that dinner would not be long delayed, left us to ourselves.

"I never knew you to fancy Scott," I could not help saying.

"Ah, Parker – Sir Walter is among the most instructive of writers. One could do worse than have recourse to him for instruction in our history. He was a most meticulous writer. Consider this novel, for instance – there are a score of pages at the rear devoted to his notes on the text, all setting forth the historical basis for this story of Elizabeth and Leicester."

He settled down in an easy chair, putting the book temporarily aside for some further study of the two papers left with him by Miss Cosby.

"Did your further enquiries add anything to what we learned from our client?" I asked before he was too deeply immersed in either the papers or the novel.

"Ah, very little of significance," he replied without looking up. "That little 'trouble' at the bank where Cosby worked before the Indo-China venture seems to have been some trivial peculations on his part. Nothing was ever proved. He left the bank quietly and went to the Orient. There he organized the Indo-China Importing Company with some assistance from his late uncle, and apparently conducted a legitimate and profitable business, occasionally making trips into neighboring countries to discover and buy artifacts, works of art, primitives and the like. Then, after seventeen years, he sold his business and came back to England to lose himself here."

After but a cursory examination, he put the papers aside and took up the historical novel he had brought from library. Thereafter he alternated between the papers and the novel until at last, after jotting down a few notes, he sat back with the book until Miss Cosby knocked on the door to announce dinner.

Over a substantial evening meal, Pons pressed his inquiry. "You mentioned, Miss Cosby, that you believed your brother to be moderately wealthy. You have had ample opportunity since his death to ascertain the facts."

"Yes, Mr. Pons, I have. He has left me comfortably situated for the rest of my life. The transfer of funds from to Indo-China together with the sale of his business amounted to a considerable sum. His accounts at the bank are in excess of ten thousand pounds. Then there are other investments. In addition, my brother occasionally hinted at certain insurance against losses or something happening at the bank. This, however, has not come to light; if he had such a policy, we have not yet discovered it. My brother was secretive, and he was also extremely parsimonious, I am sorry to say. There were many times I would have found myself painfully short of funds if I had had to rely on him; fortunately, I never had to."

"I observed a handsome bed of roses as we came in," said Pons then.

"David was very proud of his roses. He was forever tending them. He put them in himself – but then, he has never had a gardener on the grounds. He did everything, Mr. Pons – everything. Of course, it was in part to save money – but primarily was because he was convinced no one could do it as well as he."

"While he was in Indo-China, did you find him freely communicative?"

"It is odd you should ask, Mr. Pons," replied our client, "but that is one thing David could not be said to have been. He wrote very brief, terse letters."

"Did he speak of his associates?"

"Only on occasion of our uncle. Uncle helped him to get started, but my brother was evidently in complete charge of his business. Now it is conducted by a man named Goddard – Henry Goddard."

"But your brother certainly employed others. He would have needed someone to take charge of his office whenever he took trips into the interior for the works of primitive art he sold."

"I believe he employed three people. He mentioned that number. One was a clerk, one a bookkeeper – who was in charge when he was away, and one an assistant of some sort. He accompanied my brother in his buying trips."

The paucity of the food he ate betrayed the fact that Pons was hot upon some scent or other. I could not fathom, from the general nature of his questions, what it might be. He had learned nothing that he had not already discovered by inquiring about London earlier in the day. Yet his face had never seemed more feral, with his keen eyes fixed on our client, and a duo of faint lines across his high brow.

I was not, however, prepared for his businesslike manner at the end of the meal.

"Now, Miss Cosby," he said briskly. "it has turned dark. We shall need a lantern and a shovel."

Our client's jaw fell momentarily as she gazed at Pons in astonishment for an instant before she acquiesced.

"You will find both in the potting shed, Mr. Pons. Come, I will show you."

"Pray, permit me. We will be able to find our way."

"Very well, Mr. Pons. The shed is directly behind the house, at the edge of the grounds."

Once outside in the deepening dusk, Pons caught me by the arm and pressed a pistol into my hand. "It is quite possible that the house may be under surveillance, Parker. I need you to 'cover' me while I am at work. There is an ash tree on the west side of the house, not far from the rose garden. Beyond it is a clump of laurel bushes. Go now and take up your stance there. Wait upon me."

"You have deciphered Cosby's figures," I whispered.

"Alas! Sadly prosaic," he retorted, and slipped away.

I found my way to the ash tree without difficulty, and thence around the rose garden toward the growth of laurel along the stone wall at the western line of the Cosby property. There I concealed myself; I had indulged Pons' flair for the dramatic before; I would indulge it again.

I saw the light of the lantern spring up, and presently Pons came along, bearing the lantern in one hand, a shovel in the other. He came up to the ash tree and paused to take his bearings. I saw him fix his position before he stepped off five paces in a northeasterly direction. Then he took four sharply to the left in the direction of the bust of Queen Victoria, and was thus brought to the very edge of the rose garden. There he put the lantern down and dropped to his knees to examine the earth.

And there, presently, he began to dig.

He dug for a little while and paused to sound the hole he had made. Then he dug for a while again, and once more sounded the pit. And presently he must have heard something he expected to hear, for he worked far more carefully, digging around some object. And at last he brought up a tin dispatch box a trifle more than half a foot square. He put it on the ground next to the lantern and opened it. Whatever was in it shone and glittered – red.

But at that moment Pons was interrupted.

"I'll take that!" said a firm voice.

I saw standing in the lantern's glow a slender man of medium height. He had a revolver in his hand, pointed at Pons.

Leaving the box with its contents where it stood, Pons leisurely came to his feet, lifting his lantern high to reveal a man of middle age.

"Mr. Leach, I presume?" said Pons. "Known to his intimates as 'Red' Leach?"

I saw now that the fellow had a red beard and a shock of dark red hair.

"I don't know you," he said anxiously.

"My name is Solar Pons, though I doubt you have had occasion to hear it in Southeast Asia. The gentleman covering you with his gun from the laurels is Dr. Lyndon Parker."

Leach wavered a little.

"Good evening, Mr. Leach," I called out.

A wild look came into the fellow's face.

"As far as I know, you have done nothing illegal, Mr. Leach," continued Pons imperturbably. "Pray do not act on impulse now. You have come to see Miss Cosby on a matter of business, obviously of importance to you. Let us all go into the house together."

Leach stood as if struck dumb.

"But first," said Pons, thrusting forth his hand, "your weapon."

For a few moments they stood, immobile.

"Come, man, what do you say?" demanded Pons.

Slowly, as if mesmerized by the turn of events, Leach handed his weapon to Pons.

"And now, Mr. Leach," said Pons briskly, "pick up that ruby – it is certainly the largest I have ever seen – and come along."

"You'll trust me with it?" asked Leach in an incredulous voice.

"I daresay you have a claim on it," replied Pons.

"It is the Eye of Buddha," said Leach.

"Miss Cosby will want to hear about it," said Pons. "Let us go around by the front door and announce ourselves properly. Parker, put up your pistol, that's a good fellow."

Leach walked with a bad limp. Perhaps because of it he made no effort to make a break but went along docilely enough between Pons and me – past the ash tree, around the house, and to the front entrance, where Pons put down the shovel and the lantern and sounded the bell.

Miss Cosby herself came to the door and threw it open. Her eyes widened in surprise at the sight of three men, where s had expected but two.

"Miss Cosby, may I present Mr. Leach – familiarly known as 'Red' Leach," said Pons.

"Oh!" she cried, one hand flying to her lips.

"Mr. Leach is carrying what your brother buried at the edge of his rose garden on his return from Indo-China – his 'insurance' of which you could find no trace," continued Pons, pressing past her. "I believe he has a claim on it. If you are not too upset to hear his story, we will all listen to it."

"Do come in," she cried, finding her voice again. "Indeed, I *must* hear it."

Seen in the well-lit room, Leach was revealed as a man of middle age, whose grooming belied the gruffness of his voice. He had pleasant blue eyes that wrinkled at the corners, and his beard, I saw now, was affected to conceal a scar along one side of his jaw.

"I didn't mean anything but to put the wind up old Davey," he said apologetically, "to let him know I was still in the country of the living. No more than that. Except to prepare him for my coming to claim what was mine."

"And what was that, Mr. Leach?" asked Miss Cosby.

"At least the half of this ruby – and some of my back pay. You don't know?"

"No, Mr. Leach."

"Ah, well, Miss, then I owe you an apology."

Miss Cosby smiled tremulously. "Do go on, Mr. Leach. How did my brother come by this ruby?"

"I was his assistant, Miss Cosby," said Leach. "I went with him on his trips. I knew the places, you might say. I worked for his uncle – begging your pardon, your uncle too, Miss Cosby – and then I worked for him, after the old man died. We went all through that country buying primitive art pieces – like the kind he's got out there in the garden, and other work for which he could get a good price. That was the way he made his money – by getting ten times what he paid for a piece, sometimes a hundred times what he paid for it.

"We'd heard talk of the Eye of Buddha years before. Your uncle knew of the stone fixed in the forehead of a statue of Buddha lost in the jungles of Siam. There's little to tell of it, except that once, during a storm, we lost the trail, and blundered for miles through the forest and came upon it. We pried and chipped it out. That was the long of it. The short of it was that on the way out we were attacked by a party of priests and I was wounded. Then Davey said, 'It's every man for himself!' and ran for it. He got away. I didn't. But they didn't kill me. They took me prisoner, and healed me somewhat, and made me work for them. Over six years! I got away at last, and set out to find Davey. I sent him the leech to let him know, to get him ready to pay me what I had coming to me."

"You poor man!" cried our client sympathetically. "You may certainly keep that ruby. Whatever would I do with it?"

"Thank you, Miss Cosby."

"And in the morning you had better come around and we will discuss whatever back pay is coming to you."

Mr. Leach, his eyes quickening, favored her with a lingering glance, which she returned.

Pons rose with alacrity.

"You will excuse us, Miss Cosby. We will just walk Mr. Leach around to his lodgings and catch the 9:55 train for London."

"I fancy," said Pons with a smile, once we were seated in our compartment on our way to London, "Mr. Leach may have found more than back pay to compensate him for whatever misery was his in Siam."

"Bother Leach!" I cried. "What sent you to dig up the rose garden?"

"I thought that obvious," answered Pons. "It is no credit to your powers of observations that you should have to ask. Sir Walter Scott, of course."

"Fantastic!"

"Not at all. Cosby tried to tell his sister, but she, being less imaginative than he, grievously misunderstood him to be talking of the kennels and the dog, Scottie. True, he was looking in the direction of the kennels. He was also looking toward the bookshelves. Assuming that his mind had been affected, she made none but the most cursory attempt to understand him. What he was trying to say was '*Kenilworth*' and 'Scott' – Sir Walter, not a similarly named dog.

"It was *Kenilworth* that contained the solution to Cosby's simple cipher. You will recall that I directed your attention to the arrangement of the numerals. Out of a certain innate stubbornness integral to your nature, you affected not to see. Yet it was painfully evident that the cipher was based upon a book; The first line of numerals ranged from 90 to 451, the second did not exceed 34, the third did not go beyond 9. What more obvious than the pages of a book, the lines on a page, the words in a line? In all such cases, of course, however simple the cipher may be, it is essential that the book be known so that pages, lines, and words can be set down. Our client, however obtuse. nevertheless managed to supply the title of the book once I chanced upon it on the shelves. The message, thus disclosed proved to be spare and direct. 'Look under ash five steps northeast over four left toward Queen.' The Queen, in the case, being the bust of Her late Majesty, Victoria.

"Miss Cosby, I fear, is only just beginning to understand that her late brother was one-tenth a scoundrel. I should have preferred one of a dimension closer to nine-tenths!"

II

THE ADVENTURE OF THE ORIENT EXPRESS

The curious matter of the memorable duplicity of Baron Egon Von Ruber must surely represent a high-water mark in the years of my association with Solar Pons, however little it redounds to my credit. It began for me in an unlikely place, far removed from our familiar quarters – Prague, in the summer of 1938, at the close of an international medical convention which I was privileged to attend as one of His Majesty's officially designated representatives. I had wired my wife the time of my leavetaking, for the Continent was in the throes of New Germany's flexing of muscles under the guidance of a megalomaniac leader, and Pons must have learned from her that I planned to take the Orient Express late that day, for, only an hour before leaving, I received from Pons a long wire in our private code, which directed me to apply to a specified compartment and to share that compartment with Baron Egon Von Ruber; furthermore, I was to fall in with my travelling companion's every word and deed with implicit obedience. The implication of Pons' wire seemed perfectly clear to me – Von Ruber must certainly be in the service of His Majesty's Government and must be travelling to Paris on a mission of the first importance, one in which I was destined to play a part.

Yet I was hardly prepared for the fellow I found in my compartment when I presented myself a few minutes before departure time. He was a reasonably tall, thickset, broad-shouldered fellow with much touseled brown hair, a full beard and moustache of the same color. Narrow-lidded eyes peered at me from behind pince-nez on a long black ribbon, and an unlit but partially consumed cigar was clamped between his teeth. He had set up a chessboard and was sitting before it, his slender fingers drumming impatiently on it, as if awaiting my arrival.

"Baron Von Ruber?" I asked. "I am Doctor Lyndon Parker."

"Typical British middle class," he said with rude bluntness. "Come in."

I pushed into the compartment and stowed my baggage away. My travelling companion did not deign to glance at me again, but sat contemplating a problem on the board, his high brow wrinkled in concentration. I sat down opposite him, finally, at which he favored me with a disapproving stare.

"Can you play chess?"

"Passably," I said, disdaining to tell him I had taken a provincial championship.

"Excellent!" he said. "Do you mind?"

Since his attitude clearly set forth his assumption that I would play, I agreed.

He immediately rearranged the pieces on the board, his long fingers moving with singular dexterity. I saw that he kept the black pieces before him, and allowed me the courtesy of the white, and obviously the opening move.

"Will you open, Doctor?"

I had not had the chance to study the problem he had had on the board, and I had thus no index to his ability. I tried to think of what Pons would do in such circumstances, and resolved to test the Baron's response to the King's Gambit. Accordingly, I advanced my pawn to King 4, which he countered with a similar move. I moved another pawn forward to King's Bishop 4, fully aware of the potential disadvantage of the move. The game proceeded slowly, and I waited to see whether the Baron would make the suicide move of playing his pawn to King's Knight 4. It was soon evident, however, that Baron Von Ruber was too skilled a player to do so, and meant to refute my gambit with the Falkbeer Counter-Gambit.

"You are not a dilettante, Baron," I said.

"Obviously," he said. "I wish I could say as much for you, Doctor," he went on, with a wintry smile. "I was surprised at your opening. The King's Gambit is no longer often played; it is unsatisfactory on several counts."

His English was so flawless that I was persuaded to believe he had spent a long time in England.

"You have been in the diplomatic service, Baron?" I asked.

"You might say so," he replied.

"In England," I hazarded.

"I've spent considerable time in England, yes." He narrowed his eyes and added, "But now you are playing that guessing game your sleuthing friend is so fond of."

"Ah, you know Pons?"

"An amusing fellow with his devotion to ratiocination. But an amateur, Doctor, a rank amateur."

I was nettled, and it took a few moments to control my temper at this disparagement of Pons.

"Let us not forget our game, Doctor," the Baron said impatiently. "It is your move."

I swallowed my indignation, recalling was Pons' coded instructions, and proceeded with the game. It was patent that I was pitted against an opponent of unusual skill, for, though I took longer and longer to make each move, I was clearly on the defensive in a considerably shorter time than I had anticipated, and Baron Von Ruber pressed his pursuit inexorably.

I did, however, make good use of my time – particularly during the Baron's own contemplative periods – in trying to draw upon everything I had learned about Pons' deductive science. Without being too open about it, I studied the Baron's every feature. His hands told me that he was not accustomed to manual labor, yet they were not as soft as a diplomat's might be; I deduced that he must then have certain hobbies which engaged his hands, and one of them, I was certain, on the basis of some slight discolorations of his skin, must be chemistry. His beard and moustache concealed most of his face, but there were telltale patches of iron grey hair at his temples, and a few fine crow's-feet radiating from his eyes, which forced me to conclude that he was certainly not under forty-five, and not over fifty-five, very probably close to fifty, however much older his hirsute adornment made him look. The very circumstances of our being together suggested beyond cavil that Baron Egon Von Ruber was certainly a British agent, a German national recruited by one of our men in British Intelligence.

There was no clue, however, as to what role he might at the moment be playing. I had already observed that he was not overburdened with baggage. A briefcase lay on the seat beside him; a single bag on the overhead rack, and a waterproof coat hung from a hanger just inside the door.

"You are bound for Paris, Baron?" I ventured abruptly, risking his displeasure.

"And you for London," he countered blandly. "How can you bear that foggy climate? – especially since you, as a medical man, must know how unhealthy it is." Before I could reply, he began to chuckle; his shoulders trembled with withheld hilarity. "My dear good Doctor Parker, you are here on orders, and you are dying of curiosity. – Forgive me: checkmate! – You are trying to practise Mr. Solar Pons' childish game of ratiocination and floundering in these waters. Let me ease your mind. I am waiting upon microfilmed and detailed accounts of the German High Command's plan to invade Poland."

He said this in a scarcely audible whisper. Nevertheless, I was too shocked for the moment to speak, and I found the unusual benevolence of Baron Von Ruber's gaze suddenly and unaccountably sinister.

"Poland," I whispered at last. "Are you sure?"

"Quite sure," he said blandly. "We shall not talk of it. I should warn you, however, that there are counterintelligence agents who are aware that these accounts exist – microfilms of documents, letters, orders being held in abeyance – and you know the reputation of this train, Doctor. I sincerely trust you are not counting on a quiet, peaceful journey to Paris. I assure you, anything may happen. Are you armed, sir?"

I shook my head.

He clucked sympathetically. "You seem a little pale, Doctor."

"It is just surprise," I managed to say.

I would have given anything for a few minutes with Pons at this point of our journey. We were at the moment drawing out of Pilsen, bound for Marianské-Lazné less than an hour away, but we were still an interminable distance from Paris, to say nothing of London.

Baron Von Ruber sat back, the fingers of one hand still cradling a rook. "Have you travelled often by the Orient Express, Doctor?"

"I cannot say so. Once to Istanbul, twice to Prague – this being the second time, and once to Vienna."

"Georges Nagelmackers could hardly have conceived that his grandiose dream of duplicating the American coast-to-coast Pullman service with the establishment of the Compagnie Internationale des Wagons-Lits would have been so successful," mused Baron Von Ruber.

I had to confess that I did not know who Nagelmackers was.

"A Belgian engineer," the Baron said almost crossly. "At that, though he established the company in 1876, it took seven more years before the Orient Express made its first run by way of Vienna and Budapest. The date was June 5, 1883, though an all-sleeper train had established a run between Calais and Nice before that."

"Ah, the Blue Train," I said.

Von Ruber nodded. "Perhaps this train has the most cosmopolitan clientele in the world," he went on, "though, of course, it is at Vienna that the clientele becomes most varied."

He had said enough to convince me that he was a seasoned traveller; it followed therefore that he probably had more than ordinary linguistic ability.

"Yet the complexion of the clientele has altered over the years," he went on. "In the earlier decades one as frequently encountered Balkan rulers travelling incognito as valeted gentlemen, Indian maharajahs as Russian Grand Dukes, and there were certain moneyed travellers who brought their own furnishings to the cars." He smiled. "What fancies we human beings indulge! What vanities we foster!" He leaned forward once more. "There is nothing like chess to keep the mind in order, Doctor. Shall we have another game?"

I nodded. "Will you open?"

He shook his head gently. "You are my guest, Doctor. It is the guest's privilege to open." He might as well have put into words his clear inference that I needed the additional advantage of the opening.

Nettled again, I decided upon the difficult Reti's Opening, and advanced my knight to King's Bishop 3. I was gratified at the almost imperceptible raising of Baron Von Ruber's eyebrows.

But my gratification was brief. To tell the truth, the information Baron Von Ruber had offered was startling and dismaying, for implicit in it was the clear knowledge that a major war impended. He had said "waiting upon" – so patently he did not yet have the microfilms; just as patently, he expected to receive them sometime in the course of our journey, very probably after we had crossed the border into Germany at Cheb, slightly over an hour away.

Yet I was dubious about even these seemingly elementary conclusions. Would Pons have reasoned in this fashion? The microfilms might even now be on the train, and whoever carried them might only be awaiting a suitable opportunity to transfer them to my companion. I wished more than ever that Pons were at hand to deal with this contingency, for Baron Von Ruber seemed to me far more interested in his chess game than in any impending event. I marvelled at his detachment. If German counter-intelligence were aware of Baron Von Ruber's accommodations with His Majesty's Government, then almost certainly somewhere on this train lurked agents who would watch his every move. Yet it occurred to me that had Von Ruber been under such surveillance, he would almost certainly not have been chosen to carry anything to Paris. It was rather more likely that some other British agent had been assigned to pass the microfilms to Von Ruber.

Outside, the villages and countryside of Czechoslovakia flashed by; the mundane occupations of villagers and countrymen were carried on as on another planet. But, of course, it was the Orient Express that was another planet, one that was in miniature the Continent of Europe, bearing Russians, Chinese, Poles, Slovaks, Germans, Frenchmen, Americans, and my own countrymen in their pursuit of matters as prosaic as those of the tillers of the fields we passed, or as devious as that which now concerned Baron Egon Von Ruber and, at Pons' whim, myself, for it seemed all as plain as a pikestaff to me – Von Ruber had been chosen to carry the microfilms to Paris, and I to take them across the Channel.

The chestnut-clad guard tapped on the door and opened it, looking in. "Comfortable, Gentlemen?"

Baron Von Ruber nodded brusquely, but I fear, in spite of my friendly assurance, I looked upon the guard with suspicion, for, in the circumstances everyone must inevitably seem to come under suspicion.

Baron Von Ruber, however, was engrossed. He had not been content to play my game, but had rapidly taken the offensive of his own, and was clearly bent upon making it his game, which, in my state of mind, I saw little opportunity of preventing, since he maintained an aggressive attitude that brooked little countering. In his precision, he was not above a waspish aside from time to time.

"Tut, tut, Doctor," he said on one occasion, "I fear your mind wanders. You sacrifice your pieces needlessly. You offer me little challenge."

Thus stung, I rose to his taunt, but he maintained his advanage. I fought stubbornly, and for a time even forgot the reason for our enforced companionship. Marianské-Lazné was reached and passed, and it was not until we drew into Cheb and the train began to fill with swastika-banded guards and border personnel that my concern with Baron Von Ruber's mission resumed its paramount place.

The German Border officials seemed unnecessarily rough and blunt, but I had my passport and customs declaration in order, and my baggage was so slight that it did not take them long to go through it; moreover, Baron Von Ruber's arrogant superiority made its impression on them, and we were soon abandoned.

"One must know how to treat these robots," said Von Ruber philosophically. "The German mind is peculiarly susceptible to domination. It bends to positive leadership – however in error it may be – as some flowers to the sun; the step from Bismarck to Hitler is not really such a long one as you British sometimes imagine, and it is always a profound riddle to the

German mind how you people manage to fumble through without any significant evidence of political acumen."

I bridled, but bit back the angry words that rose, remembering Pons's admonition.

"Your move, Doctor," said Von Ruber, as placidly as if nothing he could say could ruffle my calm.

I brought my mind back to the game and sat pondering the board. The Baron now had me very much on the defensive, but I observed that, in contrast to his impatiently drumming fingers when I had made my entrance into our compartment, he was now almost icily detached – but alert with the alertness of one who is aware on more than one plane; only part of his attention was now given to the game; it was manifest that he sat with every sense aware, assimilating every untoward sound and interpreting it. The Orient Express was moving through Germany toward Nuremberg, but daylight still held to the countryside, though the first dusk could be seen from time to time in wooded areas and valleys from which the last light of the sun had been withdrawn.

"Ought we not to lock the door of our compartment, Baron?" I asked abruptly.

"I'm expecting visitors, Doctor," he answered, almost harshly. "I cannot say in advance in how much haste they may be."

I moved a pawn and lost it at once to my opponent, who sat looking at me, I thought, with a bored and tolerant air, as if he were now cognizant of some residual resentment in me, as I was aware of his low opinion of the British Intelligence in sending into this breach such an amateur as I. Thereafter, in rapid succession, I lost three more pieces and the game.

"Another game, Doctor?" Baron Von Ruber asked almost contemptuously.

"If you will open," I said, congratulating myself on not having revealed to him my championship, which seemed now indeed far more insignificant than I had ever conceived it to be previously, for Baron Von Ruber was unmistakably a skilled opponent a cut or two above my level, though I assuaged the thought with the assurance that the tension of the circumstances inevitably altered my game.

He chose the English Opening; I countered, and we were off once more, though I had little taste for yet another game. Darkness was now creeping swiftly across the land; the German villages loomed out of the dusk all lit like clusters of glow-worms, shining briefly in the course of our passage.

The game made progress, less swiftly than the Orient Express. This time, much to my astonishment, I gained a tentative, then a firm advantage. I noticed that Baron Von Ruber's slender fingers seemed to grip his pieces more tightly, and understood that, as the night wore on, he waited upon events with ever growing expectation, which must inevitably affect his game, even as my initial shock had affected mine. I pressed my advantage, reflecting that, after all, my responsibilities at the moment and until the microfilms were given to me were wholly passive.

At ten o'clock, and in full darkness, the Orient Express drew into Nuremberg. I looked out to the platform; it was reasonably well filled with travellers. I tried to pick out from among them someone who might attempt to reach my companion – the tall, aging Englishman, perhaps; the squat Frenchman; the bemonocled Austrian – who might all have been German citizens presenting themselves in these guises to my imagination. I smiled and turned away.

Baron Von Ruber was grim. "Something amuses you, Doctor?"

"Only fancies," I said.

"Of life or death?"

"I am familiar enough with both," I answered tartly. "You forget that I am a medical man."

"Ah, yes. We may need your services."

I was sobered at once.

After an interminable wait, the Orient Express drew out of the station, rapidly gathering steam, and once more there was a considerable movement up and down the corridor, as there was after every stop. But presently this died away, and the train sped across country toward Vienna on its absurdly winding course to Paris.

We resumed our game, myself intent now, the Baron far more concerned about matters external to the board. Perhaps, inevitably in these circumstances, I was finally able to checkmate him. "You improve, Doctor," he said laconically.

In an imprudent outburst of self-satisfaction, I said, I hope modestly, "I once took a provincial championship."

"Indeed," he said correctly. "My congratulations." His whole tone implied that he somehow believed that British standards of judgment in chess were somehow less precise and demanding than those maintained on the Continent.

"Another game, Baron?" I asked.

"As you like."

"Please open," I said.

He did so. The Ruy Lopez.

"It is an opening I fancy," he said mildly.

"I have played and countered it," I said.

Precisely at this point, there was a sudden rush of footfalls in the corridor, then a faltering – and someone fell against the door of our compartment. Baron Von Ruber was out of his seat in a bound and at the door. He flung it open.

A slender Englishman, medium in build, toppled into our compartment, gasping, I thought, "Von-s – Von-s," and clawing and reaching for Von Ruber's hands. My companion kicked the door shut and strove in vain to support our visitor, who was beyond supporting, for he collapsed and slid down along Von Ruber's body with a strangled moan to the floor, knocking over our chessboard and scattering the pieces.

"Doctor, your good offices, if you please," said Von Ruber, as he bent over the fallen man, methodically going through his pockets.

I dropped to my knees beside our visitor, but needed only a few moments to assure me that he was beyond any help I could give him.

"Baron, this man is dead."

"I feared as much," said my companion calmly. "It complicates our position, I'm afraid."

I came to my feet and turned toward the door. "I'll call the guard."

"Stand where you are, Doctor!" commanded the Baron with surprising firmness.

I stood.

"Madman!" my companion went on. "Surely you understand that the guard is the last person to call! We must fall back upon our own ingenuity. We must dispose of the body."

Silently, he indicated the window. Then he turned off the lights, plunging our compartment into darkness.

"Where are we?" he asked.

I looked from the train, my senses reeling. Pons' "obey him implicitly" rang in my ears as if he had spoken it; indeed, I seemed to hear the echo of Pons's voice even as I thought of him.

"Passing through a forest, as nearly as I can make out," I said.

"Good! Lower the window, Doctor."

I did as he had bidden me.

"Now, then, give me a hand."

Distasteful as the task was, I bent to it; there was no alternative. The body was comparitively slight, however, and between us we managed with but little difficulty to push it out the window.

Baron Von Ruber turned up the lights once more. Swiftly, he set up the chessboard again, and with what, in the circumstances, was a phenomenal memory, he replaced every piece precisely as it had been. He scrutinized the compartment carefully – for any sign of blood, I concluded – and then sat down once again, as composed as if he had but risen to stretch his legs.

"You are pale, Doctor," he said ironically.

"I'm unaccustomed to dealing with bodies in this cavalier fashion."

"Ah, one adjusts to circumstances," he said, shrugging. "A body in our compartment would only draw attention to us. We cannot afford it. The German Gestapo, of whom you may have heard, are anything but gentle in their methods. But perhaps an English gentleman would not appreciate a course so alien to the methods of your Scotland Yard."

"How did he die?" I asked.

He smiled. "Surely you should tell me that? He was poisoned, I think. There is no sign of blood here, and I felt none. Did you?"

I shook my head. "Did you know him, Baron?"

"Alas, yes! He was a British agent named Ashenten. He was really too old for service. But he accomplished many things during and after the last war, especially in the course of Russian revolution – and you British are sadly sentimental about old boys. I salute him, no less; there was bark in him still. I suspect somewhere there is a woman – he was susceptible to them. It would be easy to slip something into a drink if he trusted her."

"I should have thought a seasoned British agent would be alert to every such device," I said.

"Ah, there is always a conflict in Englishmen between caution and chivalry," said Baron Von Ruber with a little smile. He shrugged. "I believe it is your move, Doctor."

I shook my head. "How can you so coldbloodedly go on with a game of chess at a time like this?"

"Doctor, you of all people should know that life goes on no matter how often death intervenes. I regret Ashenten's death, but then, he was unmarried, he leaves no family, his place will be filled. Very probably old Colonel Somerset, who trained him, has his substitute ready to step into his place. Pray Doctor. I fear we may not have much longer to finish our game."

I bent to the board once again, while my companion rose, crossed to the door of our compartment, and looked out. He took the cigar out of his mouth, cradled it for a while in his fingers, and then dropped it into the receptacle for waste beside his seat.

"I'm sorry," I said. "I find it impossible to concentrate."

"Very well," said my companion. "Let us just put out the light and rest for a while in the dark. I should not be surprised at some further interruption soon, if – as I suspect – Ashenten was followed to our compartment."

He suited his actions to his words, and our compartment was darkened once more.

I welcomed the dark. I sought to bring order into my confused thoughts. I was still unsettled about Von Ruber's callousness in disposing of Ashenten's body, and a score of questions pressed upon me. How long would it take for the body to be discovered? Perhaps not until morning. But even at that hour the Orient Express would still be in Germany; it could be halted, searched, and everyone aboard subjected to the ungentle interrogation of the Gestapo. Yet, clearly, there was nothing to connect us with Ashenten; on the contrary, if Von Ruber were under suspicion of acting clandestinely for Britain, he would be the last person to be suspected of having a hand in Ashenten's death. It followed, inevitably, that the body of a dead British operative would quite properly be laid to German counterintelligence, and nothing whatever would be done about it.

I remained disquieted. I was at a loss to understand why Pons had chosen to plunge me into such a webwork of intrigue, and I knew that at this point the untoward events about which Baron Von Ruber had warned me had only just begun. We were now moving toward the former Austrian border, which, since *Anschluss* only a few months before, was no more; we would thus be on German territory for many more hours.

"Ought we not to make up our berths?" I asked.

"To sleep?" asked Von Ruber incredulously. "My dear Doctor Parker, it would surely be a convenience for our unknown 'friends' if we were to sleep. One of us, at least, must remain constantly vigilant. I prefer it to be both. If you must sleep, let it be by day, when we are less likely to be called upon to act."

"Forgive me," I said. "I am not accustomed to these intrigues."

Baron Von Ruber barked his brief laughter. "Give you a corpse in familiar British surroundings, eh, Doctor? And with your ratiocinative friend standing by to solve the little riddle. You ought to be familiar with Dr. Freud, sir. It has perhaps not occurred to you that your sleuthing friend may represent for you – ah, let us say – a father image?"

Whether it was my travelling companion's casually scornful air, or whether he touched upon a raw nerve, I could not say; but his retort stirred me immediately to cold fury; I did not trust myself to speak, and I had to resist the impulse to get up and leave the compartment. Admittedly, part of that fury was directed against Pons for subjecting me to Von Ruber's companionship; but he could certainly not have known of the fellow's unmitigated arrogance, and surely not of the low opinion Baron Von Ruber held of him! I simmered, a condition which Von Ruber's quiet chuckling did not abate.

I sat in smouldering silence for miles, staring out of the window. As nearly as I could determine, the Orient Express was still passing between the Bohemian forest and the valley of the Danube. The lights of villages seemed now not so many, testifying to the deepening night, and the stations through which the train passed without stopping were largely deserted. To add to my gradually subsiding irritation, I was hungry.

Yet I must have dozed off, for I was awakened suddenly by Baron Von Ruber's hand gripping my shoulder and his sibilant voice at my ear. What I would not have given at that moment to hear Pons's familiar, "The game's afoot!" Instead I heard my travelling companion whisper, "Wake up, Doctor. We are about to have company."

I snapped into complete awareness at once.

Baron Von Ruber returned to his seat just as the door of our compartment opened noiselessly and a slight figure slipped inside.

Baron Von Ruber turned on the light.

There stood an attractive, slender woman who looked hardly more than a girl, her eyes wide in the light, her lips parted. She carried one clenched fist to her mouth, and crouched back against the door, like a beautiful creature at bay.

"To what do we owe the honor of this visit, Fräulein?" asked the Baron.

"Please help me," she whispered.

"Ah, and how can we do that?" asked my travelling companion without stirring from his seat.

"*They* are after me," she almost whimpered.

"Fräulein must not expect us to understand her meaning without explanation," said Von Ruber.

"The Gestapo," she said, and shuddered.

I began to smoulder anew at my companion's utter lack of chivalry or even ordinary courtesy; he did not so much as offer her a seat; he seemed indifferent to her plight. But if I was indignant at his passivity, I was stunned by what followed.

For our visitor began to sway, and it seemed clear to me that she was about to faint. I leaped to my feet to go to her assistance – and almost simultaneously the compartment erupted into activity. Von Ruber sprang to his feet, shouting –

"Her nails, Parker. Beware her nails!"

And then – I can hardly bring myself to set it down even now – there was a muffled explosion from one side, and to my horror I saw a spot appear on that fair forehead as our visitor collapsed to the floor.

I flashed a glance at Von Ruber just as he restored a snub-nosed weapon fitted with a silencer to his pocket.

"You shot her!" I muttered in a strangled voice, my senses reeling.

"You bungler!" said Von Ruber in a voice that trembled with restrained anger. "You left me no other choice. Permit me to introduce you to Gisela Margenstein, known to everyone in British Intelligence as *die kleine Lorelei*, a notorious secret agent affiliated with the Gestapo. One of her favorite weapons was poison under her fingernails – one scratch, and death. Your country lost Cyril Woodbridge, one of the better men in British Intelligence, only two months ago in his hotel room in München – he died of a scratch on his neck. The last person known to have seen him alive was *die kleine Lorelei*. I have no doubt she pretended to faint, just as she was doing here; he leaped to her assistance and was killed for his pains. Only a month before that, it was Raoul Gerson, French Intelligence. That infernal British chivalry almost cost you your life, Doctor."

I sat down, still too shaken to stand.

My companion was now unceremoniously searching the body of the woman he had shot down in cold blood.

I found my voice. "Sir, you are a murderer!"

"True, true," he said with equanimity, never even looking up. "Say rather an executioner, for Fräulein Margenstein was known to be implicated directly or indirectly in no less than twenty-seven deaths. Now, come, Doctor," he continued as he stood up and put out the lights once more, "we shall need to dispose of her body."

"No, sir," I cried.

"Doctor, open the window," commanded Baron Von Ruber in a voice of steel.

"I am paralyzed with shock," I answered.

"As you will, Doctor," said my companion. "The alternative, however, is so singularly unpleasant that you cannot have contemplated it. In a matter of hours the body will be discovered in our compartment. Can you imagine the reaction of the Gestapo to the death of one of their most valued agents? You will never see England again, Doctor Parker, or that fellow Pons to whose little adventures you are so devoted."

I knew that, if indeed the woman he had so mercilessly slain were, as he said, *die kleine Lorelei*, what he now said was only too true. I forced myself to open the window, and, though almost nauseated with shock and revulsion, I compelled myself next to help Von Ruber dispose of the body. Then I sank down heavily in my seat.

"Who would have thought a medical man to be so shaken," said Baron Von Ruber softly out of the darkness. "Or so soft."

"I have for many of my adult years sat in, as it were, at the solving of murders," I said passionately. "I never thought I should witness so coldblooded a crime."

"Accessory to the fact, is, I believe, the term," said Von Ruber. "But were you not in the war?"

"I was."

"And did you not witness many deaths fully as violent if not more so?"

"Indeed, I did."

"One of your friends was torn apart by a shell not very far from you on one occasion," he continued.

"How could you possibly know that?" I cried.

"My dear Doctor, it is not only private enquiry agents who may be able to learn things, either by footwork or the deductive process. In this service we never employ anyone, no matter how casually, without learning everything about him there is to be learned. Shall I tell you the antecedents of your wife, the former Constance Dorrington, the details of your private practise, or the continued bondage you have to those long familiar quarters at number 7B, Praed Street? Since 1919, I believe, Doctor."

"I understand that I have been thoroughly inquired into," I said bitterly.

"You have indeed," he replied. "And we know that you are a man in whom your government can place implicit trust."

"Thank you," I said. "I had not thought that complicity in murder – "

"Execution."

" – would be demanded of me."

"Any more than it was from 1914 to 1918?"

"Ah, that was different."

"Forgive me, Doctor – this is precisely the same. Your pathetic Mr. Chamberlain may plan to arrange for peace in our time, but make no mistake about it – we are at war, not overtly, as yet, but behind the facades. The microfilms should prove as much to His Majesty's government. Not – " he added wryly – "that I put much faith in either photographs or human intelligence. But it is of the first importance that the films reach their destination – and a life like that of *die kleine Lorelei* is completely inconsequential by comparison. Think on it, Doctor. I have work to do."

The lights went up again, and my companion got down on his knees to scrutinize the floor – in search of bloodstains, I concluded. But it was soon obvious in the satisfaction of his face that he had not found anything incriminating. He got up, dusted off his knees, and sniffed the air.

"A trace of the scent she wore is still here," he said then. "We shall keep the windows open in spite of the late summer coolness. Do you mind, Doctor?"

"As you like."

He put out the lights once more and took his seat again. "I should think it reasonably safe to sleep a little, if you are so minded, Doctor," Baron Von Ruber said presently. "I rather think we shall not be disturbed for a few hours. They will want to give Fräulein Margenstein all the time she may need."

"And when her body is discovered?" I asked.

"My dear fellow, in this profession lives are traded with less compunction than stocks on the Bourse. Tomorrow it may be mine. Who knows? We shall hope, with good fortune, to spare yours."

I had closed my eyes against the fleeting landscape in its starlit darkness – but closed them in vain against the scene I witnessed only a short time ago, and which now rose up again in all its horror, so that I saw in my mind's eye still the momentary shock, the implicit recognition of death in that fair, seductive face, for the instant before *die kleine Lorelei* crumpled before me. Yet, despite the traumatic horror that lingered, the sounds of the Orient Express rushing blindly through the night eventually lulled me, and at last I slept.

II

I woke later in the following day than I had anticipated.

Across from me, Baron Egon Von Ruber was contemplating a partially smoked cigar, little more smoked down than that he had tossed into the waste receptacle the previous evening. I glanced involuntarily into the waste receptacle; the cigar was gone. My companion had parsimoniously retrieved it. Even as

I thought as much, he put the cigar back between his lips. At the same moment he saw that I was awake.

"You slept very well for having witnessed an execution," he said dryly. "But you must be hungry. A restaurant car was attached to the train in Vienna. Are you up to something to eat?"

I said that I was. "Where are we?"

"Just out of Vienna," he answered.

He waited while I performed my ablutions, busying himself with the arrangement of his briefcase on the seat of our compartment. Then we stepped out into the corridor.

"You haven't locked the door," I pointed out.

He shrugged with an expressionless face. "What good is a lock against someone determined to enter?" he asked.

The restaurant car was crowded. Nevertheless, Baron Von Ruber's natural self-importance impressed itself upon the head-waiter, who escorted us to a table and, with a flourish, laid menus before us. The food was Viennese – *Wienerschnitzeln, Zwiebelrostbraten, Karfiol, Knödl, Apfelstrudel, sole Metterrich, Ribisl* – and the dining-car crew was almost certainly Viennese. I had not eaten since just before boarding the train late the previous afternoon, and I was ravenous; perhaps against my better judgment, I ordered a lavish meal, beginning with strong, aromatic coffee and rolls and ending with a large piece of *Apfelstrudel*.

Baron Von Ruber eyed the menu more judiciously.

I looked around the car. A good third of its occupants were military personnel. Long association with Solar Pons, however, made it inevitable that I should scrutinize our fellow diners with more than ordinary care. The majority of them, apart from the military, were the customary travellers, but they were now a more cosmopolitan assemblage than I had observed either at Prague or at Nuremberg – a yashmaked Indian Maharanee and her attendant, a fez-wearing Egyptian, a burnoosed Arabian added color to the clientele in the restaurant car, and various languages fell to ear. There were, however, certain occupants of the car who seemed to show as much interest in us as I did in them – a rotund little Frenchman with waxed moustaches, whose keen eyes dwelt upon us more than once; a chunky old man, whose eyes were masked by dark glasses, and whose mouth had a bulldog tenacity; and an almost flamboyantly handsome young man clad in a sports jacket, with a Byronesque scarf knotted about his neck, who, though he was playing the gallant with a young lady met on the train, was nevertheless fully as observant as I fancied myself to be.

I watched these three people casually. The Frenchman retreated behind a newspaper; the young fellow continued to dance attendance upon his newfound friend; the old man got up and, with the aid of a cane upon which he leaned heavily, for he had, I saw now, a club foot, lumbered out of the car. And across from me, Baron Von Ruber finally made up his mind about what he wanted to eat and ordered coffee, rolls, and *sole Metternich*.

"You eat sparingly," I said.

"The better to keep my wits about me, Doctor," he replied. "I could not help noticing that you were examining our fellow-diners. You are sadly obvious about it."

I felt a flush rising to my cheeks.

"The successful way in which to accomplish your end is to appear to be casual. Observe that young fellow in the sports jacket, for example. I would not be surprised to learn that he has discovered more essential information about everyone in the car than anyone else in it, and yet he has seemed completely won by the young lady."

"I have to point out that I was aware of his scrutiny," I said stiffly.

"And the military?"

I said I had not thought them of any interest.

"Yet two of them – plainly members of the Gestapo – have hardly taken their eyes off us," said Von Ruber calmly.

At this moment, the young man in the sports jacket ushered his companion out of her seat and came down the car toward us. As they passed, a tiny ball of paper dropped gently to the table in front of me.

"Ah, Doctor," said Von Ruber softly, "you have made a friend."

I covered the ball of paper with my hand, palmed it, and unfolded it under the table. I glanced down and read:

"Take care. You are being watched by the *Polizei*. If you need help, call for – "

The message ended in a scrawled representation of an insouciant human figure, its head surmounted by a halo.

I passed it across the table to my companion. "Perhaps you know that signature, Baron?"

"I take it for the representation of some sort of saint," said my travelling companion. "And how many saints are there in 1938? Not many. This one bears a worldly look. So we may take it he is earthbound."

"In short, an adventurer."

He nodded. "Or an intriguer. He may be useful. On the other hand, he may be only another gambit ventured by the enemy."

I was about to speak, but the Baron stopped me with a quick warning, his face turned down and aside. "Be careful. Our lips are being read by a little corporal across the way."

I knew better than to turn my head away from my companion. What I said was innocuous. Baron Von Ruber did not speak again, for at the moment food was placed before us, and we were both impatient for it.

We lunched in silence, and when we had finished, made our way back to our compartment.

Baron Von Ruber opened the door and immediately threw up one hand in the German salute, saying, "Heil Hitler!"

Our compartment was occupied. The thick-shouldered old man I had seen in the restaurant car sat in Baron Von Ruber's place; a hard-faced, muscular young man sat in mine. It was obvious that our baggage had been examined and the compartment itself subjected to the most minute search. The old man had an ugly-looking weapon in one hand; it was pointed at us. He carried his heavy cane in the other hand, and leaned upon it as he got to his feet. His club foot was of such dimensions that it seemed of itself to wear an air of menace. His voice, when he spoke, was guttural; his language was German, and he addressed himself to Von Ruber.

Their conversation was extraordinary, and for the first time I began to have grave doubts about Baron Egon Von Ruber's role. Was he indeed a British agent? Or was he a double agent? The two men talked as if they were old acquaintances, and as if I could not understand the German language.

"You dropped out of sight ten days ago in Prague," said the man with the club foot. "What happened?"

"The Herr Doktor should know I was ill at the home of a friend."

"Who?"

"Count Leventrov."

"We will see him. Your mission?"

"I could not accomplish it."

"Why not?"

"British agents prevented it."

"You are travelling with the friend of a notorious British detective."

"A coincidence. He was attending the medical convention in Prague."

The man with the club foot favored Von Ruber with firming, outthrust lips and an expression of unusual doggedness, sinister to look upon. "Hans!" he said. His companion jumped to attention. "Search them."

Hans immediately subjected Von Ruber to a thorough search.

I could not witness it completely, for the man with the club foot now stood between us, but I did see Hans yank Von Ruber's cigar roughly from his mouth, pry open his mouth to look and feel around in it, then push the cigar back into my companion's face again.

All too soon it was my turn, even to the removal of my shoes.

Hans found nothing. He stood back and shook his head mutely.

"Where is it?" barked the man with the club foot.

"I don't know what *it* is, Herr Doktor, but it would be my guess that *die kleine Lorelei* has it. She will have taken it from Ashenten."

"And Ashenten?"

"Dead."

"You saw him?"

Von Ruber nodded.

"Then it was you who pushed his body off the train."

"Manifestly. I could hardly afford to be found with it. He died in this compartment after he fell against the door in the corridor."

The face of the man with the club foot grew dark with anger. He prodded Von Ruber with his cane.

"The word?"

"Poland."

He snorted, but evidently Von Ruber had given the correct password or key, and the man with the club foot was satisfied. He motioned to Hans; Hans moved to the door. The man with the club foot made his shuffling, limping way after him. Hans edged out of the compartment.

The man with the club foot, looking now hugely sinister where he hulked against the partly open door, bowed in my direction and said, "Your pardon, Gentlemen. I am in the wrong compartment."

Then he was gone.

"Wrong compartment!" said Von Ruber sardonically. "That fellow is even in the wrong train. And, if it comes to that, the wrong war."

"Who is he?" I asked.

"An anachronism. He was of service to the German High Command a quarter of a century ago. The Germans are idealists who hope to keep past glories alive. But make no mistake about it – that fellow with the club foot is still one of the most dangerous men in Europe."

"He is in Counterintelligence?"

"He lives for espionage," said Von Ruber. "I trust, Doctor, you did not receive the wrong impression from our conversation. I am quite well aware, of course, that you can speak and understand German."

"I thought it strange that you should know the password or whatever it is."

"It is my business to know it," said Von Ruber curtly. "My life would not be worth a Pfennig if I didn't."

Nevertheless, I was far from reassured. Von Ruber was altogether too glib, and the incontrovertible evidence of his previous acquaintance with the man with the club foot, described by my companion as one of the most dangerous men in Europe, suggested several possibilities, most of them unpleasant. I tried hard to think of how Pons's mind would work, how he would study the facts now before me, and to what conclusions he would come. But my natural conclusions were circumvented by the incontrovertible fact that Pons himself had instructed me to place implicit confidence in Von Ruber, and there had been that in Pons's wire that hinted at some contradictory and unaccountable behavior on the part of my travelling companion. Without that wire to fall back upon, I would unhesitatingly have concluded that Baron Egon Von Ruber was a double agent.

Even so, I was not entirely convinced that Von Ruber was honestly acting in the interests of His Majesty's Government. The object of the search instituted by the man with the club foot – as by *die kleine Lorelei* – must certainly be the microfilms to which Von Ruber had made such blunt reference the previous evening. Since there could be no doubt of the affiliation of these two agents, it followed that the microfilms had been lost; yet, Ashenten may have had them, and he must then have found some way in which to pass them on to someone else. To whom then? Could it be Von Ruber? I would have sworn that it could not; yet I was obliged to admit that in the excitement of Ashenten's entry into and death in our compartment, it was possible that the microfilms had passed from him to Von Ruber. But the search of Von Ruber and of our compartment was of such thoroughness that there seemed little possibility that the microfilms could be hidden either in the compartment or on Von Ruber's person.

"You are troubled, Doctor?" Von Ruber asked, not without a note of mockery.

"You must forgive me, Baron," I said. "I fear I have a pedestrian mind."

"Even a pedestrian mind ultimately arrives at its destination," replied Von Ruber.

He said nothing more, and there was a kind of embattled silence between us.

The train forged ahead. Salzburg came and went, and the Orient Express discharged and added passengers; München loomed two hours ahead. The woods, mountains and tidy villages of Bavaria rolled past; the landscape wore an appearance of serenity and peace, belied by the tensions of the surging events of history that went on behind that placid facade. It seemed to me that at any moment now some inquiry would be set on foot about the body of *die kleine Lorelei*, which must surely have been discovered by this time.

"What will happen when the body of the woman is found?" I asked.

"Ah, Doctor Parker, I should imagine that the authorities will conclude that someone on one of the trains passing over the route between Nuremberg and Vienna murdered her," he said. "If she was known to have been on board the Orient Express, then of course we will all be suspect. And, of course, it may have been known. They had no doubt that Ashenten was on this train, as the man with the club foot told us. They will conclude that *die kleine Lorelei* managed to kill Ashenten, and they will have some reason to believe that she, in turn, took the microfilms from him and was murdered for them.

"Now, then, Ashenten was known to have fallen into our compartment, but it is not known that he came there deliberately. He was a dying man; he could have fallen anywhere, could he not? The man with the club foot is certainly now a member of the Gestapo; he is convinced that I am still a German agent."

"Were you in fact ever such an agent, Baron?"

"Doctor Parker, the Barons Von Ruber have served the German Government faithfully up to the time it became evident that a monster – a madman ruled Germany!"

"Count Leventrov?"

"A friend. His house was a refuge. The British reached me there."

"So that, in point of time, you have only recently begun to act for my country against yours?" I pressed him.

"We have certain interests in common. And you must realize, Doctor, that my background is thoroughly known. My exploits, my accomplishments – all are in the files. I am known. The man with the club foot went through the business of searching me, but surely you understand that it is you who are suspect?"

"I!" I cried.

"Indeed, you. You are the friend of the notorious Mr. Solar Pons, who is known to act for the government at such times as his lazy brother is not inclined to do so. I, Doctor Parker, am playing a role of some consequence – I am your red herring. Thanks to the man with the club foot, they will think that I am watching you in all your pristine innocence."

"Incredible!"

"Has it never occurred to you that there is a very strong element of the incredible in all espionage? – But I digress. You asked me what will happen. By the time that all the known facts about the matter have been assessed, the authorities will conclude that someone on this train is now in possession of the microfilms. He must be found, at all costs. We may thus expect some increased police activity – very probably from München to the border. But we are likely to escape it – we have been searched."

"The weapon!" I cried. "The gun with which you shot her."

"Did they find it?" he asked coolly.

"I didn't notice."

"Of course not. The gun went out the window within ten kilometers of the spot where they found *die kleine Lorelei* . Should they find it, they will discover the registration to be in a fictitious name – certainly not that of Von Ruber."

"Your fingerprints!"

"Oh, come, Doctor! I am hardly the amateur you must think me. There will be no fingerprints."

I was chagrined, all the more so because of the mockery that danced in my travelling companion's eyes. I fell silent and turned to watch the country pass. The train, which travelled at various speeds on its route, was now moving along at which in I took to be top speed. We should soon, I reckoned, be in München, and I resolved to hold my tongue at least until then.

At München, in mid-evening, the Orient Express slowed for a long stop. The station platform, brilliantly lit, disclosed – as I had come to expect – a large number of military personnel, some standing in isolated groups, some mingling with other travellers, and several officers standing by themselves except for their orderlies.

"We are likely to be here for a while," said the Baron. "Perhaps you would care to join me in one of those little games your friend plays?"

"And that is?" I asked, I fear, somewhat coolly.

"Deduction, I believe he calls it." He pointed idly. "That fellow over there. What do you have to say of him?

I looked out and saw a middle-aged, greying man, somewhat gaunt of face, standing against a pillar. His orderly stood stiffly a little behind and to one side of him. Both seemed to be islands of solitude.

"An officer," I said.

"*Oberleutnant*, yes."

"Certainly not one of the recent bully boys. A Junker?"

"Very probably."

"He seems unhappy."

"Oh, they are all unhappy with Hitler, the Junkers. They helped create the monster under the delusion that they could control him." Von Ruber shrugged.

"Well, it is elementary that he is going on a journey, but not in our direction," I went on. "His orderly seems very young; so he is probably newly assigned, which leads me to suspect he is one of the National Socialist recruits placed to spy on the officer."

"Very good, Doctor! But there is something more."

"Oh, his uniform is spotless, and I have no doubt his manner punctilious – they pride themselves on that, do they not?"

"Go on."

"No more."

"Let me call your attention to his boots."

I looked long and hard at them. "I believe, Baron, that he has either a wooden foot or a wooden leg."

Baron Von Ruber clasped his hands together in pleasure. "You have learned well under your friend's guidance," he said. "Of course, there are a few trifling things you seem to have missed – he is a married man who has recently suffered a family death – observe the mourning band; he is arthritic – you will notice the slight thickening of the terminal joints of his little fingers; he is openly contemptuous of his orderly – he does not once look in his direction and even when his head turns toward him in the smallest measure, his expression betrays his feelings; his decorations indicate that he has been wounded in battle; so he is very probably a veteran of the World War. There are other small points, but they are of little consequence."

"Remarkable," I said, "but elementary."

Baron Von Ruber chuckled, and his eyes danced.

At this moment my gaze was arrested by a uniformed soldier striding by, a handsome young fellow who, as he passed, looked briefly into our compartment and favored us with a friendly smile. With a start of surprise, I recognized him.

"Was that not our dashing young friend of the restaurant car?" I asked.

"Indeed it was."

"But where did he get that German uniform? I could have sworn he is English."

"I have no doubt he is. He appears to be a young man of considerable ingenuity. He has a bright future if he can manage to avoid getting shot."

The man with the club foot came limping by. He did not deign to glance in our direction. His companion, however, looked at us, one after the other, with brows beetling; his gaze was profoundly suspicious.

"That fellow Hans seems to be a primitive type," I said.

But Von Ruber was troubled. "Dear me," he murmured, "Hans has some doubts about us. I fear he may cause us trouble for which we may be unprepared."

"But he is simple-minded, compared to the other," I protested.

"My dear Doctor, it is precisely because that is true that he may be a source of trouble. It is always easier to bluff and parry an intelligent man, but all the finesse and cunning one may use are of no avail against the doubt and suspicion of a man of limited mental capacity such as Hans." He paused reflectively. "But how to act before Hans blunders into our little intrigue and destroys it – and us? I dislike to expose myself by leaving the compartment any more than necessary."

A tap on the door interrupted us.

"More trouble?" I whispered.

"Hardly the Gestapo. The tap is too gentle," answered Von Ruber. He raised his voice. "Come."

The door opened and our insouciant young friend looked in. He was still clad in his German uniform.

"Come in," urged Von Ruber.

The young fellow slipped into the compartment.

"You suggested that you might be of service," said Von Ruber bluntly.

"I did."

"You saw the companion of the man with the club foot?"

"Called Hans."

"Yes. Can you devise some plan to separate him from the other long enough to keep him off the train until it has drawn out of the station?"

"That should be easy. He can be denounced as a spy – the Gestapo are sensitive about such matters. Let him have been observed slipping something to a French traveller, perhaps."

"Good! If you should be challenged, the password is 'Poland'."

The young fellow smiled engagingly and went out.

"Was that not dangerous?" I asked, in astonishment.

"Certainly. But less so than permitting Hans his suspicions. We may have convinced the man with the club foot for a few hours, but with Hans nagging at him, we cannot say how long it will last. Hans is convinced we have the microfilms."

"He won't carry it off."

"I rather think he might," said Von Ruber confidently. "Consider – both club foot and Hans were convinced we had the microfilms. Now, should your young friend denounce Hans in front of his employer, and accuse him of slipping something to a national of another, inimical country, the fellow with the club foot might well conclude that Hans may be playing a double agent's game. The conclusion may not last long – but it will last long enough to see us out of Germany. We need almost seven hours."

"And if it fail?"

Von Ruber shrugged. "I suspect our young friend can take care of himself. He has verve and daring. He is fluent in the language, for if he were not he would never chance wearing that uniform."

The activity of the station platform was continuing without cessation, and there was considerable movement in the corridor outside our compartment. Von Ruber was probably correct in his estimate of the situation, but I was far from happy. How had Pons ever come to cast me for a role in such a maelstrom of danger? Only desperation could have been at the bottom of it. At the same time, I was by no means free of my doubts about my travelling companion. The man with the club foot knew him as a German agent – and evidently one of long standing; yet Pons's wire had left me in no doubt that Von Ruber was acting for England. I had the uneasy feeling that a double agent could double again.

Moreover, a certain glibness of manner combined with little, almost unobtrusive mannerisms, convinced me that I had known Von Ruber at some previous time – probably as a moustached or clean-shaven man.

"Forgive me, Baron," I said presently, "you mentioned having been in the diplomatic service."

"Among other things."

"Could we by any chance have met before?"

"Quite possibly," said Von Ruber crisply.

"Can you recall the occasion?"

Von Ruber smiled thinly. "Do you remember the frequent engagements your sleuthing friend had with Baron Ennesfred Kroll?"

"I do indeed. You were on his staff!" I hazarded.

"I was certainly on the scene, Doctor Parker, though I managed to keep just a step or two ahead of the law."

I suppose at that point I should have begun to suspect Baron Von Ruber's duplicity, but my companion wore such an air of assurance that I was nonplussed and when, a few moments later, he referred to an incident relative to one of Pons's encounters with Baron Kroll, which only someone associated with the matter could have known, my suspicions were once again put at rest. Yet I could not help harboring, far back in my mind, the conviction that somewhere between München and Paris Baron Egon Von Ruber might quite possibly find it to his advantage to doublecross England as he was clearly now doublecrossing his native country. I recalled Pons's frequent judgment on double agents – that money could always buy them, and that not one was to be trusted. How had he come to trust Baron Von Ruber?

But essentially, I was troubled by the fact that if indeed I was intended to carry the microfilms of the German High Command's plans for the invasion of Poland to England, I still had not the slightest idea where they were, and if Baron Von Ruber had knowledge I lacked, he was being singularly uncommunicative. The man with the club foot was convinced that Ashenten had carried the microfilms; the woman known as *die kleine Lorelei* had been similarly convinced. But Ashenten had certainly not had them in his possession when we had disposed of his body. Where, then, were they? I could not help thinking that somehow Baron Von Ruber had come into possession of the microfilms and, for reasons of his own, had them in a place of concealment from which he did not intend to remove them.

He sat blandly across from me, the half-consumed cigar still clamped between his lips. Meeting my eyes, he spoke.

"I notice that the process of concentration seems to furrow your brow, Doctor."

I had not time to retort, for the train was now beginning to draw out of München, and the door to our compartment was suddenly thrust open. The man with the club foot stood there.

His eyes glowered at me, dangerously, I thought.

"What did Hans take from you?" he asked bluntly.

I shrugged. "You should ask him."

Baffled rage burned in his face. He shifted his gaze to my companion. "Von Ruber," he said in his guttural voice, "*Heraus*!"

Baron Von Ruber rose with alacrity and followed the man with the club foot into the corridor.

Though I listened, it was manifestly impossible to hear clearly the anything that went on in the corridor above the noise of train moving through the night-held Bavarian countryside. Voices were raised, then lowered, raised again and finally heard nothing more. Perhaps the two men had walked down the corridor. I was now more than ever convinced that Von Ruber was in possession of the microfilms; somehow he must have come by them from Ashenten; but where he had hidden them I could not begin to think though I suspected that he had cached them somewhere on the train away from the compartment and certainly not on his person, with the intention of picking them up just before leaving the train at the Gare de l'Est in Paris.

Von Ruber re-entered our compartment, a sphinx-like expression on his face. His eyes were lit. He sat down.

"That astonishing young fellow succeeded in implanting in the old man's mind enough suspicion of Hans to see us through Germany at least," he said.

"What happened?"

"Hans was arrested. He may very well lose his life before that fellow with the club foot concludes that he's been duped." He shrugged. "The fortunes of war. I had hoped both would be gone, but I am satisfied now that Hans is not on the train. I feared his suspicions."

"But we are not at war, Baron," I said coldly, shocked anew by his detachment about death.

"Not yet. But war is inevitable, Doctor Parker, in a year or two. That madman in Berlin will precipitate it. The British will concede regarding the Sudeten region, but the Polish invasion will be an act of war they will find intolerable since it disturbs the balance of power – though the sirenical hope of German neutralization of Russia may paralyze them for a time."

"The prospect of another war frightens me," I said.

"Does it not any intelligent man? Indeed, it does. But men are imperfect, and in the mass dangerous in their folly. We cannot stave it off." He shrugged. "I think, Doctor, we can count on being undisturbed to the border. Perhaps we can sleep a little."

He reached up and put out the light.

III

I awoke in the early hours of the morning to the touch of Von Ruber's hand on my shoulder.

"Doctor, we're coming to the border."

The Orient Express was already slowing down to draw into the station and in a few minutes came to a stop. French officials crowded aboard and came through the train. My passport was in order, and so was Von Ruber's, but I observed that though the customs officials ignored my baggage, the Baron's was carefully examined. Moreover, our compartment itself was closely scrutinized – the seats lifted and every possible place of concealment searched, by which I deduced that someone had sent word in advance to the effect that Von Ruber was to be kept under close observation.

I said as much to my companion when at last we were alone.

He only shrugged. "One's reputation frequently precedes one. It is always a question of knowing whether one must live up or down to it."

"I don't know about you, Baron," I said, "but I'm famished." He rose with alacrity.

The activity of the border officials had crowded the restaurant-car. I looked in vain for the man with the club foot, but I did not see him, though I caught a fleeting glimpse of our insouciant young friend, now back in his own clothing. The rotund little Frenchman with the pointed moustaches was very much present, and, it seemed to me, considerably interested in us, as before. He did us the courtesy of waiting until we had ordered before he came directly to our table.

"Your pardon, Messieurs. I very much fear I must have a word with you."

With a flourish he held his credentials in his hand before us: M. Hercule Poiret of the French *Sûreté*.

"Sit down, M. Poiret."

"It will be less conspicuous so, *n'est-ce pas*?" He sat down next to me. "If I mistake not," he went on, addressing himself to my travelling companion, "you are the famous – or perhaps one should say, infamous – Baron Egon Von Ruber?"

Von Ruber bowed.

"Ah, *mon ami*, my little grey cells, they tell me you are not entering France for a holiday."

"I have heard of M. Poiret's little grey cells," said Von Ruber.

"Ah, so!" The little Frenchman permitted himself a chilly smile. "I have to say to you, M. le Baron, that your every move in France will be watched. We do not tolerate the espionage."

Von Ruber smiled. "Do you imagine, M. Poiret, that France has any secrets Germany does not already know, even to the complete plans of your Maginot Line? I am in France merely to escape Germany."

"We shall see," said M. Poiret. He rose, bowed, said, "I bid you good morning, Messieurs," and strode off, twirling his moustaches.

"We shall have, in effect, a guard to Paris," said Von Rube; chuckling. "We could hardly have asked for more."

We ate leisurely, and presently returned to our compartment aware of being observed by one of the guards and, in one place, by M. Poiret himself.

We had less than five hours to Paris, and I travelled now in growing perplexity. Baron Von Ruber, breakfast over, was again nursing his cigar; he did not seem at all communicative, though he glanced at me from time to time with what I could swear was an amused glint in his eyes, as if he were aware that I was concerned about the ambiguity of my position. I found it increasingly incomprehensible that Pons should have put me in so uncomfortable a position without some good reason; I had supposed it was to carry the microfilms of the campaign against Poland to England, but Von Ruber had not said as much. He had said only that he had boarded the Orient

Express and intended to receive the microfilms somewhere en route; perhaps I had made a gratuitous assumption. But if I had, why was I sharing the compartment with Von Ruber at Pons's urgent direction? I could only conclude that the Baron – if he were in possession of the microfilms, as I guessed – intended to wait until the very last moment, and hand them to me either as we approached Paris or in the Gare de l'Est itself, and I had no alternative but to wait upon his decision – which, after all, I had been instructed to do.

"Doctor Parker is unhappy, no?" asked Von Ruber abruptly.

"Say rather I am puzzled."

"But why?"

"I have thus far seen nothing of the materials of which you spoke."

"Were you intended to? That is, did your friend say to you that your mission included sight of the materials?"

I had to admit that my instructions had not been so explicit, and added, "But I could hardly imagine anyone who is in less need of a travelling companion than you – and I have been little more."

"It does not occur to you that it has been my pleasure to enjoy your company?"

"I fear I am too modest to entertain such a thought."

Baron Von Ruber shook his head deprecatingly. "I assure you, Doctor, you represent all that is best in the English gentleman, you have all his virtues, and in that alone you are stabilizing and reassuring."

I thanked him, but I was far from satisfied.

I said no more, but turned to the French countryside sweeping past, aglow in the light of the early morning sun, and so I sat through Nancy, and Chalons-sur-Marne, and at last the outskirts of Paris in late morning. Only then did I glance again in Baron Von Ruber's direction, and since he seemed to be asleep, I did not speak.

He came to life just as the Orient Express drew into the Gare de l'Est.

"My dear fellow," he said, "there is one last request I have to make of you. If you will follow me, please."

I gathered up my baggage, and followed him from the compartment and the train.

He walked directly over to a post in the station platform.

"So," he said. "Just here beside this post. Please take your stand here, Doctor Parker, and under no circumstances move until I return."

He half embraced me, clapped me on both arms, and patted my back. I thought for a moment that he intended to salute me in the Continental manner, but such was not his intention. Even at that moment, I had no intimation of his duplicity.

"Let me say, Doctor, I am indebted to Solar Pons for the pleasure of your company," he went on. "And now, if you will excuse me..."

He turned and hurried away in the direction of the lavatories.

I looked quickly around. As I suspected, the rotund little Frenchman, M. Poiret of the *Sûreté*, was on Von Ruber's trail. But so was another gentleman I had not previously seen – a tall, broad-shouldered man carrying an overnight bag, who followed Von Ruber into the lavatory, while the little Frenchman took up his stand outside.

A latent indignation I had felt gave way to some anxiety. Lest it seem too conspicuous – though in the crowd of mixed nationals at the Gare de l'Est none could be less conspicuous in appearance than an English medical man en route to London – I did not keep my eyes rivetted on the lavatories, but tried to appear nonchalant and above all, unconcerned and aloof from the crowd.

But when I turned again to look toward the lavatories, I saw Von Ruber hastening away in another direction, Mr. Poiret hard at his heels, and, while I stood undecided about what to do, a hand gripped my upper arm, and an all too familiar voice whispered at my ear.

"Come, Parker. The game is afoot!"

I whirled. "Pons!" I cried.

"You have brought the materials?"

I began to apologize, but even as I spoke, Pons' hand dipped into the side pocket of my coat and came up with Von Ruber's unconsumed cigar!

"Von Ruber's cigar!" I cried.

"I fancy this is what we want," said Pons. "Come, now – there's a 'plane waiting to take us to Croydon."

Bancroft Pons waited in our quarters in Praed Street. His tall, imposing figure was striding back and forth across the room at our entrance, and had the appearance of having been so occupied for some time before our coming. He stopped in his tracks at our entrance.

"Ah, you have the films!" he cried at sight of Pons.

Pons crossed to the table, took Von Ruber's unconsumed cigar from his inner pocket, and handed it gently to his brother.

"You will find the microfilms in a capsule embedded in this cigar, Bancroft. Treat it gently. It was almost crushed by the assistant of that fellow with the club foot."

Bancroft seized the cigar, muttering his gratitude, and hastened away at once.

"And how did you like Von Ruber?" asked Pons then.

"An unmitigated egotist," I said, "but otherwise pleasant enough. That fellow had the insolence to deride you!"

"Indeed?" asked Pons, raising his eyebrows.

"He called you a rank amateur," I said, my indignation rising again.

Pons' eyes danced. "I am hardly more," he said. "But you, I take it, emerged unscathed?"

"Apart from suffering his boorish rudeness," I said, "I have no wounds."

"In a few words, how did you estimate him?"

"To be frank, I was convinced he was a double agent. That fellow with the club foot knew him. The German woman he called *die kleine Lorelei* knew him. He had obviously been in the service of the German government. As a person he is one of the vainest men I have ever known."

"But cool and collected?"

"At all times." I shuddered. "He shot the woman point-blank."

"Undoubtedly to save your life."

"Well, yes," I conceded. "So he said. She carried poison under her nails." I paused, and my indignation chilled suddenly under a cloud of suspicion. "But how could you know that Hans almost crushed the microfilms when he pulled the cigar out of Von Ruber's mouth and pushed it back in again?" A few moments of revealing silence fell. "Pons!" I cried. "Pons, it was you! You were Baron Von Ruber!"

"I have seldom had more appreciation for a great impersonation, Parker. I thank you!" He executed an elaborate bow. "But come now – surely you suspected more than once?"

"I swear I did not. I thought I had met Von Ruber before. Certain mannerisms – but of course, they were yours!" I sank back into my chair in bewilderment. "But the man with the club foot! *Die kleine Lorelei*! Ashenten! They knew you as Von Ruber."

"Say, rather, they knew Von Ruber, but did not know Von Ruber was a double agent," said Pons. "The facts, my dear fellow, are elementary. Von Ruber was in the service of His Majesty's Government; he had long been in German Intelligence, but he had no stomach for Hitler and all that monster stands for; so he agreed to work for us. He obtained the microfilms and meant to carry them to Ashenten in Paris. Instead, he was taken seriously ill, and sought refuge with Count Leventrov, another of our agents. He died in Leventrov's home. Leventrov then got the microfilms to Ashenten, who was being watched. So I was flown from London to assume Von Ruber's identity, which, since Von Ruber and I were not physically unalike, was not as difficult as you may imagine. I had, of course, a complete dossier on Von Ruber. Ashenten contrived to slip me the capsule of microfilms even as he fell, dying, and I secreted it at once in the cigar. Since it was certain that *die kleine Lorelei* knew he had the capsule, she had to die. I have no regret about killing her; it was her life or yours, Parker, believe me. And I would far rather a dozen *Loreleis* died than one Parker!"

For that statement, delivered as it was with such warm and genuine sincerity, I forgave Pons for his extraordinary duplicity as Baron Egon Von Ruber, difficult as it was to do.

"Of course, it was prearranged that we would have someone at the Gare de l'Est to assume Von Ruber's identity long enough for me to join you for London – if only to lead astray any secret agent who might be following Von Ruber – little M. Poiret, for one." He sighed and cried, "If only there were some way to prevent the fulfilment of the German High Command's plans, but I fear there is none, there is no way short of assassination to stop the Nazi madman – and our Government, I fear, is too soft for that course. So we must prepare, Parker, for another and even more terrible holocaust. I regret that my poor powers are so limited."

III

THE ADVENTURE OF THE GOLDEN BRACELET

"Ah, Parker," cried Solar Pons, as I walked into our old quarters at 7B, Praed Street one summer afternoon in 1939, "I see that your wife has gone on a holiday, and you have come to spend a little time with an old friend. That is not your customary medical case you are carrying."

"She's visiting her aunt in Glasgow for a week," I said, "and my locum can easily do without me for a few days."

"Capital! Capital! Put your bag in your old room, and share a pipe with me."

"Are you at leisure, then?" I asked, as I came back and took my old place at the fireside.

Pons chuckled. "You manage to time these occasional visits of yours with fine judgment. As a matter of fact, I am expecting a client." He bent and gave me a light, enveloping me in the smoke of the vile shag in his pipe, and then stood back once more in that familiar pose with one elbow on the mantel. "Does the name Simon Sabata mean anything to you?"

"That fellow is in all the papers, Pons," I cried. "He is notorious. I believe that questions were asked about him in the House yesterday, and the Government of Turkey is demanding his arrest on a charge of the theft of some of their national archeological treasures. The evidence seems conclusive as to his guilt."

"Gently, Parker, gently. We have not seen any of the evidence apart from certain reproductions of drawings he has made."

"He has freely admitted making them."

"We have so far only read of the alleged evidence in the newspapers."

"The several pages of drawings – in colour – run by the *Tempest* two weeks ago would seem to be conclusive."

"Let us wait and hear his story," suggested Pons. "I fancy that is his car that has just drawn up to the kerb."

In the silence that fell I heard the slamming of a car door, the creak of the entrance below. The steps on the stairs were those of a man of more than ordinary light weight, for they were scarcely audible.

Our client moved swiftly, for his knock sounded before I expected it.

Pons opened the door to him.

"Mr. Pons? Thank God! I am at my wits' end," cried our visitor.

"Pray come in, Mr. Sabata. We shall today also have the counsel of my old friend, Dr. Parker."

Sabata acknowledged the introduction with only a frosty, distrait nod, and sank gratefully into the chair Pons had moved forward toward the fireplace. He was a short, slender, almost dapper man. He sported a greying Van Dyke, and the marks on his nose clearly indicated that he wore pince-nez, which the black silk cord around his neck terminating in a pocket of his vest only corroborated. He had singularly intent eyes, which, after his fleeting glance in my direction, did not leave Pons's face.

"I am sure you know why I have come, Mr. Pons," said Sabata. "Your brother was kind enough to make the appointment for me. It is a delicate matter – a very delicate matter, indeed."

"Let us forget the newspapers, Mr. Sabata," said Pons. "I would prefer to hear the story in your own words."

Our client took a deep breath. "I have given an account of it so frequently that I have come to doubt the evidence of my own senses," he said. "It began, I suppose, last April on the underground. I had spent the day at the British Museum, and had worked rather late. I got on to the underground..."

"At the Museum Station – or Holborn?"

"Oh, the Museum Station. Is that important?" He was manifestly impatient.

"Go on, Mr. Sabata."

"I got on and sat down. There were not many passengers, but a young lady followed me and sat down across from me. I could see that she was of foreign parentage, but obviously, judging by her ease of manner and her clothing, she had been in London a long time or was a British citizen. She was olive-skinned, dark-haired, and her eyes were very dark and – well, yes, liquid, I should call it – like the eyes of many Turkish women I have seen. Since she sat directly in the line of my gaze, I quite naturally studied her. I assure you I had not the remotest interest in her personally, for all that she was a very attractive woman, and I am sure I would have forgotten her quite readily had I not seen her bracelet."

He paused and shook his head, as if he were trying to clear his vision of some cloud. "Mr. Pons," he went on, "that young woman wore a bracelet of solid gold. It was of a kind that is extremely rare. It has been found only at one place in the entire world – at Troy, by Schliemann. I had never seen such a bracelet outside of a museum, under guard.

"Mr. Pons, I am sure you must understand what such a discovery must mean to an archeologist."

"Particularly to one of your reputation," said Pons dryly.

"Ah, but which reputation!" cried our client bitterly. "I now have several." He sighed and went on. "It seemed to me the most natural thing in the world to introduce myself to my fellow-passenger. Caution, discretion, the behavior-patterns of a lifetime – all fell before that golden bracelet. She did not, however, take offense, and readily gave me her name – Sarah Sirit.

"'I could not help noticing your bracelet,' I said to her. 'I hope it is not an impertinence to ask where you got it?'

"She was very casual about it, holding out her arm and turning her wrist round, as women do. 'Oh, it is part of a little collection I own,' she said.

"'Surely,' I said, scarcely concealing my eagerness, 'you do not have more like it?'

"'Six more bracelets, several other artifacts, and some figurines,' she said, as if she were talking of something she had casually bought from a diamond merchant.

"Mr. Pons, I almost swooned. When I had myself under control once more, I said, 'You must know it is priceless.'

"'I collect antiquarian pieces,' she said, quite simply, as if this were some trivial occupation in which she indulged in her spare time.

"'Where on earth can you hide them?' I asked.

"'I keep them at home,' she said, with some surprise.

"Well, Mr. Pons – to shorten my story, I was impelled to ask whether I could see the rest of her collection. She was reluctant, but I overcame her reluctance, and prevailed upon her to permit me sight of her treasures at once. So we rode on past my station to Sudbury Hill, where we walked but a short distance to her home. She lived alone, and let us in with her latchkey. The house appeared to be sparely but well-furnished, and in very good taste, as I would have expected from the owner of such a treasure. I suppose that now, on reflection, I must concede that its furnishings were predominantly masculine – but I must not get ahead of my story.

"My hostess took her own time, which is consistent, as you may know, with the customs of the East. She served me Turkish coffee, and we made a considerable amount of small talk – about archeological subjects, of course, on which she was very well informed, knowing a surprising amount of data about my own excavations in Turkey and Greece – and in general establishing ourselves on a more friendly basis. But time at this point meant nothing to me; I was excited with the anticipation of what was to come, and presently she turned to a mahogany desk against one wall of the sitting-room and unlocked one of its drawers.

"There, neatly laid out on cotton wool from which the actual dust of the pieces excavated had not entirely been removed, were her treasures. She took them out, piece by piece, and placed them on the table before me. Mr. Pons, there were forty-seven pieces in all – a priceless collection. I have never seen its like outside of a museum in my life. I had, of course, seen greater but less rare collections in the course of my excavations – you will know how wide they have been – but these were extremely rare, for they were the first real proof of the Yortan culture, of which heretofore we have had only vague hints.

"I could scarcely control myself. I did not dare ask how this collection had come into the country. They were for the most part small pieces, which could easily have been smuggled in – bracelets, daggers, figurines in bronze, silver, and gold, armbands, anklets, cups – most of them in solid gold; too, as you very probably know, there is a considerable sale of antiquities on the part of the natives of the excavated areas – of pieces they have discovered, despite the attempt of the Turkish government to retain all the artifacts anyone uncovers – and all those I have uncovered have been turned over to the government for the national collection – but in the course of our conversation she offered this information herself, such as it was.

"The treasure had been taken from three tombs discovered near Mehmet, a village not far from the Sea of Marmara. By whom, she did not say, but the clear inference was that she and her brothers had taken part in the opening of the tombs. The pieces could not have been brought openly out of Turkey; so they must obviously have been smuggled into England. And certainly not all at one time.

"It was now well past midnight. I hope you will understand that I simply could not take my leave of this treasure. No Yortan tomb had ever been discovered or opened to my knowledge – yet here before me lay indisputable evidence that it had been done, and we had at last proof of the existence of a seafaring nation originating in Troy, living east of that city, sometime in the third millenium B. C.

"By this time, my hostess was patently tiring. I asked, finally, whether I might photograph her treasure.

"About this she was firm. I might not. 'But you may sketch it, if you like,' she said. 'I have sketching materials.'

"Could I return tomorrow?' I asked.

"Much to my surprise, she denied my request. 'No, Mr. Sabata, it must be now – or never,' she said. 'I do not know how long I will be here.'

"Well, Mr. Pons, the upshot of it all was that I remained there over night. She gave me a room in an alcove off the sitting-room, and the cabinet with the treasure in its drawers was not out of my sight save for the time I slept – and that was a very short time, indeed, for my excitement did not abate sufficiently to permit much sleep. And I remained there for three more days and nights – studying and sketching that superb collection, making rubbings – until I had reasonably good representations of every piece in her possession.

"I then asked whether I might publish my drawings.

"'Oh, no,' she said, with some agitation. 'It cannot be done.'

"Of course, she would say so if the collection had been smuggled out of the country. Though she was out of reach of the Turkish authorities, there might be members of her family in Turkey who could be reached.

"'Without mention of your name or address,' I said.

"Well, we talked back and forth, and I overcame her reluctance to the extent of gaining her promise that, if I had not heard from her in three months, expressly forbidding me to publish my drawings, I might do so.

"When I left the house before dawn the next morning, I was as elated as I have ever been in my life. I had seen something archeologically unique, a treasure I had dreamed some day of seeing but not actually believed I would ever have the good fortune to see – dreamed of seeing piece by piece as I discovered it in my explorations – and seen at last not in the ancient soil of Turkey but in a house in Sudbury Hill!

"Of course, I need hardly say that I expected every post to bring me a curt letter forbidding me to publish my drawings, and it was not until two months had passed that I began to hope that I might be permitted to publish them. And then, as you know, in the end, no letter came – though I waited ten days longer than the three months she had specified. And then – I published."

He groaned and covered his eyes.

"Pray continue, Mr. Sabata," said Pons softly.

"All the world knows the rest of my story," cried our client bitterly. "Within a week the storm broke. Those pieces were identified beyond doubt as having been stolen from a treasure trove acquired by the Turkish government – a trove of which no display had ever been made – and my drawings had been so precise as to make identification positive. Understandably, representations had been made to our government, and within hours gentlemen from Scotland Yard and the Foreign Office visited me.

"I had no alternative but to tell about my adventure, to give them Miss Sirit's name and address. I had no hesitation, in the painful circumstances, in accompanying them to Sudbury Hill, and led them directly to the house.

"But, Mr. Pons, no Sarah Sirit had lived in that house, according to the owner – a Mr. Leonard Harwood, whose father had built the house. No one but Harwoods for two generations had ever lived in it. Yet it was unmistakably the house in which I had spent three days and four nights; I could identify a piece of furniture, in every every room in which I had been. I needn't tell you that the cabinet drawers contained not a trace of those priceless pieces – not even so much as a thread of cotton wool! Mr. Leonard Harwood had never heard the name of Sarah Sirit and plainly looked upon my tale as a fabrication. I am afraid the police took the same view, and unhappily for my reputation, so did the Turkish government – my permit to renew my explorations in that country has been cancelled."

"Mr. Harwood, I take it, was abroad during the month of April?"

"Yes, he was! – in America," said our client eagerly. "That is the one feature that has given the police pause – though Harwood scoffs at the idea that anyone could have lived in his home during his absence, since he found nothing out of place. But I fear this is all academic – my reputation is ruined. I should never have published my drawings without the pieces to offer as evidence. It is all so baseless!"

He gazed at Pons almost in desperation. "Mr. Pons, if there is anything you can do to discover the treasure, you may name your own fee – no matter what it is – I shall not question it. Can you undertake it?"

"I shall have a go at it, Mr. Sabata."

After our client had taken his departure, Pons sat for a long minute in silence, an errant smile on his thin lips. At last he turned to me, his smile broadening. "What do you make of it, Parker?"

"I thought it a preposterous tale," I said.

"Oh, it is preposterous enough," agreed Pons. "But it is certainly true."

"How can you be so certain?"

"Because no sane man would willingly connive at the destruction of his own reputation," he replied. "In these little matters, Parker, such an account is either true or not true; in this case there can be no doubt of its truth. Someone meant to harm Sabata and succeeded."

"Ah, it is a case of vengeance."

"I submit it is."

"Why not simply hire a thug to assault or kill him?"

"You touch upon the essential point, Parker. Sabata was intended to be hurt in his field, where he has until now been highly respected. I submit that every step of this little plan was carefully worked out. Miss Sirit did not take the same train or enter the same compartment by accident. No, it was planned that she would do so, and Sabata's every movement was watched. Someone intended that Sabata should not go back to Turkey to continue his explorations – that his permit to dig be publicly cancelled under the blackest kind of cloud."

"And the discovery of the treasure elsewhere will restore his reputation," I said.

Pons shook his head. "Refurbish it, perhaps – but not restore it. For a charge of this kind to be made in itself does the primary damage. The truth will never catch up to it. The whole tale is so fantastic as to seize hold of the imagination, and nothing thereafter will diminish it. In matters of a man's reputation, it is only necessary that a charge be made for, once made, an indelible impression has been created and it can never be entirely erased." He paused and gazed thoughtfully toward the ceiling. "How did you assess our client, Parker?"

"A vain man."

"Nothing more?"

"And certainly an impulsive one. Only a man of impulse would have taken such a course as he set forth to us."

"I daresay."

"And indiscreet," I went on. "How could a man of his reputation have been so thoughtless as to spend three days and four nights in a house with a young woman whose acquaintance he had made but an hour before?"

"Ah, a man driven by passion – whether it is for gold or women or fame – recognizes no bar," observed Pons.

"Someone must have been very familiar with his habits."

"I rather think Sabata has been under surveillance for some time," said Pons dryly. "He would not have noticed it. It would have required elaborate preparations; they were made. Whoever laid this trap for Sabata knew his man well enough to know he could not resist the bait. The house in Sudbury Hill had to be got ready, and this involved the transportation from some other point of the priceless treasures Sabata saw there."

"I suppose there is no doubt that he saw them?"

"None. His drawings are explicit enough to have enabled the Turkish government to make positive identification of the pieces. What does all this suggest? Come, Parker – you have been familiar with my methods for a long time – what do you say?"

"It is plain as a pikestaff that only someone with at least as much knowledge of archeology as Sabata must have been consulted," I said.

"Capital! I am delighted to see that you have lost none of your powers since your marriage."

"But surely he must now come forward as a result of all this publicity!"

"Must he, now?"

"He could hardly have missed seeing it."

"And enjoyed every word of it," said Pons, chuckling. "Surely it is obvious that only a fellow archeologist would have devised so ingenious a revenge! Indeed, it is highly improbable that anyone else could have done so."

"No other archeologist would intrigue to so harm his own reputation!" I cried. "You said as much of Sabata."

"Unless he had already lost it," retorted Pons. "I think a little inquiry into Sabata's career might not be amiss. Such a man has certainly made enemies – any small success breeds them, and a man of Sabata's temperament, cursed with vanity and impulsiveness, is bound to have made more than the average. Let us just make a brief foray into the files at the Museum. They will certainly have a file on Sabata."

Within the hour we were deep in that venerable mecca for scholars from all over the world. Despite its ever increasingly crowded facilities, the Museum did indeed have a file on Simon Sabata who, it quickly emerged, had been embroiled in more than one intemperate episode, as the leaders on the clippings Pons scanned revealed – "Sabata Assails Peguy" – "Sabata Challenges Colleague's Findings" – "Archeologists' War of Words" – "Corum Refutes Sabata's Claim" – "Sabata Accuses Corum" – and so on, one upon another.

"This fellow seems to surface only to quarrel with someone," I whispered.

Pons's eyes danced. "Does he not, indeed!"

"He must have a dozen enemies to every friend."

"Ah, I fancy this is what we want." He sat back with a clipping dated three years previously.

"Archeologist Retires Under Cloud" read the leader, and the first paragraph told the story: "Nathaniel Corum, the well-known archeologist whose discoveries in Turkey were successfully challenged by Simon Sabata, who wrested from him the government of Turkey's permission to head a new research venture in that country, announced his retirement today. Discoveries in the area of Mehmet were proven to be spurious by Sabata."

"Sabata seems to be anything but an engaging fellow," I said as we rode back toward Praed Street on the underground.

"I fancy he is not much loved in or out of his profession," said Pons dryly.

"He seems to have sown discord whenever possible."

"All to his greater glory."

"With no concern as to the feelings or reputation of his victims."

"'Victims' is the word, Parker," agreed Pons.

"He has been acting all along like a dog in the manger."

"Indeed, he has," agreed Pons.

I came at last to the crux of what I meant to say. "He is not, I should say, exactly my idea of a desirable client."

"He does indeed leave much to be desired," said Pons. His eyes twinkled. "That is an opinion in which I am certain Nathaniel Corum concurs."

"How can you be sure that Corum is implicated in the plot against Sabata?"

"I fear it would be asking too much of coincidence if he were not," said Pons. "Consider – he is an archeologist, he has reason to hate Sabata, he excavated near Mehmet, he lives in Sudbury Hill. Now, surely, it would be a most extraordinary coincidence indeed if two men with such qualifications were to be found in any given area of London at the same time. Not impossible, admittedly, but improbable. But apart from these factors, there is one other, even more important – only someone like Corum could have got his hands on the pieces Sabata recognized and sketched, and of all the archeologists who came under Sabata's attacks, only one other, the German, Thielmann, excavated in Turkey."

"Why not Thielmann, then?"

"Thielmann has been dead two years," said Pons. He shook his head as if to shut off any further protest. "No, it cannot be anyone other than Corum. He is the author of the little drama, and his friends or servants acted it out, with Sabata as the unwitting star."

"And Harwood?"

"Undoubtedly another unwitting actor. He may have been known to one of Corum's accomplices, and so, too, his plan to visit America. It would have been a simple matter to take a wax impression of a door key. Nothing else was needed. And some care was taken to arouse no suspicions in the neighborhood of Harwood's home – you will have noticed that Sabata reached the house late at night, and left before dawn."

"But the antiquities – the pieces Sabata saw!"

"Oh, there is no question but that they were stolen. Perhaps by Corum himself. Perhaps by Turkish thieves who sold and smuggled them to him one at a time."

"Well, it proved to be an elementary matter after all, despite so promising a beginning," I said. "I suppose all that is left to do is notify the police and have them call on Corum with a search warrant."

"I rather think not," said Pons, with a little smile. "We shall use another tactic that may do as well."

"Surely you are not again going to burgle a house!" I cried.

"No, no, Parker. This matter calls for more finesse. I fancy a direct confrontation is in order. We shall call on Nathaniel Corum this evening."

Nathaniel Corum lived in a rather large house in a park-like area of land in the western reaches of Sudbury Hill. A pair of antique oil lamps glimmered yellowly in the darkness on either side of his door.

Pons lifted the knocker and sent a loud knock reverberating in a hall beyond.

We waited for a long minute before the door was opened far enough for a servant to put his head out.

"Yes?" inquired the head of what appeared to be a greying man in middle age.

"We wish to speak with Mr. Nathaniel Corum," said Pons crisply.

"Mr. Corum sees no visitors," said the head.

The door began to close.

"One moment," said Pons, putting a firm foot against the closing door. "I think he will see us. Pray take him my card."

He took a calling card from his pocket, added my name to it, and wrote something across the back.

A black-clad arm emerged from the darkness of the hall beyond the door, and a fat hand took the card from Pons's fingers. The arm withdrew. The door closed.

Within moments it was thrown open. The arm and head proved to belong to a rather tall, oversized man who was at the moment acting as butler, but had the appearance of being a general factotum.

"Come this way, gentlemen," he said.

He led us down the hall into a large room lined with bookshelves. At a table beside a reading lamp sat a man past middle age, for his hair was thinning and his thick beard was iron-grey. He regarded us out of unfriendly dark eyes. In one hand, I saw, he clutched Pons's card, and it was obvious that he had crushed it in anger and only afterward straightened it out. "You may go, Talbot," he said to his servant, then turned to us.

"What is the meaning of this, sir? How dare you! 'It is either us or the police.' What insolence. I warn you, Mr. Solar Pons, tread carefully. I am familiar with your reputation."

"And I with yours, Mr. Corum – before and after Simon Sabata."

Corum's face grew white with rage. He crumpled Pons's card once more and threw it to the table. For a few moments he fought for control; then, his chest heaving, he cried, "That is a name I have never permitted to be mentioned in my presence."

"But surely, after what has befallen him, you can hear it with less agitation," said Pons, smiling.

Corum's rage visibly cooled as he sat looking up at Pons, who still stood challengingly before him. "He deserved it," he said savagely, and a grin of malicious glee distorted his features. "He deserved it."

"I have no doubt he did," said Pons. "And it was very artfully done, too, if I may say so."

Corum's eyes grew wary.

"And now that you have had your sport with him, I have come for the Yortan treasure, Mr. Corum."

Corum threw himself back in his chair and gripped the arms.

"Incredible!" he cried. "How have you the insolence...?"

"Come, come, Mr. Corum – it won't do, it won't do at all. It will not take the police much longer to reach the same conclusions I did. There is surely only one man in all London who could have accomplished Sabata's downfall – you alone had the means to do so. Once the police move against you, they will never cease hounding you until the treasure is in their hands and presently on its way back to Turkey. Now that you have accomplished your end in Sabata's ruin, the treasure has plainly become too dangerous for you to hold. Surely it would be better found in Sabata's hands, than in your possession! At the moment, the police are of two minds about Sabata's story – once he produces the treasure, they will never believe it."

A succession of emotions chased one another across Corum's face – indignation gave way to wariness once more, wariness faded into craftiness, and presently he was eyeing Pons as if he saw him in a new light.

"You could hardly expect me to jeopardize myself, Mr. Pons."

"Your name need not come into it.

"How is that possible?"

"Unless of course you want the satisfaction of having it publicly known that you brought about Sabata's downfall."

Corum brushed this aside. "Mr. Pons, you may not believe it, but those pieces by means of which Sabata snatched my commission from me and ruined my reputation were planted among my findings by Sabata's agents."

"I believe it," said Pons.

"Yet you are employed by him?" Corum spoke scornfully.

"My instructions were to find the treasure," said Pons. "I have none beyond that. I have agreed only to 'discover the treasure' – and he has agreed to no more on his part. It does, after all, belong to Turkey, and the Turkish government has begun to make angry representations to our government. I am confident that you know the meaning of this. The treasure has now become, as our American brethren put it, 'too hot' for you to keep – whether you yourself smuggled it out of Turkey or whether you bought it is immaterial."

"How is it possible to keep my name out of it?"

"Anything is possible for me, Mr. Corum. It is not so for the police."

Corum came to his feet. He crossed the room to a bell-pull and tugged at it.

Within moments, a door at the far end of the room opened, and a dark-eyed, olive-skinned young woman stood at the threshold.

"You rang, Mr. Corum?"

"Have the Yortan pieces brought to me, Ana."

She turned at once, closing the door softly behind her.

Corum came back to the table and sat down. He said nothing. Pons and I continued to stand in silence. Corum put one hand on the book he had been reading – a new work by Henry Williamson – as if he meant to take it up again, thought better of it, and withdrew it.

The door at the rear opened again, and Talbot came into the room carrying a rectangular chest. He brought it to the table and put it down before Corum, who signalled him to leave the room once more.

"Come closer, Mr. Pons," said the archeologist.

He opened the chest. There before us lay some of the antiquities our client had sketched in a house that was not more than ten streets from the place we now stood.

"There are two other layers beneath," said Corum. "These cases lift out, as you see." He lifted one, as he spoke, disclosing another layer of the Yortan treasure. "They are all here." He replaced the case again, and closed the chest. "The chest, too, is a fine piece."

"It will be returned, Mr. Corum."

"Pray accept it with my compliments, Mr. Pons. Like the treasure itself, I bought it in good faith. It, at least, was not stolen from the government stores."

"You had not known the source of the Yortan treasure, Mr. Corum?"

"No, sir. Not until I read the account of Sabata's disgrace in the papers. I thought it taken from a tomb excavated by the natives – a common source of antiquities of this kind. Can I have the car brought around to take you home?"

"We have a cab waiting, thank you, Mr. Corum."

Our client presented himself next morning at ten, in response to a telephone call from Pons.

"You have good news for me, I trust, Mr. Pons," he said as he entered our quarters.

"Ah, well," said Pons, his eyes dancing, "there is an ambiguity in that, Mr. Sabata. Good and bad are relative matters; they depend upon more than the perspective of the individual, is it not so?"

"Hm!" said our client ungraciously.

"Pray be seated, Mr. Sabata."

"I am a busy man, Mr. Pons," said our client brusquely, as he sat down.

"I am happy to see you have quite recovered from your despair of yesterday," said Pons.

"I am trying to put the best face on the matter," said Sabata.

"But it is difficult – very difficult."

"Perhaps," said Pons, lifting the cover of the chest on the table, "this will help a trifle."

"Great Scott!" cried Sabata, leaping to his feet. "The Yortan treasure!"

He went quite pale and caught hold of the table to control his trembling.

"Forty-seven pieces, I believe you said," Pons went on. "It is all there."

"Where did you find it?" demanded our client.

"In Sudbury Hill."

"Impossible! The police searched that house from top to bottom."

"I am sure they did," said Pons.

"I will have that fellow Harwood charged!" cried Sabata. "I will break him for the dastardly scheme!"

"Breaking people seems to have been a pastime of yours, Mr. Sabata. Nevertheless, I would not advise you to have Harwood charged."

"Why not?" Our client thrust his face at Pons's like that of a diminutive bulldog.

"Because Harwood did not have the treasure in his possession. He has never seen it. He knows nothing about it."

"You said so!"

"On the contrary. I said only I found the treasure in Sudbury Hill. That is my last word on the subject."

"I demand to know where you found it!" cried Sabata.

"I agreed only to discover it. I have done so. I agreed to nothing more."

A baffled expression locked itself to our client's face. "Surely you are not going to deprive me of the satisfaction of turning it over to the police?"

"Not if you insist upon doing so."

"Then I will take it and go. Just send round your bill, sir."

"Not so fast, Mr. Sabata," cried Pons, with one hand on the chest.

Sabata threw his arms across it, as if fearful of losing it. "I will take it now – directly – to Scotland Yard."

"Not before you have given me a receipt for it."

"Such quibbling, when my reputation is at stake!" cried Sabata angrily, as he wrote out the receipt for which Pons had asked.

Then, clutching the precious chest to him, he walked with quick, nervous steps from our apartment, bound for Scotland Yard.

"If you have any pity in your heart, Parker," said Pons before the echo of our slammed door had ceased to sound, "pray spare a little of it for Simon Sabata. He is going off in white heat to hang himself."

And so it proved in the days to come, for despite Pons's admission to the authorities that he had tracked the treasure to earth at the behest of Sabata, the majority of the editorialists in the daily papers – and no doubt the majority of readers as well – left no doubt, without exposing themselves to legal action, of their belief that Simon Sabata had been in possession of the treasure from the beginning.

"Seldom is revenge so sweet," said Pons at our next meeting. "Nathaniel Corum must be hugging himself with glee! Sabata's ruin was inherent in his nature, and Corum knew how to draw it out."

IV

THE ADVENTURE OF THE SHAPLOW MILLIONS

Solar Pons looked up from the morning post, chuckling. "Have a go at that, Parker," he said, handing a letter across the breakfast table.

It came with a breath of fragrance. "Ah, perfumed stationery," I said. "From a lady."

"Elementary," said Pons.

"Mr. Solar Pons, Dear Sir," I read. "Even though I have been told you don't handle my kind of trouble in your private inquiry practise, I am sure only a cad would deny his assistance to a lady in need. If Arthur thinks he can do me out of my share of the money by just divorcing me, he's got another think coming. I've promised myself the best detective in London. I'm not going to give up my share without a struggle. He thinks because he's a Major in the Second Regiment of the King's Horse Guards nobody can touch him, but we'll see about that, and Mr. Pons, I believe you're the man to do it. If it's all the same to you, I will call on you at ten-thirty tomorrow morning." The letter was signed in a flourishing hand, "Mrs. Rosie Shaplow." She appended an address in Chepstow, Monmouthshire.

I looked into Pons's twinkling eyes. "You are surely not going to demean yourself by exploring the lady's marital affairs," I cried. "Matters of divorce are beneath a man of your calibre."

"Ah, let us not be hasty, Parker," said Pons. "It involves no commitment to hear what the lady has to say. Moreover, there is an intriguing little note in the letter – apart from some mystery about 'the money' – that interests me."

"It is no more than a sordid divorce proceeding," I said.

"You observed nothing else about Mrs. Shaplow's letter to give you pause?"

"Except that Mrs. Shaplow would appear to be a vulgar woman, given to saturating her stationery with cheap perfume..."

"On the contrary," interrupted Pons, "it is costly – a cloying and much advertised perfume from Paris."

"The principle is the same. She can hardly write a coherent letter."

"True, she becomes increasingly indignant at the thought of losing a share of 'the money'. But there is at least one other little point."

"I fail to see a facet of interest beyond the commonplace. Yet Mrs. Shaplow is so specific I have no doubt she has been impressed time and again with her husband's importance."

"It is a role husbands play without effort."

"While I have no interest in Mrs. Shaplow's marital difficulties, I confess to a tickling of curiosity about a fellow who vaunts his membership in the Second King's Horse Guards. In any case, it is far too late to put the lady off. She will be here within the hour."

In half an hour before the appointed time, our client presented herself. She proved to be an attractive blonde in her mid-thirties, dressed in the height of expensive bad taste, and wearing a furpiece around her neck, though the weather was much too warm for it. She flashed no less than five gaudy rings and reeked of perfume; as if that were not bad enough from my point-of-view, she had a singularly annoying habit of fluttering long, and, I was sure, artificial eyelashes over her cold blue eyes. "I said to myself that Mr. Solar Pons would take my cases," she announced with easy self-confidence, as she settled herself in the chair Pons proffered and fluttered her lashes at him where he stood leaning against the mantel. "I can pay – and if I get my share of the money, I can pay well – as well as you've been paid, Mr. Pons."

"Indeed," said Pons, keeping a straight face with difficulty.

"As soon as the suit is settled, that is."

"Ah, there is a suit before the courts?"

"Oh, yes, I should say so, Mr. Pons. Over seven million pounds! And he can't lose it, I should say, with a Certain Personage in it with him. They are the two parties to the action, as my husband puts it." She seemed to be proud of the circumstances, but in a thrice her indignation boiled up again. "But if he thinks he can up and divorce me without even going to court – just by having his important friends stamp the papers, why, I'll not stand for it, I certainly won't."

Pons's face, I saw, was now alight with interest. "Pray start at the beginning, Mrs. Shaplow," he urged.

She was momentarily stopped in her flow of words, but not for long. With a little laugh, she said, "I suppose it began when I married Arthur three years ago. He had already started the suit then. Not that, as you might say, he needed the money – he was that good a provider, he never left me in want of anything – but with one thing and another, I suppose we were apart too much, he was always having to go in to London, and he still does to this day, takes the 8:17 for Paddington every morning, as regular as you please, five days a week, always on the watch for new investors, because of course he never had so much money to fight the bank with over so many years, and the sum's worth it, indeed it is."

I was surprised at Pons's willingness to permit our client to go on so, but he seemed, if the evidence of my senses were not to be distrusted, to be engrossed in her account, which was delivered in a very rapid manner, as if Mrs. Shaplow were utterly unfamiliar with commas or periods. Indeed, his eyes glittered in their intensity, and he caressed his earlobe in such a manner as to denote unusual interest – and in nothing more than the customary details of the prosaic sordid story of a divorce action!

"But the suit isn't *my* story," she went on without interruption from Pons. "I suppose it's the old story. I suppose Arthur met another woman in London and took a fancy to her. He was always the one to give in to quick like or dislike – that's Arthur. Naturally, he wouldn't say anything to me. Not that I didn't notice anything. I could tell he was cooling on me, but it didn't worry me at first. Three days ago he told me, we were all through – divorced, and he put the divorce decree in my hands."

She opened her purse as she spoke, and, producing the document, thrust it at Pons, who leaned forward from his position at the mantel and took it. With but a cursory glance at it, he laid it on the mantel next to a packet of letters.

"Mr. Shaplow has left you?"

"He has, indeed! Taken a room at the *George*, in Chepstow."

"Ah, he has not transferred to London?"

"No, Mr. Pons, he has not."

"But he continues to come up to London five days a week?"

"I believe so," she answered. "It's that matter of the suit. And, Mr. Pons, I mean to have my share of that money when the suit is won. The bank is fighting it, naturally – with seven million pounds at stake, I'm not surprised they would." She gave another decided nod and added, "I'd fight, too!"

"He left you without funds, Mrs. Shaplow?"

"Oh, no, not that, Mr. Pons. He gave me a bundle of notes."

"How much, precisely?"

"Well, I didn't count it," she said carelessly. "But I'd say it was close to a hundred pounds."

"Ah, then you are temporarily provided for."

"It's not money I need right now, Mr. Pons," said our client. "I need someone to follow him and find out what he's doing and who he's seeing. And you're the man for it, Mr. Pons, I'm sure of it. I know all about you. They don't call you 'the Sherlock Holmes of Praed Street' for nothing. I brought along a photograph of him. It's three years old, but he looks about the same now."

The purse next gave up the photograph. This in turn was handed to Pons.

He scarcely glanced at it before he laid it on top of the document on the mantel.

"I propose to pay you a little something now, and more when you've found out for me what I want to know," said Mrs. Shaplow. "And then, of course, when I get my share of the money, you shall have a handsome fee."

"Mrs. Shaplow, I will undertake to make some inquiries in the matter," said Pons gravely, standing now with his hands clasped behind him. "At this point, however, I prefer not to accept a retainer."

"Well, that's very satisfactory, Mr. Pons," answered our client, bouncing to her feet. "I won't argue with that. All I want is something to hold over his head so that I get what's coming to me."

"Ah, you don't want Mr. Shaplow back?"

"With me, Mr. Pons, it's all or nothing. I won't share a man and if Arthur's found someone he fancies more – why, goodbye Mr. Shaplow! That's the way I feel. I was never one to cry over spilt milk. Life's too short for that. Rosie Shaplow never shed tears over anything very long. If it's another woman, she can have him. If it isn't, he'll be around one of these days."

With a proud flourish of her blonde head, she bade us good-day.

Listening to her tripping down the stairs to the street, Pons glanced whimsically over to me. "What do you make of that, Parker?" he asked.

I fear my voice betrayed a certain indignation and pain. "I can only say that I am shocked – there is no word for it – at the fact that you are about to become involved in a vulgar divorce action."

"Ah, I regret disappointing you, Parker," said Pons, smiling. "But the action, it would seem, has been concluded."

"Well, its aftermath, then," I said. "A suit for alimony."

"I do not recall that our client mentioned 'alimony'."

"She ran on without end about her 'share of the money'."

"Seven million pounds," said Pons reflectively. "It give one pause. The action instituted by Mr. Shaplow appears to have been directed against a bank. Mrs. Shaplow has lived with its details for three years."

"But if the action had not been concluded at the time of the divorce," I pointed out, "she is not entitled to any share of the amount awarded, unless, of course, she is a direct party to it. She doesn't seem to be."

"Let us just have a look at the decree," said Pons.

So saying, he slipped the document out from under the photograph and opened it. I came up and looked around him. The document was a formal decree of divorce, properly signed by Lord Merivale, the President of the Divorce Division of the High Court. The decree was absolute.

"There is no provision here for alimony," I said.

"And no record of a court hearing," said Pons. "An extraordinary document! Are our legal processes now so simplified that a divorce can be obtained so freely?"

"She may not have contested," I pointed out.

"True."

"And evidently no children were involved.

"Mrs. Shaplow did not impress me as a lady eager to encumber herself with the care of children," I said. I could not help adding, "Pons, why – *why* did you choose to have any part of this?"

"It does not strike you that there is something of more than ordinary interest about Mrs. Shaplow's problem?" he countered.

"It is common, disgusting – nothing but possible adultery and a lust for money!" I cried.

"I submit there is more here than meets the eye," he said imperturbably. "Indeed, I am even more intrigued than I was by her note, now that I have heard her story."

"You cannot mean it!"

"I was never more serious. Let us have a look at the object of Rosie Shaplow's ire."

He exchanged the divorce decree for the photograph our client had left. It was that of our client and her husband, taken, I deduced, quite possibly on their wedding day, for the background looked suspiciously like a registry office. Our client had assumed a pose I could only call simpering, while her husband gazed out at the world with calm, level eyes, the gaze of a self-assured young man. Moreover, he was dapper in appearance, almost elegantly well-dressed, and with what I should have described as a commanding presence which was not in any way diminished by what I took to be a monocle dangling from a cord about his neck. He wore his hair pomaded, and his upper lip was decorated with a closely-clipped moustache.

"He appears to be a man of means," I said.

"She would seem to have got much the better of this bargain," observed Pons dryly.

"I don't doubt it."

"I have a fancy to know the major," said Pons.

"You need only meet the 12:40 at Paddington tomorrow."

"Dear me! How unimaginative! I should prefer to be more subtle. What do you say to a week or so in Chepstow?"

I was astonished. "Why go to Chepstow when he comes to London daily?"

"I would prefer to have him come to us," said Pons enigmatically.

"I must admit I don't follow you, Pons."

"Rely upon your increasing skill at ratiocination, my dear fellow," replied Pons. "Just hand me that *Railway Guide*, will you?"

I gathered, from the place to which he turned in the *Guide*, that he was looking up Chepstow; in a few moments he glanced at the clock on the mantel, and confirmed my deduction.

"We can take the 3:55 for Chepstow, if you are willing. I have one or two little things to do by way of preparation, while you, if you will, can wire the Beaufort Arms for quarters for the week, and apprize Mrs. Johnson that we will be in for a late luncheon every day, and for no other meal."

When I returned from these errands, Pons was behind the locked door of his room. I heard his voice from time to time, as if in conversation, and it was presently manifest that my companion intended to play a role not his own in the course of his inquiry. In an hour there emerged from his room a bent, crabbed old fellow who bore no resemblence to Pons, save in the aquilinity of his nose and the piercing glance of his eyes. He wore a thick ulster, and carried a steam rug and cane, while his face was concealed behind carefully composed lines of age, framed by white sideburns, moustache and a tuft of neatly trimmed beard.

"What on earth are you up to?" I cried.

He made a little bow, clearly enjoying himself. "Colonel Septimus Barr, at your service," he said. "And you, Parker, will serve as my companion. You need not change," he went on, magnanimously. "You are so much the gentleman that you will fit into any such role with ease."

I acknowledged the compliment, but not without a touch of uneasiness. "Have I not heard you speak of Colonel Septimus Barr?" I asked.

"You may well have done so. There is, indeed, such a person, but he will not in the least object to my borrowing his name and personality for the nonce."

"I know your fondness for disguise," I said, "but I fail utterly to understand the need of it in this matter. Surely the best course would be to trail our client's husband and, since this is clearly beneath a man of your talents, it can be done simply by retaining an agency that specializes in that sort of thing."

"I daresay I ought to bow to your superior knowledge in marital matters, but I am eccentric enough to prefer my own way," he replied, chuckling. "But you need not burden yourself."

Pons knew full well that I would not hold back, no matter what his plans, and once I had arranged for a locum to take care of my few patients, we were on our way.

By nightfall we were ensconced in the Beaufort Arms at Chepstow, on the west bank of the beautiful winding Wye just above that river's junction with the Severn. Our quarters looked toward the ruined castle near the river, in the south east tower of which Henry Marten, the regicide, was imprisoned for two decades, and beneath which he was buried at his death in 1680. The grim ruins and the derelict slipways of the now abandoned national dockyards, constructed for use in the recent war, dominated that bank of the river, but all else was serene and singularly beautiful, perhaps all the more so in the soft twilight that held the countryside around Chepstow.

And, as Pons had planned, next morning we were on the 8:17 train, bound for Paddington. We rode first-class and Pons spent his time poring over the financial pages of the *Daily*

Mail, leaving me to enjoy the most attractive river scenery in England as the train advanced up the Wye, bound for Ross before turning toward Gloucester.

"What can you hope to accomplish by this?" I asked presently.

"It is a gambit, no more. It may fail," said Pons. "But I rather doubt it. I submit that our client's husband may be in search of just such passengers as we seem to be. If that assumption is correct, he will invariably be attracted by the attention I pay to the financial pages."

"Assuming that he sees you," I said.

"I rather doubt that he sits still," said Pons with a self-satisfied smile.

"Why do you say so?"

"I am persuaded to believe that Major Shaplow does not report for work in an office in London, particularly not one in which he is subject to the orders of someone else," said Pons.

"Well, that is certainly plain as a pikestaff," 'I retorted . "He could hardly take a train that would not bring him into London until after noon, if he had to report for work somewhere."

"So it follows that the Major is self-employed," continued Pons.

"Pressing his lawyers to push his suit, most likely," I said.

"Ah, I wonder," murmured Pons, and resumed his scrutiny of the paper.

For over four hours thereafter we rode through the countryside; and, after three hours in London, we rode back to Chepstow the way we had come. Though I forebore to say so, it seemed a kind of madness to me. Pons devoted himself to the financial columns, though I fancied that from time to time he flashed a bemused glance in my direction. I endured the almost nine hours of riding in an increasingly crowded train stoically enough, but on our return to Chepstow, I could not restrain my protests.

"Pons, this is unlike you. I have grown accustomed to more positive action."

"Ah, well, Parker, as any angler will tell you, different fish respond to different baits," he said blandly.

"What has fishing got to do with it?" I cried. "Mrs. Shaplow has set forth her case and expects you to act upon it."

"To obtain for her, if I recall correctly, her 'share' of 'the money'," prompted Pons. "Surely you will grant me the same ambiguity of which she was guilty? I assure you we will play this gambit no more than a few days."

"That is a crumb to be grateful for," I said, I fear, ungraciously.

Pons only smiled in that superior fashion that never failed to nettle me.

In the morning we were once again aboard the 8:17. All was as before, save that the day was more cloudless than yesterday. But already I was tiring of the landscape, for all its singular beauty – of the winding Wye, whose surface I scanned from time to time in search of coracles, now fast disappearing from England's rivers – of the Twelve Apostles and Wyndcliff and even Tintern Abbey in its lovely meadow – of Symonds Yat and the Welsh marches and the Severn Tunnel, so rapidly growing familiar; and I was little drawn to the book I had brought with me to read, perhaps because of the vexation I felt at Pons' oblique course to his end. I began to find the prospect of three more days of such traveling infinitely wearying.

We had gone past Gloucester on this morning, however, when I was suddenly conscious of someone's having paused in the corridor to look into our compartment – a bemonocled gentleman, expensively dressed, whose glance seemed to be directed first at the object of Pons's scrutiny, and then at Pons himself. He stood so for only a few seconds; then he was gone.

"Major Shaplow, of the Second King's Horse Guards," murmured Pons dryly.

"I recognized him," I said. "A trifle older than his photograph."

"But even more appropriately dressed," observed Pons. "I fancy we have not seen the last of him."

"I have seldom seen you so confident and for so little reason."

"Ah, it is not confidence, Parker. I submit it is the science of deduction. The Major and I share a common interest at this point. Money. He has seen me poring over the financial columns. In half an hour or so, he will return this way to see whether I am still engrossed in these columns. I will be. He will then presume to introduce himself. Apart from a suspicion natural to my identity, I will not find his intrusion unwelcome. We shall hope to enjoy his company."

An unpleasant premonition began to take shape in my mind.

"Pons, you are surely not planning to separate the Major from some of his money by trickery!"

"Perish the thought!" cried Pons, laughing heartily.

In the course of the next forty minutes, I observed Major Shaplow passing our compartment twice. When he appeared for the third time he did not pass, but paused diffidently, tapped on the frame of the door, and stepped in.

Pons looked up indignantly.

"I trust you will pardon my intrusion, gentlemen," said Major Shaplow rapidly. "I could not help observing your devotion to to the financial columns, sir," he went on, speaking directly Pons, "and it occurred to me that you might be looking for a promising investment."

"I happen to be doing so," said Pons stiffly.

The Major took out his card, and with a low bow presented it to Pons, saying, "Permit me, sir."

Pons took it with ill-concealed suspicion, gazed at it for a moment, and then muttered aloud what he read on it: "Major Arthur Howells Shaplow. The George. Chepsto, Mon." He handed the card across to me.

"Major," I said, perceiving that Pons meant me to, "this is Colonel Septimus Barr of London. My name is Parker."

"My pleasure, sir," said the Major, bowing punctiliously.

"Well, well, sit down," said Pons ungraciously. "You don't seem to be an investment counsellor."

"Colonel Barr is forever looking for a high return on his investments," I put in.

Pons flashed me a sudden keenly appreciative glance. Major Shaplow smiled. "Surely we all are."

He was indeed a handsome fellow, and I found it easy to believe that the ladies found him irresistibly attractive. He had a youthful appearance that surely belied his age; he appeared to be one of those fortunate men who age very slowly, who maintain the bloom of youth well into middle age. Moreover, his hands were manicured, his hair, though pomaded, was not offensive, his moustache waxed. I detected about him the faint astringence of a cologne or lotion, possibly used after shaving, but a trifle too feminine for my taste. He had to decide where to sit, and chose to sit next to me.

Opposite him, Pons favored him with a searching and still somewhat hostile stare. "You spoke of investments?" he said finally.

"You may have heard of me, Colonel," said the Major cautiously.

"Can't say I have," said Pons curtly.

"Ah, well, they try to keep matters as quiet as they can," said the Major lightly.

A gleam of interest shone in Pons' eyes. "'They,' sir? Who are 'they'?"

"I should say, Colonel, that this is as yet a highly confidential matter – viewed from both sides of the issue," said the Major with annoying caution.

"Dammed, sir, I don't know what you're talking about," said Pons in well-feigned vexation, his lips and beard atremble with impatience.

"I refer to the subject of the investment, Colonel," said the Major with simple dignity, "but I prefer not to broach the subject unless I can be certain of your interest."

"What rate of return?" snapped Pons.

"It may go as high as twenty percent," said Major Shaplow levelly.

"Indeed, indeed," replied Pons with obviously mounting interest. "What is it – utilities, steel, foreign bonds?"

"Colonel, forgive me – nothing so prosaic," demurred the Major.

"Come, come, man – we'll be in London before you get around to saying."

"Colonel, it is unique."

"Ah, I have heard such words before, sir."

"You have never heard of an investment like this."

"What the devil is it?"

"Colonel, may I bank on your complete confidence? And yours, Mr. Parker?"

"Of course, of course," said Pons testily.

"Very well, then – Gentlemen, it is a suit against the National Shires Bank. The sum involved is seven million pounds."

He said this in a hushed, conspiratorial voice which carried great conviction.

Pons fell back and sat for a moment open-mouthed. Then, leaning forward eagerly, he asked, "Can you win it?" In a masterly touch that conveyed more than anything else an old man's greed, he ran his tongue avariciously out over his lips.

"I cannot lose it," the Major answered, almost in a whisper. "I have been joined in the action by a person of the highest rank."

"Names, sir, names!" cried Pons.

"May I show you the papers, Colonel?"

"By all means!"

Major Shaplow rose. "Excuse me, gentlemen," he said, and darted out into the corridor.

"Pons, what are you up to?" I asked.

"I am after the money, Parker," he answered, chuckling. "And so is Major Shaplow."

"Twenty percent!" I cried. "Small wonder!"

"Hist," whispered Pons. "He will lose no time."

In less than a minute Major Shaplow returned, carrying a laden briefcase. He now carefully closed the door of our compartment before sitting down again, this time next to Pons, and opening his briefcase.

"Pray bear with me, Colonel," he said, as he began to take documents from the case. "I want to show you the papers in the matter so that there cannot be any doubt in your mind."

"I should warn you, Major," said Pons, "I'm a cautious man."

"Had I not concluded as much I would not have risked intruding upon you," said the Major.

Pons grunted eloquently.

Major Shaplow now drew from among the papers taken out of his briefcase one that he allowed Pons to look upon only briefly.

Pons gazed down. His eyes widened. His jaw dropped. "His Majesty!" he murmured, awed.

"No less, Colonel. It appears that the institution in question refused to handle war loans in the recent war, and His Majesty is determined to avenge this insult to our country. He has joined me in the suit."

Here Pons held up one hand imperiously. "Stay, Major. I do not yet know the basis of the suit."

"Four years ago the bank dishonored a cheque of mine drawn upon it. There were funds in the bank to meet it. I inaugurated the suit for damages; understandably, the bank fought it, and with every delay the sum has risen. With His Majesty's entry into the matter, the sum was fixed at its present figure."

"How long can the bank fight it?" asked Pons.

"Not more than another year."

"And you propose that I invest in your claim at a return of twenty percent?" said Pons.

"I believe I said it might come to twenty percent."

"Twenty percent," said Pons inexorably.

"Colonel, let me show you some of the other documents."

Thereupon he passed them to Pons, one after another, and Pons in turn passed them across to me. They were indeed amazing and impressive, for many of them bore famous signatures, among them those of Lord Sankey, Lord Hewart – the Lord Chief Justice, and many other dignitaries of the Royal Courts of Justice and Somerset house, as well as of the world of banking. One was clearly signed by His Majesty. There were also official paying-in slips of the Bank of England, one for as high as twenty thousand pounds; on several of them was the signature of the chief cashier, long familiar to me, since it appeared on our treasury notes.

"I wanted you to understand the magnitude of the suit," said Major Shaplow quietly. "I have exhausted my own funds. I cannot apply to His Majesty, for obvious reasons. So I must appeal to investors – and I am forced, by the exigencies of the matter, to make the appeal privately."

"These documents appear to be in order," said Pons, impressed.

"I assure you, Colonel, on my honor, they are. You have seen the signatures and the official seals. They are on record at Somerset House and the Courts of Justice."

"I am surprised that the bank has not offered to settle," said Pons.

"Oh, they have – but for a sum far, far below that I asked. They have made a settlement offer several times. At first it was for but a few thousand pounds, but as the principal named in the suit rose, so did their offer. It is now at a hundred thousand pounds."

"Ah!" cried Pons sharply. "So that even if the suit were not pressed and the settlement offered accepted, an investor could not lose!"

"No, sir," said Major Shaplow. "That is precisely the point."

Pons took a deep breath, bestowed a narrow-eyed look of intent calculation upon Major Shaplow, and said again, bluntly: "Twenty percent."

"On one condition, then," said the Major, conceding.

"Name it."

"That the sum invested be in banknotes."

"Agreed," snapped Pons. "How much?"

"Colonel, I need five thousand pounds."

Pons took a deep breath and exhaled it slowly.

"But if you do not have that much to invest, I shall be grateful for whatever you feel you can put into the suit," the Major went on.

"Three thousand," said Pons.

Major Shaplow hesitated only momentarily. Then he nodded.

"We shall have to have an agreement," said Pons.

Once more the Major nodded, "Of course. I will draw it up and bring it with me whenever you say."

"I will have time to go to my bank when we reach London," said Pons, choosing his words carefully. "Make a note of that, Parker. Three thousand pounds for Major Shaplow's action. Meet me tonight at seven, Major. I have a flat in Bayswater. My name is in the directory. Colonel Septimus Barr."

I found my voice at last. "Perhaps Major Shaplow will permit me to invest a thousand of my own?"

"And do you, too, insist upon twenty percent?" asked the Major sadly.

"Come, come, Major," put in Pons testily, "one can hardly make exceptions between friends."

"Very well, gentlemen."

"If I were a drinking man, Major, I'd ask you along to the refreshment car and drink to your millions," said Pons. "Good luck, sir! We'll meet tonight."

Major Shaplow closed his briefcase on his precious documents, rose, clicked his heels, and bowed. "Until tonight, Colonel Barr – Mr. Parker." Then he let himself out of our compartment.

"Extraordinary!" I cried. "Small wonder that Mrs. Shaplow wants a share of the proceeds!"

"I daresay it is safe to venture that she has been living on the anticipation for some time," agreed Pons.

"Twenty percent. You drive a hard bargain, Pons."

"So do you."

"I followed your example. I am a novice in these matters." I could not help adding, uneasily, "But I confess I do not see how you are acting for Mrs. Shaplow in this."

"At this point, Parker," said Pons, " – I should have thought it evident – I am not acting in her interests, but in my own." He chuckled. "I have seldom had the pleasure of meeting so engaging a fellow."

"Yet you were positively churlish."

"By design, Parker. I venture to say that any association between Rosie Shaplow and us is remote from his thoughts!"

"An astonishing action," I said. "And the mass of detail in the documents!"

"These matters demand care," said Pons. "We are nearing, London. I fancy we ought to have a witness to tonight's transaction. Perhaps Jamison is off duty and can be persuaded for us."

Once back in our quarters, Pons busied himself for a while on the telephone. Disdaining the luncheon Mrs. Johnson had prepared, he was in and out of 7B, without troubling to remove his disguise – paying a visit to his bank, and another

Colonel Barr's Bayswater flat, to assure himself of the Colonel's acquiescence in our use of his address and his absence that evening.

Then he sat down and wrote a brief note to our client.

"Ah," I cried, when I saw the address on the envelope, "I see it all now. You mean her to be here, tonight, and take possession of some of the money after it has changed hands!"

Pons favored me with an astonished stare. "This letter could hardly reach Mrs. Shaplow until tomorrow," he said dryly. "There are times, Parker, when you have marked relapses from the level of ratiocination to which you have progressed!"

"Perhaps I had better get over to the bank," I said then.

"I fancy a cheque will do. I do not recall Major Shaplow's having insisted upon bank notes from you."

"Well, that is a relief," I said. "I will just prepare a cheque."

By half before seven that evening we were in possession of Colonel Septimus Barr's Bayswater flat. Inspector Jamison, off duty, had met us there, his ruddy face disclosing his perplexity. He made several pointed comments about being asked to witness a transaction for Pons and demanded to know what the matter concerned.

"I was retained to obtain some money for a lady," said Pons, with a bland smile.

"Ah, and you need someone with legal standing to witness it," concluded Jamison. "I warn you, Pons – no shadiness, no skirting the law."

"I defer to no one in my respect for the law," said Pons crisply. "I think, though, that until the matter is concluded to our mutual satisfaction, we shall just keep you in the adjoining room, out of sight. Once money has changed hands, I'll want you to meet Major Shaplow."

Promptly at seven, Major Shaplow rang. I opened the door to him and he came in – still as dapper and fresh as he had been on the train this morning. He carried his bulging briefcase self-confidently into the room, and, reaching the place where Pons sat in an armchair, clad in the Colonel's dressing-gown, he bowed with a decidedly military air that bespoke his experience in service. His eyes merely flickered to the table nearby, on which Pons had arranged the bank-notes, beside which I had put down my own cheque.

"I trust, Colonel, you've not changed your mind," he said.

"Never change my mind once I make it up," said Pons brusquely. "You've brought the agreement?"

"I have, sir."

Major Shaplow opened his briefcase and drew forth four pages, comprising two sets of agreements – one to be signed by Pons, one by myself. He handed one to each of us and settled back to wait upon our reading it.

I read it with care. Major Shaplow appeared to have left no detail to chance, for the agreement was plainly and carefully worded and incapable of misconstruction in any particular. It assured the investor of a twenty percent return on his investment at the expiration of one year from date, or the successful conclusion of the pending suit against the National Shires Bank, which ever came first. Major Shaplow had already signed.

"This is admirably drawn up, Major," said Pons affably.

"Colonel, where money and honor are concerned, I prefer to leave nothing to chance – to avoid all possibility of error," said Major Shaplow.

"A commendable attitude," said Pons.

Thereupon he signed the agreements in a simulated crabbed hand and at the same time pointed to the money on the table.

"There is your money, sir. Three thousand pounds. Pray count it."

The Major went carefully through the bank notes and examined my cheque as I in turn signed the agreements.

"Perfectly correct," said he, packing the money away into his briefcase. "And the agreements, I believe, are in order," said Pons, folding one and slipping it into the pocket of his dressing gown.

Major Shaplow flashed a glance at the paper Pons handed him. He began to fold it, paused, and opened it again, his eyes glinting suddenly, his face tautening.

"Why, this is not the signature of Colonel Septimus Barr," he said. "I can hardly make it out."

"Ah, it is Solar Pons, Major," said Pons amiably. "I think your little game is up." He raised his voice. "Come out, Jamison."

Major Shaplow stood as if rooted to the spot, still holding the signed agreement in his hands, as Inspector Jamison came from the adjoining room.

"Inspector, I want you to meet Major Arthur Shaplow, one of the most accomplished confidence artists in all England. Major, this is Inspector Seymour Jamison of Scotland Yard."

With a single convulsive movement, Major Shaplow dropped both his correct poise and the paper he had been holding, swept up his briefcase, and bolted for the door. Unhappily, I had got up to come closer, and he ran full tilt into me, knocking me to the floor and sprawling on top of me – and with Jamison within seconds on his back.

By the time I had recovered my breath, both Jamison and Major Shaplow were gone.

"The sheer magnitude of Shaplow's fraud beggars the imagination," said Pons on our way home. "A suit for seven million pounds against the National Shires Bank – with His Majesty as party to the suit! And the care and detail with which the whole thing was worked out! What a waste of effort! That fellow could have achieved higher goals had he put his mind to it. His extraordinary conception proves again that the more grandiose the tale, the more readily people are taken in by it."

"But the documents," I protested weakly. "Those stamps and seals were certainly genuine."

"Ah, yes, Parker – the stamps and seals were, but the signatures were skillful forgeries. The average Englishman does not realize how easy it is to get a document stamped at Somerset House. The forms are for the most part obtainable at any law stationer's; one need but fill them out, hand them in with the amount required for stamps, and the documents are duly notarized or stamped. The documents are seldom read. I'll wager that, if I couched the decree in the appropriate verbiage, I could tomorrow go to Somerset House and present you – as Major Shaplow did his wife – with a decree of divorce from Mrs. Johnson!"

"Then Mrs. Shaplow is not, after all, divorced?"

"That was the burden of my note to her."

"But how did you proceed from her divorce to the Major's colossal fraud?" I asked.

"Ah, Parker, you will recall my reference to an intriguing little note in Mrs. Shaplow's letter. You failed to observe it. There is not and never has been any such regiment as the Second King's Horse Guards. I was confident that any man who could vaunt himself as a Major in a nonexistent regiment must be capable of even more imaginative ventures, and I suspected that 'the money' in the endless suit might be one of them."

V

THE ADVENTURE OF THE BENIN BRONZE

When I entered the quarters I shared with my friend Solar Pons at 7B, Praed Street one wild autumn evening late in our first decade together, I found my companion standing at the mantel with an opened letter in one hand. He had evidently just come in himself, for his deerstalker had been carelessly dropped on the table, and his Inverness was still on his shoulders.

"Ah, Parker," he said, without looking up, "the exuberance of your gait suggests the successful conclusion of another case."

"You may say so," I replied. "Old Jabez Black has taken a marked turn for the better. I have seen him through the worst."

Pons turned from the mantel, slipping off his Inverness. "We have the offer of a promising problem," he said, handing me the letter he had been reading.

The letter was a folded double-sheet of linen paper with a single embossed line at the top, announcing Mrs. Aaron Morley. Below yesterday's date, written in a manifestly hasty script, was:

> Dear Mr. Pons,
>
> "Unless I hear from you I hope to call on you at eight o'clock tomorrow evening. Uncle Randall will do

nothing – he treats the matter as a joke, but my intuition tells me it is not. No such frog is native to England, and that cannot be denied. Forgive me. I am frightened.

Miriam Morley

I looked up. "If that isn't just like a woman! It is all a-scatter."

"But intriguing, is it not?" said Pons, his eyes dancing. "And I fancy it is perfectly plain to our client. Something menaces her uncle and, however incredible it may sound, a frog not native to England has something to do with it. That is surely simple enough. What do you make of the scent?"

I had been conscious of the not unpleasant fragrance that rose from the notepaper. "Perfumed," I said.

"I submit it is rather a pungence than a perfume," said Pons.

I raised the letter to my nostrils.

"Yes, you are right," I agreed. "It is the pungence of bayberry.

"Is it not a curious scent for a woman's stationery?"

"Women frequently have very odd tastes in these matters," I said.

"I defer to your judgment," said Pons.

"I see she has given you no chance to refuse her an appointment. There is no return address."

"Posted at Basingstoke late yesterday," said Pons. "She is scarcely an hour away by train or car, and perhaps she can afford the loss of a couple of hours should she fail here. It is now close upon the hour and I fancy we will presently hear of the problem that besets her."

"She has written this in some agitation," I said, surrendering the letter to Pons at last, "and in haste."

"Ah, that is elementary," said Pons, smiling. "You will also have noticed the slanting of the script peculiar to left-handed people as well as those trivial affectations – such as the circular dot above the i – common to younger writers. Even her agitation was not great enough to permit their omission."

"I believe I hear a car at the kerb," I said.

Pons stood listening.

The outer door opened below. In a few seconds a woman's light step sounded on the stairs. Within moments a gentle tap at the door brought me across the room to throw it open, revealing our client.

Mrs. Aaron Morley was a woman of perhaps thirty – a sharp-featured blonde whose vivid blue eyes at once fixed upon Pons, the sight of whom brought a tremulous smile to her thin but beautifully-shaped lips. Her skin was fair, and the clothing she wore was costly.

"Pray come in, Mrs. Morley," invited Pons.

"Thank you, Mr. Pons."

"That is Dr. Parker at the door," he went on. "We have been intrigued by your message and were waiting on your arrival."

I sprang forward to pull out a chair for her. She thanked me and settled gratefully into it, drawing off her gloves, and beginning without preamble to speak. It was immediately evident that such composure as she had was false, for she launched into her account at a point clearly several removes from its proper beginning.

"I have tried and tried to tell Uncle Randall Creighton that he must ask for help," she said, "but he's so stubborn, Mr. Pons – why, the very mention of your name threw him into a rage, and he will not hear of the police. Of course, the servants are at the Hall – but the house is so surrounded by shrubbery and trees that anyone could hide there for some time without being discovered. He will not see how dangerous it is."

"Forgive me," interrupted Pons. "Surely it would be best to begin at the beginning."

She stopped short, blushing, took a deep breath, and said, "I suppose it would. But I can't be sure when it began, unless it was with the post one day last July, when my uncle received a letter with a drawing in it. Nothing else."

"What kind of drawing?" asked Pons.

"I have tried to make a sketch of it. He destroyed it, after studying it for a while and showing it to us; but I remembered it."

From her handbag she took a folded paper – another piece of her stationery, I saw – and flattened it on the table before Pons. I could see it as clearly as he. It looked like a design of some kind. Across the top of the paper there were three globular objects, like dewdrops; these crowned what was clearly the drawing of a human eye enclosed in lashless eyelids; and below this representation there was a small V of perfectly executed little circles.

Pons looked at it in silence for a long minute. Then he gazed at our client. "He said nothing of this?"

"Not to me. Not to Aaron. I overheard him mutter just one word. It was 'Benin'."

Pons's eyebrows rose. "Ah, he was in Africa?"

"He was in military service there just thirty years ago. He took part in some battle or other which was hideously bloody. Indeed, Mr. Pons, he was so affected by it that for many years he fancied he could smell the blood, and ever since he has burned incense ...."

"Bayberry," said Pons dryly.

"Yes, that is it. Everything in the house reeks of it—though I have tried with little success to get the reek out of our quarters. Uncle Randall burned it, of course, to take that other smell away. But there was no other smell. Laburnum, perhaps, rhododendron in season – nothing more."

"Proceed with your story, Mrs. Morley."

"I suppose he received other drawings like this—I saw some of the envelopes; they were like the first one, without a return on them, written in what appeared to be a very strong hand, but with a foreign appearance – "

"Postmark?" put in Pons.

"London. Of course, I couldn't be sure, he showed me nothing, just destroyed them as they came. Then, sometime in August, we began to hear the frog. I was in the study with Uncle Randall one night when we heard it the first time. I didn't know what it was, of course. He did. He named it right away – some kind of hairy frog not native to England."

"*Trichobatrachus robustus*?" ventured Pons.

"Yes, that's it, Mr. Pons—that's what he called it."

"Did he seem alarmed at the cry?"

"No. More puzzled and surprised. Later on, though, I thought him distinctly uneasy. We kept on hearing the call."

"Every night?"

She shook her head. "Only now and then."

"How often?"

"Well, perhaps twice a week. Uncle Randall finally went out to look for it – he and Michael, the gardener – and once Aaron went out on a Sunday afternoon to go over the grounds with him. That frog is rather a large one, I understand – larger than our native frogs, and they would have seen it, as thoroughly as they hunted. They didn't. My uncle finally refused to consider that it might actually be the frog because it would not survive at liberty in this climate. He said the cry of that frog was also used as a signal by members of an African secret society before the turn of the century. The British had put an end to it at Benin city. In the past fortnight, every time Uncle Randall has heard the frog call he has become dreadfully restless and disturbed – he would turn up the phonograph to drown it out, and pace about muttering – that sort of thing. Or dash outside in an effort to find the source of the call. I cannot help feeling that there is some sinister danger threatening him, Mr. Pons, and I would like you to look into the matter."

Pons took a turn about the room before he replied. "I very much fear, Mrs. Morley, that without his co-operation there is little we can do. But tell me – if he was at Benin in 1897, where were you?"

She smiled. "Mr. Pons, I was born a little later. Both my parents went down on the *Titanic*. Then for five years I lived with my mother's sister. After her death, I came to live with Uncle Randall, my father's brother. That was – let me see – about 1917. He has been like a father to me. Even after I married two years ago – my husband is an officer of the Merchants' Bank in Basingstoke – he insisted that we should live with him. My uncle is rather reclusive by nature, and it is rather more as if he were our guest than otherwise."

"The three of you make up his family?"

"Not entirely. My brother Paul also lives there. Paul is a solicitor in Basingstoke. He has not married, but it is understood that when he does so he will make his home elsewhere."

Pons tugged at the lobe of his left ear as he frequently did when deep in thought. "Is your uncle accustomed to speak of his military service?" he asked then.

"Oh, no. Quite the contrary, Mr. Pons," cried our client, leaning forward a little, wide-eyed. "It was altogether such a horrible experience that he has always refused to talk about it. I do believe this harassment – for it is that – disturbs him because he is reminded of those terrible events."

"No doubt," said Pons. "Now, tell me, Mrs. Morley, do you know whether your uncle brought back from service in Africa the typical souvenirs many soldiers do bring home?"

"Oh, yes, indeed. He has some particularly ugly pieces. They are on a shelf in his study – not really very visible, to tell the truth, as if they too reminded him of those bygone events."

"Thirty years ago! I submit that is rather a long time to be disturbed, Mrs. Morley."

"My uncle is an uncommon man, Mr. Pons." She clasped her hands suddenly and cried, "Oh, I hope I have not done the wrong thing in coming here!"

"I assure you, you have not," said Pons gravely. "I only wish there were some way in which I could be of immediate assistance. Perhaps we had better come down to Basingstoke tomorrow and pay your uncle a visit."

"He is in danger, then?"

"I fear he is in the gravest danger, Mrs. Morley," said Pons.

Our client sprang to her feet, her clasped hands pressed to her breast. "Oh, Mr. Pons! I knew it! It's what happened in Africa – I know it!"

"Why do you say so?"

"Because we have seen a strange black man in the vicinity," she said. "Aaron saw him first. Then one day when we were both in Basingstoke, we caught sight of him slipping into a side-street. Aaron said at once, 'That is the man I saw at the wall.'"

Pons shook his head slowly from side to side. "Pray implore your uncle not to go again in search of that frog, Mrs. Morley."

"Oh, he is so stubborn, so stubborn!" she cried.

"You have given us no address, Mrs. Morley," said Pons then. "Though I assume that you live in the country."

"It is Creighton Hall, Mr. Pons, on the London road. You will have no difficulty finding it. It is a large estate. Ten acres with a substantial copse, a garden, and extensive lawns. A brick wall separates it from the road, and the name is on the gatepost."

"Thank you, Mrs. Morley. We will call just after noon tomorrow."

Once our client had departed, I took up the drawing she had left on the table. "What do you make of this, Pons?" I asked.

"That is a drawing of African facial decoration," he said at once. "The three droplets above the eye – which would be repeated above the other eye, were the face full – represent tribal marks. The V of concentric circles below the eye – which would similarly be on the other cheek – are typical African decorations."

"Found at Benin," I ventured.

He nodded.

"Then we may assume that something Creighton did there has come back to haunt him," I said.

"We may indeed. Does not everything point to it? But it is strange, is it not, that Creighton is not more disturbed by the events at Creighton Hall? Mrs. Morley reports no fear, no alarm, no panic – only surprise, perplexity, and at best a little uneasiness and perturbation."

"Why, that is simple," I said. "Creighton evidently committed some crime against that African society of which he was not aware – you remember Mrs. Morley's saying that the call of that frog was a signal used by a secret society of Benin."

"I do."

"They have finally caught up with him."

"What would you say they want of him?" asked Pons.

"Perhaps the return of what he took."

"Some 'particularly ugly pieces,' I think Mrs. Morley said."

"What is ugly to us may not be ugly to them. It is as simple as that."

"I submit it would have been far simpler to break in and take what they want," said Pons. "No, though that is a splendidly imaginative concept of yours, Parker, I fear more is wanted of Randall Creighton than some artifacts or works of primitive art. I daresay nothing short of his life will do. But are they not taking an interminable time in going about it?"

"I would say so," I agreed. "And what is so horrible in Creighton's experience that he cannot bear to recall it?"

"If he was in West Africa in 1897, it could hardly have been anything other than the reduction of Benin city. We have been in Benin since 1853, and a rewarding trade has grown up with Benin – in ivory, palm-oil, and pepper. But we were appalled by the custom of human sacrifices that prevailed in that country. Sir Richard Burton, when he was British consul at Fernando Po in 1863, went to Benin in an attempt to end that custom, but he failed. Since 1885 the coast of Benin has been under our protection, and at that time every attempt was made to placate the king, though it was not until 1892 that King Overami agreed to a treaty. He did not live up to it. Two years later it was necessary to banish Nana, a Lower Benin chieftain. Then, in 1897, our consul-general, J. R. Phillips, together with eight Europeans, was brutally slain while on the way to visit Overami. As a result Admiral Sir Harry Rawson led a punitive expedition of over a thousand men up the Benin river to fight their way into Benin city. The annual 'customs' had just been celebrated, and the city was found to be filled with the bloody remains of many human sacrifices. Six chiefs were executed, and Overami was banished to Calabar. I daresay Creighton was in that punitive expedition, and it is the sight of Benin city, reeking with gore and the cannibalistic saturnalia that took place before the arrival of the expedition, that he does not wish to remember."

I shuddered. "And, of course, we don't know what some of our men, in the heat of outrage, may have done to the surviving celebrants."

"Precisely," he agreed. "But there are two or three little points about Mrs. Morley's narrative that disturb me."

"The whole thing disturbs me," I retorted. "About those pieces Creighton brought back from Benin – they are surely of no value."

"I would not say so. A Benin bronze went for five thousand pounds recently at Sotheby's."

"You don't mean it!"

"I am not in the habit of saying what I do not mean," he replied testily.

"Then we have a possible other motive."

"You are only fishing, my dear fellow. These waters may be deeper than we know." He picked up the drawing I had dropped to the table a few moments before and studied it in contemplative silence.

I waited in vain for him to speak. "Couldn't it be possible that these tribal marks refer to a tribe associated with that secret society in Benin which came to some harm because of some action of Creighton's?" I asked finally. "That sounds logical to me."

"I am sure it does," said Pons.

"A warning of what is to come," I went on.

"Why? Why send any warning at all? Is that not the stuff of fiction rather than of life?"

"Life is often stranger and more dramatic than fiction, so much so that fiction often fails to reflect it," I replied.

"*Touché*," said Pons. "And it must be admitted that life occasionally imitates fiction," he added. "But we have too few facts to support any meaningful speculation and it is rather those we have not yet had put to us directly that are likely to solve the problem. Let us just wait until we can call upon Creighton tomorrow."

But our plans were not destined to come about as we had expected, for it was not yet dawn of the following day when I was awakened by the telephone, and, thinking one of my patients had suffered an emergency, I answered.

"Mr. Pons, Mr. Pons – please, *please* come at once!" The voice was that of our recent client. "Aaron has disappeared. I've sent a car for you."

I was still attempting to explain that I was not Pons when she rang off.

Pons was up and standing at my elbow when I turned from the telephone. "Mrs. Morley, I take it," he said. "Something has happened to Creighton."

"No – it is Aaron who is gone. Mrs. Morley is sending a car for us."

"Aaron!" cried Pons, his face a mask of perplexity.

"Yes – they have got the wrong man," I said.

Pons said nothing at all. His face was an inscrutable mask.

Creighton Hall, seen in the early morning sunshine, proved to be surprisingly impressive, for it was obviously the home of a wealthy man – a country house of two storeys, a mansard roof, and many gables and rooms set in the midst of a lush green estate.

Our client met us at the door.

"Oh, Mr. Pons!" she cried, "I was too late coming to you."

"We shall see," said Pons, glancing at the man who stood behind her – a thick-necked man of upper middle age, who was visibly keeping his hostility in check.

"This is my Uncle Randall," said our client hurriedly, and introduced us.

"Now you're here," he said ungraciously, "come in." He stood aside and drew his niece close to him so that we could pass.

Pons, however, made no move to enter the house. "Your husband has not returned?" he asked our client.

"No, Mr. Pons. And there has been no word from him. It is unlike him."

"Forgive me," he interrupted. "There is one little detail I must see to while the dew is still heavy enough."

So saying, he turned abruptly, and strode rapidly down the path to the gate. He vanished between the gateposts, only to reappear within moments, walking rapidly along the brick wall separating the grounds of Creighton Hall from the road.

Turning, I saw that Randall Creighton's bushy eyebrows were quizzically raised; our client was no less puzzled. I could hardly explain that Pons's erratic behavior was integral to his methods.

Pons was now out of sight, screened by the thick growth of trees farther along the boundary wall. Our client looked in the direction he had gone, stepping out over the threshold, one hand pressed against her lips. She turned her head slowly and looked at me.

"Wherever is Mr. Pons going, Dr. Parker?" she asked, with a helpless gesture.

"I suspect, Mrs. Morley, that he is on the scent," I said.

I could not help observing a flicker of amusement on Creighton's face – a barely perceptible twitch.

A second man came to join our client and her uncle, a young man not yet thirty, with yellow hair, blue eyes, and a slightly outthrust jaw that made him look somewhat pugnacious. He was undoubtedly our client's brother, and so he was introduced. "We're waiting for Mr. Pons, Paul," explained Mrs. Morley, adding ingenuously, "He has run off."

"I've telephoned the police," he said.

"Oh, you shouldn't have," cried Mrs. Morley.

"Quote proper," I put in. "The thing to do."

Creighton harrumphed.

It was almost a quarter of an hour before Pons reappeared between the gateposts. As he came up, I saw that his shoes were quite wet with dew.

"That black man you and your husband saw, Mrs. Morley," he said, "can you describe him?"

Mrs. Morley was somewhat taken aback. She paused to introduce her brother, then said, "Why, I caught only a glimpse of him. To tell the truth, I couldn't even say for certain that he was black. I took Aaron's word for it. Black men all look alike to me, in any case."

"They are as different, one from another, as men of any other color," said Pons patiently. "Was he tall or short – thick-featured or fine?"

"He seemed taller than the average – stouter, too. Aaron spoke of him as very thick-lipped and with a broad flat nose. He had seen him before, as I told you."

"Ah," said Pons. "Large of foot?"

"Aaron said so, yes."

"And did he say that he walked with a kind of loping gait – like someone accustomed to making progress over rough land, perhaps?"

"I believe he mentioned something of that kind," said Mrs. Morley.

"I thought as much," said Pons grimly.

To this dialogue Randall Creighton listened with undisguised amazement. Clearly he had not been told of the black man's presence in the village. He looked at his niece, obviously puzzled.

"I submit, Mr. Creighton, that there are some questions you might answer, if you will," said Pons.

"I suppose so," assented Creighton ungraciously. "We'll go into my study."

He led the way as he spoke. The book-lined study was clearly Creighton's den. It had his burly look in its appointments and its atmosphere. I saw that a book lay face down on the end table next to an easy chair, and I read its title with quickening pulse; it was Major John Mellanby's *The Campaign in West Africa*.

"Sit down, gentlemen," invited Creighton and himself sat down where the book lay open. Seeing the book, Creighton gave it an explicable glance of annoyance, shut it and thrust it out of sight.

"Your reluctance to speak of the Benin campaign is quite understandable, Mr. Creighton," said Pons, choosing to stand rather than sit. "But we hear of a West African frog – *Trichobatrachus robustus*."

"Yes, I heard it. No question about that," answered Creighton. "We all heard it, if it comes to that. The point is, it shouldn't have been heard. Not in these latitudes. It cannot survive here, to my knowledge. I don't make a point of being a biologist, but certain things are elementary."

"A nocturnal caller?"

"At least here, sir," said Creighton. He gave Pons an oddly defiant stare. "You may know that the call of that frog was a signal used by members of a secret society of Benin."

Pons nodded.

"All the members of which were destroyed in the campaign against Overami," added Creighton flatly.

"All?" asked Pons.

"All," said Creighton categorically. "I was part of that sickening campaign, sir. I know what I'm talking about."

"Yet everyone here heard it?" pressed Pons.

"Except Meadows," answered Creighton. "His hearing isn't what it ought to be."

"Meadows is our house man," explained Mrs. Morley.

Pons turned to Paul Creighton. "Can you imitate it, Mr. Creighton?"

"I can try," said Creighton.

His attempt was roughly cut off by his uncle. "No similarity at all. None whatever. And what has it to do with Aaron's not coming home? And what, if I may make so bold to ask, has all this interference to say that Aaron just hasn't for reasons that seem sound enough to him chosen not to come home?"

"You have a collection of Benin artifacts, Mr. Creighton," said Pons, turning upon the older man.

"Had," said Creighton crisply. "Had them over in that cabinet against the near wall."

The cabinet was manifestly empty.

Paul Creighton broke in. "There's no mystery about their being gone. Uncle Randall asked me to take them to Sotheby's when I went into London yesterday. He has decided to put them up for sale."

"That's right," said the elder Creighton.

"I don't know how you could stand them for so long, Uncle Randall," said our client. "They were hideous – hideous!"

"Yes, perhaps they are," said Creighton. "It depends on the point of view."

Pons turned to the older man once more. "You received certain drawings in the mail, Mr. Creighton."

Creighton shot a glance of baffled anger at his niece, as much as to say, "This is your work!" He said only, "Child's play. They were supposed to represent Benin art. Crudely done. I don't wish to speak of them."

A diffident cough from the threshold attracted our attention.

An elderly servant stood there, waiting for us to turn toward him before saying, "Constable Miles Danbury is at the door."

"Thank you, Meadows," said our client.

Mrs. Morley started for the door, followed by her brother.

"I'd like a word with you, Meadows," said Pons, making it clear by his demeanor that he preferred to speak with Meadows privately.

Randall Creighton grunted, nodded permissively to Meadows, and left the room.

Meadows came cautiously forward, his dark eyes uncertain.

"How long have you been with Mr. Creighton, Meadows?" asked Pons.

"Twenty-five years, sir."

"What kind of man is he?"

Meadows hesitated, searching for words. "Firm, sir – very firm," he said finally.

"Harsh?"

"Only with those who needed it."

"As, for example?"

"Well, for one, Alan Garston. Garston drove for him until Mr. Creighton discharged him last spring."

"Anyone else?"

"Garston was the only one he ever discharged, sir." The old servant did not intend to say more.

"How large is Mr. Creighton's family, Meadows?"

"He has just Miss Miriam and Mr. Paul, sir."

The sound of voices moved upon the study from the hall.

"Thank you, Meadows," said Pons.

"Ordinary fishing," I murmured. "It is unlike you, Pons."

"One must have all the facts in order to reach any conclusion about them," he replied imperturbably. "But the police are now here; the search can begin."

Constable Danbury followed our client into the room. He was tall and slightly stooped, as if in protest against his height. His plain features lit up with a smile at sight of Pons, and he came striding over to him with hand outstretched.

"Danbury, Mr. Pons," he said. "You've not heard of me, but I've heard of you."

"Now you are here, Danbury, we can get on with the search for Mr. Morley. I take it you've been given the details?"

"Yes, Mr. Pons."

"Good. I fancy the copse is the primary object for searching. I daresay Morley will have been drawn to the rear of the house rather than to the front, which is at least partly in sight of the road. I think, Mrs. Morley," he went on, turning to our client, "you had better remain here, in the event Mr. Morley returns to the house."

So saying, he led the way out of the study and unerringly through the house to the door that opened to the garden, beyond which the thick copse loomed. Through the garden he went, following a well-defined path, and to the edge of the copse.

"Let us just walk in ten feet from one another," proposed Pons. "We will go along the farther edge there, turn when we have gone through the copse, and come back, following this pattern until we have covered the ground."

We struck into the wooded area of the property, which covered perhaps seven acres of it, but was considerably overgrown. I took the edge of the woods, adjacent to the grassy pasture. Next to me walked Randall Creighton – then Pons, then Constable Danbury, and finally Paul Creighton.

"Why do you say Morley was *drawn* from the house, Mr. Pons?" asked Danbury.

"By the call of a frog," said Pons, explaining.

"It goes back to Uncle's service in Africa," volunteered Palk Creighton. "Aaron constantly urged Uncle Randall to talk about it. He felt it troubled Uncle."

The elder Creighton harrumphed again, as he vanished into the copse.

"There has been someone thrashing about in here," said Danbury. "Look there – and there." He pointed to broken and turned branches. "Somebody used to the jungle would move easier than that."

"Quite right, Danbury," agreed Pons. "We may take it Morley is more likely to have gone through here.

"Have you seen any strange black men in Basingstoke, Constable?" asked Pons.

"From time to time. I don't know that I'd call them 'strange' except as they're strange to me," answered the Constable soberly. "I can't pretend to know everyone in Basingstoke. And the market brings in many people from outside."

"Black?"

"Some."

We reached the far end of the copse, swung around, and made our way to the garden once more. There were further signs of someone's traveling through the copse, this way and that. I could imagine Morley out here in the dark, blundering after an elusive frog call that led him one way and another.

From the garden, we turned back again. By this time we were in the other half of the copse. We went in silence now, intent on our task. Pons, I saw, was unnaturally grim, and the Constable took his cue from Pons.

We had gone a little more than half way through the copse on our third run when a sharp, half-strangled cry rang out.

"*Christ*!"

It was Paul Creighton, who stood immobile, frozen in shock, staring down at the earth before him.

Pressing forward, we saw what lay there – the body of a young man, literally hacked apart. Blood spattered a wide area – one arm was cut away – the head was almost severed from the body – at least a score of brutal cuts had gone through clothing and flesh. Protruding from beneath the body was the curious bronze head of a Negro.

Paul Creighton began to back away.

"Aaron Morley, I have no doubt," said Pons.

"Yes, that's what's left of him," said the Constable. "I knew him. This is savage work – no civilized man could have done this."

Randall Creighton, swallowing hard, pointed tremblingly at the bronze head and looked accusingly at Paul Creighton. "You said – you took them to Sotheby's."

"I did. Six of them. That's all there were."

"There were seven."

"I took six." He turned and ran blindly back through the copse toward the house.

"Mr. Creighton, I fear it will be your unpleasant duty to inform your niece," said Pons.

Creighton turned and stumbled away.

"That bronze head, Danbury, is a work of primitive art from Benin, the British Protectorate in West Africa where Creighton fought thirty years ago," said Pons. "It represents an *oba* or chieftain of Benin. Though I doubt that you will find any fingerprints on it, handle it with care."

The Benin bronze was a superbly savage piece, approximately sixteen inches in height. The head rose out of a high choker that carried all the way to the thick lower lip; it was framed in six strands meant to resemble coral along each side of the face. A reticulated headdress, decorated with coral beads, crowned the head. What struck me instantly, however, apart from its brutal strength as a primitive work of art, was the facial decoration – the Vs of concentric circles beneath the eyes, the three tear-like bronze globules ranged above each lashless eye – the same pattern drawn upon the strange message sent to Creighton. "That black fellow must have left it here," said Danbury. "How can we be expected to find him!"

"Do not look for him, Danbury," said Pons quietly.

The Constable glanced at Pons as if he thought his ears had betrayed him.

"There is no black man, Danbury. He is the product of one man's vivid imagination. I commend him to your attention."

Danbury flashed a curious look at Pons. "I don't follow that, sir."

"Let me draw some facts – however trivial they may seem – to your attention, Constable. It was the late Aaron Morley who saw the black man, who pointed him out to his wife. The calling of the frog, designed to point to the kind of crude and bestial African ritual murder common to nineteenth century Benin, was meant to lure Randall Creighton to his death ...."

"They killed the wrong man," cried Danbury.

"Not 'they', Constable. An examination of the terrain indicates clearly that only one murderer was involved. Morley was murdered after midnight; by that time the dew had formed. A quick walk around the estate on our arrival revealed no break in the dew – no one walked away from the grounds since midnight. It will be your task to establish a motive, Danbury.

I submit that you ought to look into the victim's background as well. Leave no stone unturned.

"Murder was intended here. There was elaborate preparation. So much is patent. I leave the investigation in your hands."

"I have never known you to be so ambiguous as in your charge to Danbury," I said on our way back to London. "If anything, you only added to his perplexity."

"The commission of murder," answered Pons, "apart from that capital crime committed in passion – anger or a jealous rage – or that committed in reaction to being surprised at or escaping from some other crime, like burglary – is not readily embarked upon. The preparations indicated in our client's account pointed clearly to the murderer's plan to lure Randall Creighton from the house, strike him down in the dark, and lay the blame on the black man Morley had conjured up."

"Our client saw him too," I pointed out.

"She saw a black man her husband said was the same man he had previously claimed to have seen lurking about the wall along the road at Creighton Hall. But so incredible a motive after as we were expected to believe – a murder for vengeance after thirty years – was so improbable that the stage required extensive setting. The imitation of the frog call over a period of time. The black man deliberately conjured up. All this demanded imaginative care – and a powerful motive."

"Pons, you are speaking in riddles," I protested.

"Come, come – it is plain as a pikestaff. You should have noted other discrepancies – our client, for example, told us her uncle disliked to talk about his African experience; Paul Creighton said, on the contrary, that Morley 'constantly urged' the elder Creighton to talk about it. Our client and her brother had no reason for lying – Morley did. The motive, of course, must have its origin in Morley's pattern. Morley has been embezzling money from his bank and couldn't wait until

Creighton died and at least half his estate came to Mrs. Morley, whose visit to us undoubtedly precipitated the crime, with its simulation of African ritual murder. A quick auditing should determine the state of Morley's accounts."

"But it was Morley who was murdered!" I cried.

"So it was," said Pons enigmatically. "I am not sure I should call it 'murder'. If Danbury follows it through correctly, the plea will be 'self-defense', I have no doubt."

"You can't mean that Randall Creighton..."

"Who else? He was set upon by Morley, but he was ready for him. The old man obviously had his suspicions. The attack incensed him. Moreover, he very probably knew that, thwarted in this, Morley would try again. He did to Morley what Morley meant to do to him. In matters of this kind, one either accepts the premise laid down, or one does not. The premise implicit in our client's account required too much credulity. Consider – in order to believe that some black from Benin would exact vengeance upon Creighton, it would be necessary to believe that in some manner the black had chanced upon the identity of a given British soldier engaged in the reduction of Benin city, that he had so imbued his son or some younger relative with the desire for vengeance that he had induced him to undertake the long journey from Benin, learn Creighton's whereabouts, and carry out his mission. That is asking too much of anyone. Small wonder our client's uncle was puzzled and not frightened! The drawing he received in the mail was meaningless – simply something Morley had fatuously copied from the bronze he intended to use. And, having no sense of personal guilt because of that horrible Benin affair, there was no reason for Creighton to be disturbed.

"Since vengeance and passion seemed very improbable motives for doing away with Creighton, one had but to fall back upon such all too common motives as greed or the removal of someone who constituted a danger to the murderer. Creighton surely menaced no one, but his wealth was an obvious temptation. Finally, Morley, with his uncertain hours, thought he had ample opportunity to carry out his plan, which included the imitated frog calls, the previous secreting of that Benin bronze – with the intention of plainly connecting Creighton's death to his involvement in Benin – and the laying out of that book Creighton certainly wouldn't have been reading, to judge by our client's account of him. I do not recall a crime more sanguinary in all my years of involvement in these little inquiries."

"But, Pons – how could you fail to tell Danbury!"

"I submit he has the facts – or he will get them. It is not my purpose to interfere in the course of justice. It must be admitted that Morley got what was coming to him – he sadly underrated Randall Creighton and became his victim instead of his murderer. I am merely a private enquiry agent. I do not look upon myself as an agent of justice, which in this case seems to have been served."

VI

THE ADVENTURE OF THE MISSING TENANTS

In the early hours of a winter night within the first decade I shared with my friend, Solar Pons, I was awakened by his hand on my shoulder, and his voice at my ear, "We are about to have a visitor who will not be put off. You may care to sit in, Parker."

"What time is it?" I asked, struggling awake.

"Two o'clock."

"Two o'clock!" I cried. "What is it, then?"

"Some little crisis at the Foreign Office," replied Pons. "Bancroft is on his way."

I was just emerging into our sitting-room, tying the cord of my dressing-gown, when Pons's brother, Bancroft, having come noiselessly up the stairs of 7B, opened the door and stepped into our quarters. He was an impressively tall, formidable man, with a mind far keener than my companion's, for which I had had Pons's word on several occasions.

He nodded in my direction and said to Pons without preamble. "Ercole d'Oro, the Italian consul, has disappeared. The Italian government has begun to make some inquiries, and the situation is delicate."

"You ought to have called in the Pinkertons," said Pons. "They never sleep."

"They can afford not to; the Foreign Office cannot," said Bancroft. "You are needlessly waspish. We have not seen fit to apply to the Yard. There is good reason here for the utmost discretion in this inquiry."

"I fancy there is a woman other than the Countess involved," observed Pons.

"Elementary. Spare me these trifling exercises of yours," said Bancroft testily. "But, of course, there may be some involvement with a woman, since d'Oro was last seen entering the house in Orrington Crescent which he had been using for some months as a rendezvous for his amatory exploits."

"Ah, these Italians," mused Pons. "I fancy their Foreign Office could be demoralized by an attractive woman."

"You know of Count d'Oro?"

"I met him socially some years ago. Since 1921, he has been the Italian consul. Born in 1882. Now forty-four. Privately tutored, some study at the University of Genoa. At one time rumored to have some connection with the Mafiosa. His hobby: entomology. One of his monographs is used as a standard reference in the field. Married in 1900 to Harriet Jackson, niece of the Earl of Ellenbroke. No children."

"Yes, yes," interrupted Bancroft, "I know these details."

"Of the house in Orrington Crescent, however, I know nothing," said Pons. "Presumably you do." Suddenly a light broke upon Pons's face. "Unless, that is, it is number 27."

"It is."

"Ah, that puts a different light on the matter. A house notorious in the annals of London's unsolved mysteries. Let us now have the details."

"D'Oro left home three days ago, early in the evening, bound for the house in Orrington Crescent. His wife was told his destination, of course – she had been given to understand when d'Oro leased the house a month ago, that it was to be used for clandestine meetings concerned with the affairs of government – bluntly, espionage. I rather think the woman is convinced that some foreign agent is at the bottom of d'Oro's disappearance. It is not impossible."

"Which means that someone at the Foreign Office – characteristically – entertains the same suspicion."

Bancroft brushed this impatiently away. "D'Oro was reported missing two days ago, after a full day during which he had not appeared either at his home or at his official quarters. No doubt the facts of his vanishing had also been transmitted to his government, for since yesterday we have had representations made to His Majesty's Government about d'Oro's safety.

"We have naturally examined the house. He had certainly reached it, and he was alone there – one does not customarily engage in this kind of dalliance in the company of a third person – and he had made some preparations to receive the lady – a Miss Violet Carson of Upper Hampstead, a secretary by profession. The hour of their rendezvous had been set for ten o'clock, and the lady – in accordance with the usual arrangements – arrived by cab at that hour, and let herself into the house. All evidence plainly indicated that her arrival was expected – the house was lit with subdued lights, d'Oro had bathed and was clad only in dressing-robe and slippers. All was as usual, except that he himself was not there. This was Miss Carson's seventh rendezvous with d'Oro. She said, on interrogation, that she had 'got ready' – by which I take it she had undressed and got into bed, which had been turned back, and lay there waiting for d'Oro to make his appearance. She thought that perhaps he had gone below stairs for champagne or something other to serve her, as was his custom, but presently, hearing no sound in the house beyond the ticking of a clock, she got out of bed, slipped into the robe d'Oro kept for the use of such women as shared his nights there, and went to look for him. She searched the house. There was no sign of him. His car – a small Fiat – was in the adjoining garage, and the garage locked; it is still there. Some of our people have been through the house. Nothing untoward has been found. No sign of forced entry. Nothing. It is as if d'Oro simply vanished all in an instant. Miss Carson waited for an hour; then she dressed again, called a cab, and went back to her flat.

"A significant factor – if we can rely on Miss Carson – is that d'Oro telephoned her at a quarter to nine to let her know he had reached the Orrington house. Between that hour and her arrival a light snow fell. Miss Carson says that there were no footprints in the snow on the walk leading to the house, which suggests that d'Oro either left soon after he had telephoned – which is unlikely in view of his having bathed and shaved after he had telephoned – presumptively – or went by another door. Of course, by the time his absence had been reported, the snow had thawed away.

"But you shall see for yourself. I am going home. The car will return for you within the hour. That will give you ample time to dress and take breakfast, if you need it. Here are the keys."

He threw them to the table, and took his leave as noiselessly and unceremoniously as he had come.

"We are all presumed to be at the instant services of His Majesty's Government, Parker," said Pons, smiling. "Come, let us get dressed."

"You said it was a house 'notorious in the annals of London's unsolved mysteries,'" I said.

"So it is. A writer in the *Chronicle* – one of those devotees of that vein of fantasy known as science-fiction – scarcely three months ago wrote a sensational article about it under the heading, *Orrington Crescent House Hole in Space?*, speculating about a favorite gambit of investigators of curious, unexplained facts – like Charles Fort – that strange, motiveless disappearances – of, for instance, persons seen walking in at one end of a street and never seen to emerge at the other, vanishing utterly – as having stepped into 'holes in space' or into other dimensions, or some such phenomenal 'openings' in time or space. Number 27 lends itself very well to such an article for the press. D'Oro is the fourth resident of it to disappear in the course of less than five years. All, if memory serves me, vanished in very much the same fashion, without motive, without trace."

He crossed the room and took down one of the files in which he kept cuttings about crimes and criminals. As I dressed in my room, I could hear his going through clippings that were never in the best of order, though Pons maintained a loosely alphabetical arrangement frequently disorganized by the hasty addition of new data. From time to time I caught muttered references to crimes he passed over – the case of Williams, the owl burglar, the Van Houtain murder, the multiple murders on Illington Moor.

"Ah, here we are!" he cried as I came back into the sitting-room, his keen eyes rapidly scanning the clippings before him. "The house appears to have been built in 1920, by Dr. Roland Borstad, son of the one-time ambassador to Germany, Henry C. Borstad. The younger Borstad was a surgeon with an interest in psychoanalysis. Author of three published papers on psychoanalysis, and one monograph on Dr. Sigmund Freud. He appears also to have had some ability in architecture and undertook part of the building of his home. Overwork brought on a nervous breakdown, after recovery from which he went to live in the Orrington Crescent house, from which he vanished on December 17th, 1921. The papers made much of the fact that Borstad had evidently been planning a journey, for he had withdrawn a large sum of money, and his bags, already packed, were standing in the vestibule in preparation for his departure."

"I know the Borstad papers," I put in. "A brilliant young man. His death was a decided loss to psychoanalysis. As I recall it, he had some very advanced, unorthodox theories, and there was conflict with his peers. They fell out about his radical theories and experiments in the domain of pain and pain therapy, and this ultimately brought about a break in their relations, endangering his position in the hospital where he was briefly the resident, and ultimately brought on a nervous breakdown."

"The house stood empty for over a year. Then it was turned over to be let, though its ownership remained in the Borstad family where it presumably still is. The second disappearance was on February 24th, 1923; it was that of Clyde Lee, son of and Duke of Dunwich. After Lee, Mr. and Mrs. John Tomlins and their family took the house. They remained for only five months, complaining that now and then distant sounds disturbed them. They made no charge against the house as 'haunted'. Tomlins, an engineer, said that the house obviously lay in a place that echoed sounds from far away – chiefly mechanical. The third disappearance was that of Howard Eliot, a writer of short stories and sensational newspaper pieces on occult subjects; he had taken the house because of its reputation and meant to lay its ghost, as he put it, since there had been occasional reports of ghostly figures in the grounds. He vanished on May 17th, 1925. As in this fourth disappearance, investigation disclosed no motive for any one of the disappearances. Dunwich waited on the arrival of ransom notes; none was received."

"That is certainly a curious record!"

"Is it not!" He stood for a few moments tugging at an earlobe. "It has, however, some parallels. None of the missing tenants at the Orrington Crescent house was married. Except for Lee, who had a man-servant and had the house done by an occasional cleaning woman, each of the missing tenants lived alone; and Lee disappeared on his man's night free. What does this suggest to you, Parker?"

"A necessary condition," I said.

"Which in turn implies a related plan."

"What connection, if any, was there among the men who disappeared?"

"Other than the common tenancy of the house in Orrington Crescent, none has been turned up. They were not known to one another." He shrugged. "But it is idle to speculate with so little knowledge available. Bancroft will have a dossier on d'Oro in my hands by the time we return. Let us just have a look at the house."

He crossed to his chamber to dress.

The house in Orrington Crescent was, for lack of any classification, modern Victorian. It was without the ornateness of many Victorian houses, but its lines – what could be seen of them through the massed foliage of many bushes – though suggesting the Georgian, were a far remove from the classical. It struck me, in the wan light of a post set in the street outside the bordering hedge, as very much an expression of the undisciplined architectural preferences of its builder. Perhaps the late Dr. Borstad had designed it himself.

Its interior, however, was essentially simple. The front door opened upon a vestibule; this in turn opened directly upon a sitting-room, adequately but not richly furnished, dominated by a fireplace which bore no signs of recent use. A table lamp was lit on a reading table next to a stuffed chair; on the table a book lay face down, as if someone had been interrupted at reading. It was, I saw, not surprisingly, a collection of Leopardi's poems, in Italian – clearly the book the Count d'Oro had been reading while he waited upon the arrival of Miss Violet Carson.

This room, in turn, led to two bed-chambers, a bath, a kitchen and adjacent pantry, a study or library, and a compact little room that might have served at one time as a laboratory – something which the original owner of the house might well have put to use, though of all its original contents only a small microscope, a retort, and some of the lesser paraphernalia of the surgeon stood on shelves in a small glass case on one wall. The furnishings in the house were sturdy, useful pieces, all for the most part ordinary, severe, and entirely unornamented.

There was no basement beneath the building, though there was a rear entrance to the house, and an enclosed stairway led to the top floor. This floor consisted of one large room, just above the study, a bath, and two other rooms of almost equal size, opposite the larger room. None of the rooms bore any evidence of ever having been furnished, though all were scrupulously clean, even to the obvious scrubbing of the variegated width oak flooring. The chimney leading up from the fireplace below stood apart from the wall, which was set back from it, and was windowless, with some shelving boards piled beside the uncommonly massive chimney, as if Borstad had meant to line this wall, too, as the wall below had been lined, with books.

Pons examined each room cursorily, then returned to the head of the stairs and stood in deep thought, carressing the lobe of his left ear.

"Does not this cleanliness surprise you, Parker?" he asked presently.

"I can't say that it does."

"Curious. Most curious. Are we to believe that Count d'Oro scrubbed down the floors of rooms for which he had no use before taking his mistress to bed?"

"Hardly. It strikes me it is you who are now doing what you so frequently accuse me of doing – overlooking the obvious. He had some charwoman in to do it."

"Possible, if improbable," said Pons.

He led the way back downstairs and once more made a tour of the rooms, pausing to examine each room more closely. Everything was in order, save in the bedroom, where the bed still stood as Miss Carson had left it – turned carelessly back and disarranged as it would be had someone lain in it for a while, as Miss Carson had testified she had done while waiting on the appearance of her lover. Only one pillow showed any indentation, and that slight.

"I never cease to marvel at the sexual habits of my fellowmen," said Pons, as he gazed at the bed. "To go to so much trouble and expense for a little casual dalliance!"

"Spoken like a true abstainer," I said. "We are not all so abstemious."

"Why not install her here permanently?" mused Pons, though it seemed to me that he was not really concerned with this question.

"Elementary!" I replied instantly. "Because d'Oro did not always meet the same woman here."

"Ah, Parker – you are wiser in this aspect of the world," said Pons, his eyes dancing.

"I will not deny it," I said.

"But let us look into the scene with more care," said Pons, then, leading the way back to the sitting-room. "It is evidently from this room that d'Oro took his departure, either voluntarily or involuntarily. Now it is patent that d'Oro was interrupted at his reading, for the Leopardi is turned face down. He could have risen to go into another room – to go outside; he could have simply lain back to rest; he could have grown tired – the possibilities, while not endless, are varied. On the other hand, he may even have become aware of some unusual sound – or smell."

At this, Pons flashed a curious glance at me. "Is there not an uncommon odor in this room? Perhaps my use of the weed has troubled my sense of smell."

"I noticed how clean the room smells," I said.

"Antiseptic?" ventured Pons.

I agreed that the room had an antiseptic odor, as if it had been thoroughly cleaned. But there was nothing to meet the eye that gave evidence of anything more than ordinary cleaning. Pons now began to walk around the room. He made a circuit of the walls, paused at the fireplace, and came back to the chair d'Oro had left. He dropped to his knees, took his magnifying glass from the inner pocket of his coat, and began to examine the floor around the chair, crawling about in an ever widening circle. His glance darted here and there; from time to time he bore down upon a chosen spot, putting his glass to use, his keen eyes missing nothing, his face, feral in appearance when he was engaged in such intent at examination, betraying nothing. When he came to his feet again, his face was a study in perplexity. "This room is a marvel of cleanliness," he said reflectively. "I submit that that is extraordinary indeed."

"Why should it be? D'Oro," I said, gesturing toward the Leopardi poems, and the books on the shelves crowding the fireplace wall, "is obviously a man of taste. Such a man would hardly want to receive his mistress in a setting lacking for cleanliness."

"That is surely well put, Parker," agreed Pons. "However, I submit you have forgotten something – this house was surely examined with some care by men from the Foreign Office; Bancroft inferred as much. There is everything to show that this room was thoroughly cleaned since then. I have not found so much as a grain of sand in the carpet."

"Incredible!"

"You may well say so," said Pons.

"On second thought," I put in – "wouldn't it be likely that investigators from the Foreign Office may have vacuumed the carpet in search of some clue in the dust?"

"Such matters are usually too mundane for the Foreign Office."

"Even under pressure from the Italian government?"

Pons was lost in thought; he did not answer. Having completed his examination of the floor, he was now gazing at the walls of the room. He crossed to the street side of the house and scrutinized the window sills and frames; he did the same with the opposite wall. Neither the fireplace wall nor that opposite, which was a partition dividing the house, contained windows. Then he gave his attention to the hearth; this gave him pause.

"What do you make of this fireplace, Parker?" he said, from his position on his knees.

I crossed and bent. "It is as clean as everything else in the room," I said.

"Nothing more?"

"It must have been scrubbed with the same antiseptic thoroughness we've already noticed," I said. "The smell of it is even stronger here. And it doesn't have the look of having had much use. D'Oro apparently goes to no more than minimal trouble to satisfy the appearances."

"Other than scrupulous cleanliness," said Pons. "I put it to you that the romantic setting ought to have more than subdued lights – a fire on the hearth, music, flowers or some pleasant scent – which, I submit, ought not to be antiseptic in essence."

I laughed, I fear, with some cynicism. "For the purpose of seduction, perhaps, Pons. But once an arrangement has been made, I assure you that most ladies are as interested in getting to the heart of the matter as the men."

"Ah, I must defer to your greater experience in these matters, Parker. I am naive enough to have believed that the ladies are invariably partial to the romantic accoutrements."

He came to his feet once more. He stood for a moment examining the bookshelves. Then he began to remove the books from the shelves. "Lend me a hand, Parker," he said. "These shelves at least do not appear to have been cleaned recently." I followed his lead in piling the books on the floor, seeing as I did so that the shelves behind the books were covered with dust and lint.

"These can hardly be d'Oro's books," I said, looking at some of the titles.

"Capital, Parker! I am always delighted at evidence of your growing inductive skill," answered Pons.

"Surely some of these books must have been the original owner's," I went on. "Medical books and case histories. And they've not been disturbed for years."

"I fancy d'Oro had no need to maintain a library here," said Pons. "Half a dozen books should have served him. These d'Annunzios and a set of Proust are probably d'Oro's; there is some disturbance of the almost uniform dust here."

"And here," I said. "Behind two textbooks used at Guy's – which certainly cannot be of much pertinence any more, considering their date."

Pons came to my side. He stood looking thoughtfully at the shelving from which I had removed the books. I saw for the first time a neat round hole in the wall behind, as if a knot had fallen from the wood, though the knot was not in evidence. Pons gazed in silence at the dust that had so manifestly been disturbed behind the books from Guy's; then he stepped back from the shelving and surveyed the wall in its entirety, after which he returned to a spot at a point on his side of the chimney approximately uniform with my position.

He removed books from the shelves, and stood with a small sound of satisfaction to contemplate the empty shelf.

Joining him, I saw that here, too, the dust had been disturbed – he still held in his hands the compact little German books he had removed from the shelf – and here, too, another knot had come loose.

"It was folly on the part of the builder to put in knotty pine so close to a chimney," I said, as he bent to examine the shelving there.

"Was it not!" agreed Pons. "Let us return the books to their proper place."

His demeanor baffled me. He said not a word as we restored the books to the shelves. After we had finished, he returned to the enclosed stairway and went up the stairs on his hands and knees, scrutinizing the steps and the adjacent walls with the aid of his glass, making almost inaudible muttering sounds as he went along. Now and then he took from the stairs or the rough plaster walls something invisible to me, inserted it into one of the glassine envelopes he invariably carried, and went on. From the top of the stairs he backed down, still examining every stair. Once more down the stairs he said, "The stairs have also been carefully cleaned." He shrugged. "But I fancy we are all but finished here. It is growing light outside, and I want to have a look at the exterior of the house."

So saying, he made his way to the front entrance.

Outside, he stood back from the stoop and viewed the facade looking out upon the street, where, I saw, the Foreign Office car in which we had come still waited, though the driver appeared to have fallen asleep. Pons stood but a few moments so; then he made his way rapidly around the house, myself at his heels.

On the fireplace wall of the house, he gestured in passing, "The chimney is completely inset. That is somewhat of an architectural novelty apart from our country houses, I daresay." He paused at the rear entrance and subjected it to a brief examination that had to be cursory in the absence of any but the dawn's light. Then he went on around the house, and, without pausing again, made straight for the car at the kerb.

Pons maintained a thoughtful silence all the way home. At No. 7, he asked our driver to follow us up to our quarters, and that young man, accustomed no doubt to orders, obediently trailed us up the steps to 7B, and stood just over the threshold waiting while Pons scribbled hastily on a sheet of notepaper.

He folded this presently, slipped it into an envelope, which he sealed, and handed the envelope to the driver.

"Deliver this to Mr. Pons at once. He must be awakened if he is sleeping – though I fancy he is waiting to hear from us."

"Yes, sir," said the driver, and slipped out of the room.

"There is just time for a spot of tea," said Pons then, rubbing his hands together in that annoyingly self-congratulatory way of his, quite as if he had solved the puzzle of Count d'Oro's disappearance. "What do you make of it, Parker?"

"There are several possible explanations," I ventured cautiously.

"I am glad to hear it," he said. "Pray enlighten me."

"Consider first, the woman." I said.

"A classic consideration," interrupted Pons, nodding and smiling.

"A jealous lover may have preceded her to Orrington Crescent, summoned d'Oro to the door, struck him down, and carried him away."

"Leaving no footprints in the snow. A remarkable accomplishment, indeed!"

I ignored his thrust. "D'Oro may have rushed from the house for some powerful motive unknown to us."

"Powerful, certainly, to take him into the snowy night clad only in bathrobe and slippers."

I abandoned my effort and sought to divert him by pointing to a sealed manila envelope on the table. "Surely that was not here when we left."

"I saw it," said Pons. "It is the dossier on d'Oro, sent over by Bancroft. I fancy we have no need of it."

"Ah, you know where he went?"

"Say, rather, I have a grave suspicion."

More than this he would not say. Instead, he turned to his microscope. There he emptied the glassine envelopes and put what I saw now were strands of some substance on glass panes for examination. There were three such strands, and two of them did not long occupy Pons's attention. He studied the third for some time before he turned from the microscope.

"Well, what have you found?" I asked.

"Fragments of cloth. Two are almost certainly from the kind of cloth commonly found on bathrobes, and the third from a cloth with cleaning oil on it. The first two came from the wall, the last from one of the steps."

"Then d'Oro must have been on the stairs at some time that night."

"He has occupied the house for months," replied Pons, "but he or his bathrobe was certainly present on the stairway at some time during his tenancy."

We were interrupted at tea and the crumpets our good Mrs. Johnson had brought up to us by a ponderous step on the stair and an equally ponderous knock that followed.

"Inspector Jamison," said Pons, and opened the door to him.

"A fine thing, Pons," he grumbled, walking in. "To be routed from bed at this hour of the morning and sent over here by the Foreign Office!"

"I sent for you," said Pons. "I have decided to reward your invariable courtesy and graciousness by presenting you with what I hope is the solution to a remarkable mystery."

Lowering his portly body into a chair, Jamison settled his bowler on his knee, touched his dark moustache with an index finger, and viewed Pons through eyes narrowed in suspicion. "I will listen," he said in a voice that dripped cautious doubt.

"Though it has been kept strictly under wraps – you know the Foreign Office, Inspector – Count Ercole d'Oro, the Italian consul – has vanished from a house in which he had an assignation."

"When?"

"Three days ago."

"And now the trail's cold, they call on the Yard!" Jamison said bitterly.

"They've not called on you, Inspector. I have."

"Where's the house?"

"In Orrington Crescent."

Jamison's eyes widened with sudden interest. "Not Number 27?"

"Number 27," said Pons.

"So. Another one. That makes the fourth disappearance from those premises. So we are to be troubled by such a matter again!"

"Not for long, I trust," said Pons, as a car scraped to the kerb outside. "But here, if I am not mistaken, is the car from the Foreign Office." He crossed to the windows, and drew aside a curtain. "Are you prepared, Inspector?"

"I was ordered to come armed."

"Good. Let us go down."

He snatched up his deerstalker and ulster as he spoke, and made for the door.

The house in Orrington Crescent was to all appearances exactly as we had left it. The subdued lights were still burning, and so far as it was possible to ascertain at a casual examination, nothing and no one had disturbed the setting.

"Moore, follow us with the materials," said Pons as he left the car.

"Yes, sir."

Glancing behind us as Pons stood unlocking the door to the house, I saw that the driver was coming up the walk carrying two wrapped objects; a rubber hose dangled from one of them.

Once inside, Pons moved with dispatch. "Help me clear this shelf, Parker," he asked.

We dumped books unceremoniously on the floor, and in but a few moments we had cleared the chosen shelf – that which we had last cleared. Over his shoulder, Pons said, "Now, Moore, if you please."

The driver now came forward. He had uncovered "the materials" and disclosed two metal canisters, hoses dangling from their nozzles, canisters much like oxygen tanks, with which I was, of course, familiar. They were marked in large letters: HM War Mag W.

Pons grasped one of them, laid it on the shelf before him, pushed the hose into what I had taken for the open knothole behind the shelf, and turned the nozzle. Then he applied the second canister to the hole on the other side of the chimney and turned the nozzle. I could hear their contents hissing into open space behind the bookshelves.

Pons took a revolver from the pocket of his ulster and pressed it upon the driver. "If by any miscalculation of mine, a stranger to you should appear in this room, hold him at bay. And do not hesitate to shoot, if you value your life, young man." With a sweep of his arm as he turned, Pons said, "Come," and hurried over to the stairs leading to the floor above.

He bounded up the steps and into the room directly above the sitting room where Moore waited upon the canisters to empty themselves. He took his stand facing the wall behind the chimney.

"To arms, Inspector," he said crisply.

The three of us stood there in silence, waiting upon events which Pons showed by his confident expression that he expected to take place. Two minutes, three – five – while below us the canisters were emptying into the wall.

Then there rose from within the wall an urgent, scrabbling sound. And suddenly the entire wall behind the chimney began to slide noiselessly downward to recess behind the wall of the storey below, disclosing a passage leading down.

But we had only a moment in which to become aware of this, before a disheveled figure in a white surgeon's gown came struggling up the steps of the passage and stumbled gasping into the empty room.

"Watch your nostrils," said Pons sharply, covering his face with his handkerchief.

"Stand where you are!" shouted Jamison.

But his admonition was needless, for the man who had come up out of the wall collapsed upon the floor, senseless.

"Inspector," said Pons, "let me introduce you to Dr. Roland Borstad, the author, if I am not mistaken, of the Orrington Crescent disappearances – and, I fancy, of others that have gone unrecorded and equally unsolved. Handcuff him hands and feet, Jamison, and drag him to the car as unceremoniously as he dragged his victims up the stairs after drugging them with gas through those same holes in the wall that served to turn the tables on him." He flashed a glance at me. "Not, Parker, with antiseptic, but with some form of anesthetic very probably of his own devising.

"Now, then, that gas we've sent below is a harmless but effective soporific developed by the scientists in the War Office. We'll give it time to settle, and then go down to learn what diabolical matters have engaged Borstad all these years. Pray that we find d'Oro still alive. Moore will give you a hand with Borstad, Jamison."

And in half an hour we descended – to find below the house fully equipped living quarters and an elaborate laboratory, on an operating table in which lay Count Ercole d'Oro, strapped down, unconscious, showing marks of torture, but alive and not in critical condition, despite Borstad's experiments.

On a desk not far away lay a thick manuscript in Borstad's hand – sickeningly annotated, detailing accounts of his experiments, not only on Clyde Lee and Howard Eliot, but on others – the hapless victims Borstad had lured out of the London night into his devilish laboratory, some of those whose names set down by Borstad Jamison recognized as among

London's undiscovered missing persons. His manuscript bore the revealing title of *Beyond the Threshold of Pain*.

As we rode back to 7B, with the still unconscious Dr. Borstad slumped in the front seat beside Moore, and d'Oro on his way to the nearest hospital by ambulance, Pons answered Jamison's impatient questions.

"Quite apart from the fact that there was no manifest motive for d'Oro's disappearance – the Foreign Office's almost paranoid view of espionage as the inevitable explanation of all such events involving any diplomat, even one of the minor status of Count d'Oro, could be discounted at once – the matter devolved basically upon one of two alternatives: d'Oro – and his predecessors, whose bones have long since been buried when Borstad had finished exploring their reactions to pain – disappeared either from the house or within it. I chose to act upon the latter alternative, and made such examination as I could on that assumption.

"Your remembering, Parker, that Borstad's difference with his superiors was rooted in his audacious experiments with the response of the human body to pain suggested a tenable, if horrible motive for Borstad's disappearance, which was obviously carefully planned, as the house he built at No. 27 was planned in its entirety to serve as a trap for his victims, such as he did not take off the streets by night – the derelicts and drunkards to be found in any city during the hours of darkness. 'Nervous breakdown' is one of those ambiguous diagnoses which covers everything from fatigue to madness.

"Once the assumption of the victim's disappearance within the house was acted upon, certain corroborative evidence was readily found. It was not the Foreign Office that cleaned the house in Orrington Crescent – it was Borstad himself, making sure that every trace of his work was eliminated. Save, of course, the threads from the bathrobe that caught on the plaster when he dragged d'Oro, unconscious from the anesthetic seeping into the room from the openings in the bookcase wall, up the stairs to the cleverly concealed entrance to his sub-surface quarters. You ought to have noticed, Parker, that the difference in the disturbance of the dust on the bookshelves was marked – where books were withdrawn and put back, the marks of withdrawal were in the dust; in the vicinity of the openings the dust was disturbed as by air, not by the withdrawal of books."

He shook his head grimly. "The dedicated scientist is constantly in danger of losing his humanity, and forgetting that he too is as integral to nature as the ant or the tree. Borstad's work in progress might better and more pointedly have been titled *Beyond the Threshold of Sanity*."

VII

THE ADVENTURE OF THE ALUMINIUM CRUTCH

During the early years of our association, a rare few of the problems laid before my friend, Solar Pons, were brought through the offices of our good landlady, Mrs. Johnson. One of them was a curious affair that appeared to be little more than a case of illegal entry, but proved to be one that took on an added dimension which perhaps no one but Pons could have foreseen.

Among the ladies who came to visit Mrs. Johnson from time to time was a widow of some sixty years of age, Mrs. Fiona Porteous. On that October day, Mrs. Porteous arrived at No. 7B, Praed Street coincidentally with the arrival of Inspector Seymour Jamison, who came for no other purpose than to stop for an idle, purposeless visit, which was uncommon for him. Mrs. Porteous vanished into our landlady's quarters, and the Inspector mounted to ours and sat down. He customarily occupied an hour or two of Pons's time with vaunting successes or asking Pons's advice in matters under investigation; but on this day he had come rather to give vent to his disappointments.

He inquired whether Pons were at work at some criminous matter, and seemed to be aggrieved that Pons was not.

"I take it, however," said my companion, "that you are busy, as usual."

"You may say so," said Jamison in a voice laden with dissatisfaction. "We have several problems on which we're not making any significant progress. Oh, we caught Alfred Fletcher, the forger – though it took us seven months; and we managed to collar Rodney Stanyan, that effete young poet who had been plagiarising his betters. Nothing much to either one – more or less simple matters of searching until we found them. And we'll convict the Russell Street murderer. But we haven't made any progress on the Midlands murder – or the thefts and substitutions at the galleries and museums – and we're as far as ever from a solution to the murder of Sidney Lowell, that crippled artist, in Bessborough Street, or the Aylesbury triple murder."

"You were looking for the son-in-law, I believe," said Pons.

"Yes, since he was estranged. But last night we found his body, too – miles away, and clearly murder too, not suicide. But once we uncover a motive, we might be able to solve Lowell's murder."

"Beaten to death with his crutch, was he not?" asked Pons. "I recall reading about the affair."

"Perhaps. Perhaps not." Jamison did not elaborate. "The crutch was all bent up and torn apart – that is, the ends were torn off and the middle part looked as if it had been used to beat Lowell to death, but it hardly seemed heavy enough for that, and Spilsbury's not inclined to agree that it alone was used, though some hairs adhered to it."

"Then it was not of wood," observed Pons.

"No, of aluminium – and rather light for a weapon."

He went on at some length, while Pons sat quietly listening, Inspector Jamison was manifestly making no appeal for suggestions from Pons, and Pons made none, only asking a question now and then in the interests of clarification.

I noticed, however, that he had one ear cocked, as it were, on the premises beyond Jamison; every little while a sound came up from below – the opening and closing of a door, I made it; undoubtedly it was this that had divided Pons's attention.

The Inspector finished at last, and, having said all he meant to say, he made his departure, looking relieved, though Pons had offered little in the way of advice, scrupulously maintaining his own counsel unless asked – and Inspector Jamison had not asked. The door had hardly closed behind him when Pons turned to me, his eyes alight.

"I fancy Mrs. Johnson will look in on us within minutes, It was certainly her door that opened and shut several times."

"I heard it."

"Perhaps some trifling matter is troubling her visitor this afternoon," ventured Pons.

The outer door opened and closed. Almost immediately Mrs. Johnson's door opened, and her familiar steps sounded on the stairs, followed by other, heavier steps. Pons glanced at me and smiled.

Mrs. Johnson reached the landing. "Mr. Pons?" she asked beyond the door.

"Come in, Mrs. Johnson," invited Pons.

He strode across the room and opened the door. Behind our landlady loomed the imposing figure of her friend, Mrs. Fiona Porteous.

"It's not me, Mr. Pons, begging your pardon. It's Mrs. Porteous would like to talk to you, if you can spare the time."

Mrs. Porteous was already engaged in pushing our landlady into our quarters; her buxom figure was so formidable that she needed only to lean forward to impel Mrs. Johnson across the threshold. It was evident that a consultation with Pons had been suggested by Mrs. Porteous, and not by our landlady, whose diffident reluctance was only too patent.

Mrs. Johnson introduced us all around, forgetting that she had done so on a previous occasion, and ended with, "Mrs. Porteous has had a spot of trouble, Mr. Pons. She would be obliged to you if she could mention it."

"By all means," said Pons, with whimsical enthusiasm. "Pray sit down, ladies."

"Good of you, I'm sure," said Mrs. Porteous in a deferential tone of voice which was, however, immediately lost as she continued. "It's this way, Mr. Pons, somebody's been in my house. Twice! Mrs. Johnson says to me I'd ought to talk to you about it – " this she quickly revised at sight of Mrs. Johnson's quick expression of dismay to " – or I says to her maybe you'd look into it for me." She smiled ingratiatingly.

Pons's smile was somewhat less than enthusiastic. "What was taken, Mrs. Porteous?"

"Oh, nothing was took – that's it. And mine wasn't the only house in the street, either, that was entered."

Pons's interest quickened as readily as it had waned. His eyes lit up. "Ah, how then did you learn that your home had been entered?"

"Well, Mr. Pons, you may know how it is with people who live alone. You get used to everything in its place. You know just how the umbrella stands in the vestibule, and how you left the book lying face down you were reading, and which way every chair faces, and which door was open and which was shut." She glanced down apologetically. "A bit fussy, you may say, but that's how it is. Maybe it's for lack of anything else to do. The one time the door to my late husband's room was standing open; it was never open before. The next time – well, I mentioned the umbrella because it was the umbrella that was moved. I left it in its stand, with two canes that belonged to John.

"Two nights ago, when I came from a card party, I found the umbrella lying on the chair nearby. So somebody's been there, taken it out, and forgot to put it back. I know where it was when I went out, and I know where I found it when I got back; there's no use trying to tell me I did it myself and just forgot about it." Her implication clearly was that Pons had better not try to do so. "Besides, the one back window I'd left open was pulled shut – as if somebody came in that way and shut it going out."

"So what did you do, Mrs. Porteous?" asked Pons.

"Well, sir, I says to myself, when I saw the umbrella, if there's somebody been here, he might still be here, so, Fiona, my girl, I says, I'll just have a look around. I took John's leaded cane and I went from one room to another, I turned up all the lights and looked under and behind everything. Nobody. Nobody was there. But two of the chairs in my parlor had been moved, and a sofa was out of line. Oh, somebody'd been there, all right.

"Then I looked around to see if anything was took. Nothing was. Somebody'd been in the large drawers, but not the small ones. And next day when I asked Emma Jaggers – she's on my right – had she seen anybody about? – I found out that her house had been entered, too – and the house across the street, that's Mr. Harvey Bertrand's – had been got into. Each the one time. And like my own house, nothing was took. I've got the feeling whoever it was will be back, Mr. Pons. What I want is for you to look into it. I can't pay much, but I can pay some."

Pons sat for a few moments in silence, his eyes closed, his fingers tented before him. It was impossible to divine from the passivity of his features what he might be thinking. Presently, however, he opened one eye and fixed it on our client.

"And where do you live, Mrs. Porteous?"

"At Number 127 Lupus Street. I own my house. John left it to me. It's early Victorian. We bought it just five years ago."

Something in her prosaic account had plainly quickened Pons's interest. "And the umbrella, Mrs. Porteous – had it been opened?"

"Opened. The umbrella?" Mrs. Porteous was manifestly disconcerted. She flashed an indignant glance at Mrs. Johnson. "Why, I never..." she began, ruffled, then composed herself and said instead, "I never looked. It's bad luck to open an umbrella in the house, Mr. Pons."

"I see," said Pons, the hint of a smile on his thin lips. "But I am not adept in arcane beliefs, Mrs. Porteous. When you reach home, pray examine the umbrella attentively, take it outside if need be, and open it. I am on the telephone. Call me promptly and let me know what you find, if anything."

"Am I to look for something?" Mrs. Porteous asked, with another glance at Mrs. Johnson.

"You are positive nothing was taken from your premises. Are you equally as certain that nothing was left?"

"Left, Mr. Pons? And what would be left?"

"Only you could know that, Mrs. Porteous. You know your premises. I do not."

"Humph!" said Mrs. Porteous expressively. "If anything was left there, I'd know it. Nothing was left. Everything in that part of the house John lived in mostly is the same as the day he died; from the hour he came in last time from the Tate and hung up his crutch a year ago, nothing's been disturbed there except for the dusting. And so with my part of the house."

Pons's eyes were now positively dancing with delight, whether at our client's delivery or for some other reason I was unable to ascertain.

"Your late husband was disabled, Mrs. Porteous?" he asked.

"He was that, Mr. Pons. Bad lame in his left leg. He came home that way from the war. Walked with a crutch the last years of his life. We lived on his pension. And I had a little inheritance of my own from an uncle. John used to like to go to the galleries and study the paintings. He once dabbled a bit in painting himself. Oils and watercolours."

"I will look into the matter, Mrs. Porteous."

"There now," said our client, with a glance of triumph in the direction of Mrs. Johnson. "I knew Mr. Pons was a gentleman!" She turned again to Pons. "And what am I to do, Mr. Pons?"

"Examine the umbrella," he answered.

She blinked. "And then?"

"Nothing more. We will call on you in good time."

So saying, Pons came to his feet. Clearly dismissed, Mrs. Porteous rose also. She extended a well-muscled arm and shook Pons's hand firmly. Our landlady favored Pons with an apologetic glance, which Pons answered with a reassuring smile.

"You are surely not going to spend your time looking into a case of ordinary illegal entry!" I protested, when the ladies were descending the stairs.

"'Ordinary'? I think not. I submit there were some points of interest that escaped you, Parker."

"I saw none. And that matter of the umbrella! You don't mean to say you meant it?"

"On the contrary, I did. It is relative, however; it will give Mrs. Porteous something to do."

"What on earth difference does it make if it was opened or not?"

"Umbrellas have been known to conceal small articles," said Pons enigmatically.

"You don't really believe that something was left in that umbrella," I said indignantly. "If so, wouldn't it follow that something was left in each of the other houses entered?"

Pons smiled. "That is presumptive, certainly, but I would be inclined to doubt it."

"What is it then?"

"You have all the facts, Parker. A few trifling deductions should present you with a tenable solution."

"You are surely striding far ahead," I said.

"Say rather that I am making a daring assessment of coincidence. You know my feeling about coincidence. We have heard one so glaring that I cannot understand your failure to see it at once."

"Enlighten me."

"My dear fellow, within an hour we have had propounded to us two mysteries..."

"Two?" I cried.

"Yes, two. One by Inspector Jamison, the other by our client. Pray permit me to continue – two mysteries, then, in each of which there figures a man who gets about with the aid of a crutch, and who is a frequenter of art galleries. This suggests nothing to you? I submit it should."

"A case of mistaken identity?" I ventured.

"Oh, fie! By Mrs. Porteous's account, her husband has been dead for a year. One could hardly mistake someone for him."

"You raise some tantalizing points," I admitted. "There are similarities, indeed – but you will yourself admit that life frequently presents us with the most astonishing coincidences. These two late gentlemen – Mr. Porteous and the murdered Sidney Lowell – may have frequented the galleries and museums – after all, the Tate is not far from Mrs. Parteous's address – but there is no evidence that they ever met, or even knew each other."

"Nor is there any evidence to the contrary. I fancy there is more to the former. I submit that, even if they never met they were aware, one of the other. How could it be otherwise? In the account of Lowell's life in the press, it is set forth that he was a copyist who spent many hours at the galleries copying some of the masterpieces there – a man of some modest skill, apparently, for he seems to have had a ready market for his wares, according to the accounts. It is highly probable that at some time during his visit to the galleries Porteous encountered Lowell at his work. Both carried a crutch. Does it not seem likely that they may have spoken to each other? A common affliction is a credible ground for striking up at least a speaking acquaintance."

I conceded this, withal grudgingly.

"Very well, then. Carry on from there. You know my methods."

With this caustic advice, so usual for him, Pons turned to occupy himself with the writing of some short work. He drew up several drafts before he was interrupted by the telephone.

I could hear our client's voice coming in over the wire. "Mr. Pons? Mrs. Porteous here. I don't know how you ever knew it, but that umbrella had been opened. It wasn't folded back together as carefully as I fold it. What do I do now?"

"We expect to call on you at noon tomorrow," said Pons. "One word of caution, however – under no circumstances open your door to anyone until we arrive. Tomorrow morning's papers will carry a notice over your name; I will have inserted it. Pray take no telephone calls in regard to it."

"What is it? What are you about, Mr. Pons?" Mrs. Porteous's indignation and curiosity boomed into the room.

"You will have to trust me, Mrs. Porteous," said Pons, and thereupon hung up before our client could protest further.

"Notice?" I asked.

Pons did not reply until he had finished a final draft of his notice. "I fancy that will do," he said, and handed it to me. I read it with growing astonishment.

"Will the gentleman who last month left on my premises an aluminium crutch please be so kind as to claim it? Apply to Mrs. John Porteous, 127 Lupus Street, at any time after noon."

I looked up. "This is utterly fantastic. I don't recall hearing Mrs. Porteous say anything of the kind."

"Nor did she."

"Pons, this is the sheerest intuition!"

"I respect intuition in the fair sex. I am wary of it in our own. No, Parker, it is ratiocination at its most unassailable."

"You cannot mean it!"

"Indeed I do. I fear, though, that you are taking my little notice a trifle too literally. Read it with more imagination, my dear fellow." And with that he left me to my own thoughts while he buried himself in his files of recent criminal events.

When I came in from a round of calls late in the day, I found Pons still absorbed in study. He had put aside his clippings and was now poring over a dossier. When I had removed my light topcoat, I stepped around and gazed over his shoulder; he was reading the Yard dossier on Sidney Lowell.

"Ah, Jamison has after all sought your help," I said.

"A reasonable deduction," answered Pons, "but faulty in this instance. I asked him to have this information sent around. He was good enough to do so."

"Expecting your assistance in return."

"Possibly. There were one or two points about Lowell's death that interested me."

"For example?"

"I submit that there is something a trifle odd about a presumably impecunious artist's being beaten to death. The motive certainly cannot have been robbery – though it is true that his painter's case was not found at the scene; yet there is no definite evidence to show that he carried it at the time, though he had it with him when he left the Tate within the hour. The manner of his death suggests that he was slain in a rage – perhaps by more than one person. I have studied these notes carefully. They deal not only with the evidence at the scene of the crime, but also in some detail with the life and habits of the late artist."

"What has all this to do with the invasion of our client's home?" I could not help asking.

"Gently, gently, Parker! All in good time. We are not due at Mrs. Porteous's home until tomorrow noon. Meanwhile, this little problem of Jamison's challenges me. I am interested in Sidney Lowell, who turns out, by the way, to have been not so impecunious as I had imagined; indeed, he had considerable in the way of investments in very sound stocks, and his artistic skill seems to have been greater than merely passably good. He is on record as having sold an excellent copy of a Canaletto to Cardinal Fonseca at a quite respectable fee, and only six months ago sold a copy of Vereer's *View of Delft* to Lord Farringdon. – An excellent work; I took time this afternoon to go around and look at it."

"The original was recently stolen, if I recall," I said.

Pons nodded and went on. "He sold some highly praised copies to collectors on the Continent, and particularly to the Americans, who are always so casual with their wealth. He was apparently a most painstaking copyist, and an artist at least high in the second rank on his own."

"Odd that he should not have perfected his own talent rather than copy the masters."

"Ah, well, copying the masters is a way toward perfection. Perhaps Lowell recognized that he lacked certain qualities of greatness and did not labor under the illusion of genius, that curse of the creative artist that too often precludes a healthy objectivity about his work. Lowell was the only son of a poor collier in Westmoreland. A teacher undertook to send him to study art and so launched him on his career, which an unfortunate accident interrupted – hence his disability. He had been haunting the art galleries for over a decade, and was well known to the curators and many of the regular visitors, all of whom regarded him with esteem both as man and artist. He seems to have entered but one contest fifteen years ago, and his work aroused some curiosity by failing to take first place, some critics charging that the judges were inclined toward the second-rate performance of a first-rate artist over the first-rate performance of an unknown. This is rather more often the case than one supposes, and virtually all prizes and awards in the creative arts are suspect. Consider the Nobel Award in Literature, for instance – bestowed upon such minor figures as Carducci, Gjellerup, and Pontoppidan, while such literary giants as Proust, Hardy, and Conrad have been ignored."

"Surely his work was subsequently recognized."

"He never again entered a contest, claiming – with some justification – that they were 'rigged'. He pursued a relatively reclusive life in bachelor quarters in Park Lane."

"What was he doing in Lupus Street?"

"That does not appear to have been shown in these reports," said Pons dryly.

"Are you planning to look into the murder?"

"It interests me," said Pons thoughtfully. "But it is Jamison's responsibility, not mine, and the Yard seldom looks appreciatively on my little efforts unless someone with authority there initiates them. Since no one has done so, I fancy that they may well be on the trail. They may on occasion be guilty of extraordinary stupidity, but in the main they are conscientious and not without skill, however plodding they may seem to be. I have, by the way, asked Jamison to go around to our client's home with us tomorrow."

"He won't thank you," I said, chuckling.

"I would be astonished if he did," replied Pons.

Pons had given Inspector Jamison a summary of our client's case over the telephone, for on his arrival at 7B just before noon next day the Inspector huffed and trumpeted about the invitation.

"I don't usually look into matters like this, Pons. Illegal entry. Petty theft – and that's not even been established in this case. Pickpocketing. And that like. Nor do you. I don't understand you, Pons." He looked at my companion as if challenging him to reveal his motive in asking Jamison to accompany us.

Pons remained noncommittal, save to observe that little crimes were often the precursors of capital offenses.

"I would regard this as minimal indeed. Nothing has been reported as taken," said Jamison. "The whole matter has the sound of some sort of hoax."

"Does it not!" agreed Pons imperturbably.

"And so does this," added Jamison, throwing to the table a copy of the morning *Clarion*, with the advertisement Pons had had inserted in our client's name circled in red crayon.

"It is bait," said Pons. "I hope to net a fish with it – one to your taste, Inspector."

Jamison flashed him a sharp glance but held his tongue.

We set out presently for our client's home, not in Jamison's police car, but by cab, at Pons's insistence. Nor were we deposited at the door of Number 127 Lupus Street; we were taken around the corner and left in the middle of Bessborough Street.

"Mrs. Porteous's house may be under surveillance," explained Pons. "We'll make our way to the rear of the house."

Jamison stood briefly and looked around. "Just over there," he pointed, "is the spot Lowell's body was found. He was killed sometime before midnight and found by a cab-driver soon after."

"A curious place for him to be," observed Pons. "Has it been determined why he was here? It is not on the way to his quarters."

"We've conjectured that he had an assignation with someone," said Jamison. "Incidentally, his painting case and paraphernalia have been found on the bank of the Thames. Perhaps, after all, robbery was the motive."

Our client was astounded when we presented ourselves at the back door of her home. She made no effort to conceal it.

"I saw that notice, Mr. Pons," she said at once, as she admitted us, plainly disgruntled. "I can't imagine what you meant by it." Patently the opinion she had held of Pons's abilities had suffered a decline.

"Time will tell, Mrs. Porteous," said Pons. He gestured toward Jamison. "This gentleman is from Scotland Yard."

Mrs. Porteous was further taken aback. She knitted her brows and looked Jamison up and down, clearly not forming any advantageous judgment, and finally fixed unwavering eyes on his bowler until the Inspector, somewhat abashed, removed it. "A highly irregular thing to do," murmured our client. "Do I understand that you gentlemen intend to wait until someone calls here and asks for that imaginary crutch?"

"Ah, Mrs. Porteous," said Pons, "I assure you the crutch is not imaginary. It hangs, I believe, in your late husband's quarters – very likely in his clothes cabinet. Do us the favor of fetching it."

Our client's jaw fell, but only momentarily. She bridled. "It is my late husband's crutch, Mr. Pons," she said, and made no move.

"So you told us, Mrs. Porteous," said Pons. "Let us have it brought out so that your visitor, when he comes, may see that there is, after all, an aluminium crutch on the premises."

"Well, I never..." began our client truculently.

"Madame, we wish to see the crutch in question," said Jamison heavily.

Our client finally gave way. She turned, muttering, "You may as well use the parlor; it is adjacent to the front entrance." And, having led us there, she vanished in the direction of the stairs opening out of the lower hall. The sound of her climbing the stairs was determinedly audible.

"A tartar!" murmured Jamison.

"Small wonder her husband spent so much of his time at the galleries," I said.

"Women living alone can do with a bit of aggressiveness," observed Pons quietly.

Mrs. Porteous returned presently, carrying her late husband's aluminium crutch. "Here it is, Gentlemen, though I don't know, I'm sure, what you want it for."

Pons took the crutch and shook it gently. He smiled. Then he placed it against the wall of the room opposite the entrance. "Now, Mrs. Porteous, we will just wait upon events," said Pons.

"Events!" she cried. "Who in the world is interested in John's crutch besides me?"

"My methods may be a trifle unorthodox," began Pons.

Our client broke in. "That is hardly the word, sir, hardly the word. I hope you're not intending to surrender my husband's crutch to any jackanapes who may call for it!"

"If our notice has been seen by the person or persons who will be interested in it, you may be sure, Mrs. Porteous, that someone will call – perhaps the very person who invaded your house and other houses in the street. You will show him into this room, where we will make certain that he sees the crutch before he catches sight of us. That is all you need do."

Mrs. Porteous, I fear, thought Pons mad and made no secret of it. Pons's tone, however, clearly dismissed her. Quite obviously irritated, she retired from the room.

"Pray examine that crutch carefully, Jamison," said Pons then.

The Inspector crossed the room and picked up the crutch. He subjected it to a careful scrutiny, but his face betrayed no discovery. "It's a plain aluminium crutch, well worn down at the bottom."

"Newly capped, is it not?"

"I see that. Still, though, worn. The cap was put on – let us say – not more than six months before Porteous died."

"Six months more or less," agreed Pons. "The precise time is immaterial. Is there nothing more that strikes your professional eye?"

Jamison shook his head even as his eye fell upon what Pons had intended him to see. "Why, there are spots of what seems to be oil or watercolor. Small, yet distinct. Did Porteous paint as well as visit the galleries?" Before Pons could reply, Jamison's eyes widened. "Pons!" he cried, "this is Sidney Lowell's crutch!"

"Ah, Jamison, you make progress, however slowly."

At this moment the sound of the doorbell came to our ears.

"Hist!" cautioned Pons. "Let us move over to the wall away from the door."

We took our stand along the near wall, opposite the crutch Jamison had hastily put down against the far wall in line with the door. Mrs. Porteous, meanwhile, had come from the rear of the house and now walked past toward the front door. She opened it.

A man's voice sounded. "Do I address Mrs. Fiona Porteous?"

"You do, sir."

"My card, Madam. I saw your advertisement in this morning's papers."

"Mr. Adam Forsyth," read Mrs. Porteous in a voice that was intended for our ears.

"I have come for my poor friend's crutch. He was set upon by hoodlums in the street nearby and carried off – his crutch was evidently thrown on your premises. Do you still have it?"

He betrayed a certain anxiety not unmixed with eagerness.

"I do. Please come this way."

Mrs. Porteous appeared in the doorway and, catching sight of us pressed against the wall to the right of the doorway, stood off to that side to block her visitor's view. He was a well-dressed man of perhaps forty; he wore a neatly clipped moustache and carried gloves. His appearance exuded confidence. He saw the crutch at once and strode directly over to it without a glance to either side.

He seized the crutch and turned to look into Jamison's revolver.

"If you don't mind, Mr. Forsyth, we'll have Lowell's crutch," said Pons.

"A trap!" exclaimed Forsyth in disgust.

He surrendered the crutch to Pons. Without delay, Pons carefully unscrewed the top. He turned it upside down. From the hollow stem slid a cardboard tube. Pons caught it, dropped the crutch, and uncapped the tube, tipping this up too. Out slid a tightly rolled canvas. Jamison's captive watched with a scornfully amused expression.

Pons unrolled the canvas and held it up. "A Cezanne, I believe. Its theft may not yet have been discovered, because the copy Lowell left in its place was designed to deceive the experts for whom Lowell had nothing but contempt."

On our way to our quarters in the police car – once Adam Forsyth had been given into the custody of the men from the Yard for whom Jamison had sent – the Inspector grumbled, "that was a long shot, Pons – as long a one as I've ever known you to make."

Pons demurred. "I think not. The coincidences in the problem were too many to be accounted for by any other explanation. It was rational conjecture. Spilsbury's conclusion that the crutch was probably not the murder weapon struck me as crucial. If not – and the crutch seemed to me fundamentally too light a weapon for such use – why was it torn apart? – if not because someone expected something to be concealed in it. What was most likely for an art copyist to conceal in a hollow crutch but a rolled-up canvas? And if that were indeed the object of his murderer's search, what more likely than a stolen canvas of some value, particularly since London has been plagued for some time by thefts and substitutions of excellent copies for the genuine canvases?

"I fancy you will find that Lowell was engaged for a long time in more than just copying art masterpieces; he was also forging them, and with singular skill. He was certainly not operating alone, and his murder may very likely have been a matter of thieves falling out. What turned Lowell to this kind of criminal activity suited to his talents? Very probably vanity. I submit it was his rejection by the 'experts' – those so often self-appointed arbiters of taste and quality whom the history of art, literature and music have so frequently proved wrong. Lowell played a kind of game that pleased his vanity – but his collaborators were not playing a game. I suggest, Jamison, that you take along one of those experts – Duveen, perhaps – Sidney Lowell so heartily despised, and examine all those 'copies' bought recently by collectors here and abroad. I daresay you will find that many are genuine, and that the works hung on the walls of many a gallery in their place are copies, to be stolen only when suspicion of their authenticity arises.

"What brought about a rupture between Lowell and his collaborators, the differences that ended in Lowell's murder – and whether Forsyth himself had a hand in it, or whether it was done by others at his behest – I leave to the Yard to discover. What seems certain is that some time either before or after Lowell left the Tate on the day of his murder – I would venture to guess that it was after – he discovered that he was being followed, and concluded that his former collaborators were after the Cezanne they must have known he had in his possession. He conceived the plan to conceal the stolen canvas, and sought out the late John Porteous's home to exchange crutches. He most certainly knew Porteous; the circumstantial evidence permits of no other conclusion. He was fortunate enough to find no one at home, and he very probably remained hidden in the house for some time – the hiatus between the Tate's closing and the time of his murder suggests the likelihood – but his pursuers undoubtedly had the street under observation and waited on his reappearance. Lowell very probably did not anticipate being slain, certain that he was ultimately too valuable to his cronies. Put Forsyth through it, though he may remain silent and not betray any other members of the organization, which, I fancy, ranges to the Continent.

"It seemed to me certain that the presence of a disabled art lover in the vicinity of the premises of another just prior to the former's murder was part of a design and not just an outrageous coincidence. Lowell undoubtedly hoped to recover the stolen Cezanne at some later time. Since he did not live to do so, his murderers, knowing that the painting must have been concealed after he had temporarily eluded them, narrowed their search to one of the houses in Lupus Street. They did not know precisely where to look – a canvas lends itself to many places of concealment – until my conjectural notice in this morning's papers informed them that an exchange of crutches had taken place. They were undoubtedly aware of the fact that Lowell had on occasion used his crutch in which to carry canvases.

"Though, as Dr. Parker is wont to say, coincidences abound in life, I make it a rule to suspect the too fortuitous. I commend that course to you, Inspector."

VIII

THE ADVENTURE OF THE SEVEN SISTERS

Whenever Inspector Seymour Jamison was annoyed by my friend Solar Pons's obvious deductive skill, in the earlier years before he was ready to acknowledge that skill without reservation, he made some sly reference to the complex circumstances surrounding the death of Lionel Ruthel, a crime which remains officially unsolved in the annals of Scotland Yard. Presumably, since Jamison had once pointed to the case as Pons's "greatest failure", this unsubtle reference was intended to unsettle him. Pons, however, took a different view of that singular matter, and with reason; he invariably maintained an inscrutable silence, wearing a tolerant smile, which nettled Jamison. But the affair had more ramifications than the Inspector knew.

It began one autumn afternoon not long after Pons's successful solution of the adventure of the Obrisset Snuffbox. I had come into our quarters to find Pons pasting clippings into his scrapbook of criminal events. As I divested myself of hat and ulster, Pons sat back with a clipping in his hand, an expression of bemusement on his lean, hawklike face.

"Now here is a curious matter, Parker," he observed. "'Murder on the Underground'," he read. "But see for yourself."

He handed the clipping to me.

I found it to be nothing more uncommon than an account of the strangling of an as yet unidentified man whose body had been discovered in a compartment of the Underground at the Willesden Green Station the previous night.

"I see nothing unusual in this," I said, handing it back.

"'Garrotted,'" he said. "A point seems to have been made of that. In itself, perhaps it is not curious. I seem to remember, however, that this is the third garrotting in London within the past seven or eight months."

"That may put a different face on the matter," I conceded.

"Does it not!" He smiled. "I should not be surprised if the case is brought to my attention before very many hours have passed."

So saying, he reached into the pocket of his mouse-colored dressing-gown and thrust at me a piece of obviously expensive notepaper, across the top of which, once unfolded, I read the name Norris Ruthel, and below it, "Lord Warden of the Pontine Marshes."

"Dear Mr. Pons," I read, "I trust it will be convenient for you to see me this afternoon at four, regarding the death of my brother. If you have not sent word by two o'clock to deny me this privilege, I will take the liberty of presenting myself at the hour named." Message and signature were in a crowded, if legible, script, each letter pressing close upon the other. I looked up. "It came by messenger?"

Pons nodded. "Not long after you stepped out this morning. What do you make of it?"

"Other than the manifest conclusions to be drawn from embossed rag paper," I said, "it is surely highly ambiguous."

"He may assume that I know about his brother's death."

"Do you?"

"There is no mention of it in the press as of this moment," replied Pons, "but I've not seen the afternoon papers. Lionel

Ruthel – presumably the brother to whom he has reference, for I find no other Ruthel on the telephone – was a wealthy art collector living in the west end. Unmarried, reclusive. His specialties lay in the domain of ancient African and Chinese art."

"And you think his the body on the Underground?"

"I daresay it is likely. The victims of the past week's other capital crimes have been identified."

"And our client? Where are the Pontine Marshes?"

"Oh, come, come, Parker."

"Not Italy?"

"Why not? I submit that Mr. Norris Ruthel may well have been until recently one of the numerous British expatriates belonging to the English colony in Rome. That appellation may be only a fanciful affectation. However, he writes in a good clear hand – nothing affected about it, and keeps a precise, even line. I look forward to his visit."

"Ah, but if he has but recently come back to England, his brother's death may have taken place years ago."

"That is a *non sequitur*, Parker," said Pons sharply. "You know my interest in the criminal activities in Britain, and you have seen my files many times. There is no Ruthel murder in that compilation."

So saying, he resumed the filing of his clippings.

Promptly at four a motor drew up at the kerb and discharged our client, who was preceded to the door of our quarters by Mrs. Johnson, who brought up his card. Like his notepaper, it too was embossed. Our client himself followed hard upon her announcement and came into our quarters past Mrs. Johnson, diffident almost to the point of apology for having invaded Pons's domain. He was a slender man of middle age, thin of face, with an air of inquiry in his pale blue eyes. His long fingers fondled a cane crowned by an ivory head, and he was impeccably dressed, with that taste which conceals the costliness of clothing and yet permits its quality to show.

He took a seat at Pons's invitation and waited on Pons to open their dialogue.

"I take it, Mr. Ruthel, that your brother's was the body found last night on the Underground."

"Yes, Mr. Pons. My brother, though a wealthy man, was somewhat eccentric and parsimonious; he chose to ride the Underground rather than use his car. Quite naturally, when I learned of his death, I assumed – very probably like the police – that its motive was robbery. I am no longer so certain of that. I began to go through his things this morning – I should say, Mr. Pons, that I've been all over the world in the past twenty years, and never once back in England in all that time; so, actually, I know very little about Lionel's life during that period, save only what he chose to write to me – and he wrote sparingly – or what I read in the papers of his purchases at some auction at Sotheby's or elsewhere – and I found something very puzzling. I am frank to say, Mr. Pons, it unsettled me."

He handed Pons a purple envelope. "This was stuck away in a locked desk drawer. It came from Marrakesch – that is, the first one did, since that is its envelope."

Pons drew from it two fragile pages of purple stationery. I went around to look over his shoulder.

The messages on the pages bore no superscription of any kind. Each was brutally terse. The first read: "10,000 pounds. In currency P.O. Box 8, West Central Post Office. Addressee, Mr. Simon Fance will call. You have thirty days. Remember Elena." The second was almost precisely similar, except that the name "Elena" had given way to "Jasmine". Each was signed with a curious little cluster of what appeared to be asterisks. Neither was typewritten and, curiously, each was in calligraphy; the asterisks were clearly brushed in with singular delicacy. Glancing at Pons, I saw that his eyes were aglow with interest.

"Scented, I observe," he said. "Very probably these came at different times, though your brother preserved but one of the envelopes. A pity."

"I suppose that is the case," said our client.

"The obvious course would be to examine his accounts."

"I have done so, Mr. Pons. I found that ten thousand pounds had been withdrawn on June second. I could find no record that a second such sum had been withdrawn. I could not but conclude that Lionel must have died after failing to submit to this second threat. For it *is* a threat, is it not?"

Pons nodded.

"And not reported to the police," Mr. Ruthel went on. "That is certainly most odd. I can only surmise that there must have been a very strong reason why Lionel should have wanted to avoid their existence. I do understand that collectors are sometimes tempted to use unorthodox methods in pursuit of their enthusiasms – but frankly, if I may say so, this matter would seem to have something to do with the fair sex."

Pons was noncommital.

"And what passes for signature – those asterisks..."

"Stars, I submit, Mr. Ruthel," said Pons reflectively.

"I can make nothing of it – nothing," said our client, throwing up his hands. "I trust you will be able to do so, Mr. Pons."

"I will look into it, Mr. Ruthel."

Our client promptly came to his feet. Still, he hesitated for a moment. "Ought I turn these messages in to the police?"

"I will undertake that task, all in good time," said Pons. "You may expect to hear from me."

"I am at my brother's home," said Ruthel. "I have no residence of my own in London, and have been with him for the past month."

"Did he seem to you in any way disturbed during that time?" asked Pons then.

"I couldn't say so, no. Preoccupied, perhaps. To tell the truth, Mr. Pons, there was no very great communication between us. He never mentioned these messages, and he certainly didn't seem worried about them. Indeed, the only event to quicken his interest was an auction at Sotheby's, offering a Ming piece he hoped to add to his collection."

"Were you ever in Burma, Mr. Ruthel?"

If our client was startled at Pons's abrupt change of subject, he concealed it well. "It is strange you should ask, sir. I spent six months of this year in Rangoon."

"Thank you, Mr. Ruthel. Pray wait upon word from me."

Our client bade us a formal goodbye and took his leave.

"I submit that the exact number which occurs on both notes signifies the involvement of seven women in the matter."

"My word, Pons! How can you say so? Why not men?"

"These seven stars appear to be similarly grouped in each case, do they not?"

"Yes. Almost like a distorted figure."

"If indeed they represent stars, does nothing further follow for you?"

I shook my head, I fear, impatiently, well aware of Pon's little game.

"But perhaps astronomy was not one of your studies, Parker. Surely you must remember something of Greek mythology."

"I have learned more of myths of various kinds since I took up quarters here than I ever knew before," I retorted.

"A distinct touch, Parker!" said Pons, smiling. "Atlas and Pleione had seven daughters – Alcyone, Asterope, Electra, Kelaine, Maia, Merope and Taygete – all of whom were translated into the heavens as stars by Zeus, supposedly to escape the amorous designs of the hunter, Orion, who with his dog, also became stars. They are to be found in the constellation Taurus, appearing in fall and setting again in spring. They have been estimated at a hundred parsecs from our own planet and appear as a little cloud of luminosity in the winter sky – six of them are clear enough to the eye; the seventh – presumably Electra mourning for Troy – is always dim, sometimes invisible. Of them Alcyone is the brightest. They do indeed appear to the eye in the shape of a crude dipper, clustered closely together, and thus tiny by comparison with Ursa Major, commonly known as the 'big dipper'. I submit, therefore, that seven women are allied in this matter."

"Sisters?"

"I should be inclined to doubt it. Very probably they are simply banded together in this common aim."

"That is surely unique in the annals of blackmail. What could be their motive?"

"Whatever it is, their names must have had some significance to Ruthel. The evidence is that he paid the first levy made on him without any obvious attempt to avoid doing so. There is nothing in either note to suggest why the demand was made – except a woman's given name. This must then have been of immediate significance to him – and of such meaning that he was impelled to pay without question."

"But he balked at the second."

"Evidently." Pon's eyes danced. "I cannot remember when such a curious combination of challenging facts has been laid before me."

At this point, unhappily, I was called to attend a patient. I left Pons sitting at the cluttered table, caressing the lobe of one ear in that familiar attitude of contemplation, the late Lionel Ruthel's scented notes under his eye.

When I returned two hours later, I found Pons once again at work on his scrapbooks – but now poring over them, rather than arranging his clippings. He looked up at my entrance.

"I am sorry to see by your revealing expression that your patient is in a bad way," he said.

"He is recovering from an apoplectic seizure, but his condition is not good and the prognosis not promising," I replied. "And what progress are you making in the case?"

"I have not been idle," he said, waving one hand toward the columns laid before him.

I leaned over and glanced at the clippings. "What possible clues can you find applicable to Ruthel's murder in papers dated four and five years ago?"

He answered by tapping one of the clippings pasted into the scrapbook under my eye. It was a mere paragraph setting forth the fact that the police confessed themselves baffled by the disappearance of a young lady, Miss Elena Brown.

"I have also found a Miss Jasmine Struthers, similarly vanished, without any record of her reappearance. Surely it is more than a coincidence that two young women, among the many who disappear every year, seldom to be seen again, should bear such comparatively uncommon names as 'Elena' and 'Jasmine'?"

"Ah, I see," I said. "They were murdered and someone has traced the crime to Ruthel. That would account for his paying the first blackmail levied upon him with such speed."

"That is certainly possible," agreed Pons, though with a manifest lack of enthusiasm. "However, I could find no evidence that their bodies had been recovered. That seems to me significant. Both young women appear to have had difficulties at home. One vanished without any trace. The other – Miss Jasmine Struthers – confided to a companion that she was off for Paris to meet a friend. Neither was ever seen again. Of course, there are scores of similar cases recorded annually, and I may be being led astray – but the coincidence cannot be overlooked."

"What other motive – if not the threat to disclose murder – could have prompted such swift payment from Ruthel?"

"That remains to be disclosed. You will recall my reference to the other two men who were slain in similar fashion – Henry Bresham and George Stoner. I have looked back into accounts of these crimes in my files. Both were murdered at night, one on the street, one in his home. Both were wealthy men. And in the accounts that dealt with Stoner, mention was made of Stoner's one-time association with the ownership and management of a rather extensive importing business, conducted under the heading of 'Ruthel's, Inc.'. This was sold four years ago. That the method of death should have been precisely the same is unmistakably significant, particularly in view of the character of the warnings sent."

"Why?"

"It suggests nothing to you?"

"Except that the same agent must have been behind each."

"You may have struck closer to the central point than you know," Pons said, with an enigmatic smile. "Nothing more?"

I shook my head testily. "If there is something other to be observed, I fail to see it."

"I submit that both warnings and method of murder are distinctly Oriental."

"But both of the woman – if indeed you have established a connection between them and the references in the notes – were English."

Pons raised his eyebrows. "You are convinced they are dead, then?"

"Well," I said doggedly, "there is no stronger motive than the threat of exposure of murder. Moreover, the warnings sent to Ruthel were certainly not written by them."

"Calligraphy is predominantly an Oriental art," agreed Pons. "Oh, yes, but one of the women – you hold for seven – might have learned the art," I protested.

"And presumably also the skill required in garrotting. One of them must then be of exceptional strength."

"It is not impossible."

"A skill much practised in Asia, in such countries as Burma and Indo-China. The only source we know for the warnings, however, is Marrakesch."

"It is certainly a mixed bag of facts," I said.

"Is it not!" cried Pons with manifest delight. "And we shall hear more of them in a matter of minutes, for if I am not mistaken, the street door has just opened and closed. It is no doubt Inspector Jamison. I asked him to step around if time permitted – and, as usual, his curiosity has impelled him here without delay."

Inspector Jamison's heavy tread on the stairs was indeed audible as Pons spoke. In a brief space, he tapped on our door, then opened it to permit his portly body entry into our quarters. "What is it this time, Pons?" asked the Inspector, looking at Pons suspiciously, his face somewhat flushed from the effort of climbing the stairs.

"Pray sit down, Inspector. A little problem has come to my attention and I need your help."

"A bit of a turn, that," said Jamison as he took off his bowler and laid it on the table. He sat down, smiling. "The Yard does have its uses, eh, Pons?"

"Indeed it does," Pons agreed.

"What is it, then?"

"Last night the body of Lionel Ruthel was discovered on the Underground at Willesden Green. Garrotted."

Jamison nodded. "Spilsbury's examined the body. In his opinion Ruthel was strangled with a braided leather thong."

Pons considered this information thoughtfully. "In April, Henry Bresham was killed. In July, George Stoner. Both garrotted." Hard on Jamison's brusque nod, he added, "Motive?"

"We've not uncovered any. It wasn't robbery, as far as we know – in any of these three murders. If there is any connection among these men, we've not come upon it yet, though they knew one another. Stoner was a partner in Ruthel's, an importing business that sold out four years ago. Both Stoner and Ruthel belonged to a social club – 'Hunters & Anglers' – but seldom attended."

"Was there ever made to the police by any one of these victims any complaint of blackmail?" asked Pons then.

Jamison's eyes narrowed. "What are you getting at?"

Pons leaned forward and tapped the notes Ruthel had received.

Jamison picked them up.

"Lionel Ruthel received these prior to his death. You'll note the date on the envelope. He paid the first demand. He failed to pay the second. He died. Presumably, since he had thirty days, the demand was made at least a month ago."

"Marrakesch," mused Jamison.

"The Yard can institute inquiries there through Interpol," said Pons. "It would be interesting to learn whether Bresham and Stoner withdrew any substantial sums of money at any time during the past year."

"If they received any demands like these, we found no trace of them."

"Destroyed, no doubt."

"I'll have to take these, Pons," said Jamison.

"I have no further need of them. You'll have noticed their Oriental character. Further to this matter – it might be instructive to look into the disappearance of two young ladies – Miss Elena Brown of Fulham, and Miss Jasmine Struthers of South Norwood. I have the newspaper accounts; there may be further details in your files. I've come upon no continuing reference to either girl. No word of bodies. Nothing.

I put it to you, Jamison, that there is surely some connection between these missing girls and the garrottings."

"Possibly," agreed the Inspector. "There could be a connection. But bodies aren't always discovered, you know."

"That's what I pointed out," I put in. "Somebody knows – or found out. That would be motive enough for no one's complaining of blackmail."

"I submit that the character of the demands made on Ruthel hardly supports the contention," said Pons. "It is quite possible that these demands were preceded by letters setting forth details known to the blackmailer, designed to leave the victim in no doubt about the blackmailer's knowledge, though no such letter was turned up by Norris Ruthel, the dead man's brother, who applied to us."

"Nor was anything of that sort found at either Bresham's or Stoner's," added Jamison.

Pons sat for a few moments in contemplative silence. "Has the Underground carriage in which the body was found been put back into service?" he asked then.

"It's still being sequestered, but I believe it will be released in the morning."

Pons came to his feet with startling suddenness. "Then there is no time to be lost. I shall want to examine it."

As Pons threw off his dressing-gown and got into his Inverness, Jamison reached for his bowler, complaining indignantly that Pons could hardly hope to learn anything more than the Yard had already learned, for the car had been thoroughly gone over, nothing had escaped the experts from the Yard.

"We shall see," said Pons. "Come along, Parker."

Still under guard on an unused line at the Willesden Green Station, the scene of Lionel Ruthel's death in the carriage was indicated by Inspector Jamison, still visibly disgrunted. There was nothing to be seen to set it out for the inquiring eye. Since

Ruthel had been strangled, no blood marked the spot. Indeed, the strangling had evidently been done with singular efficience, for no disturbance whatsoever marked the area where Ruthel had been sitting.

"Had he fallen?" asked Pons.

"No. The body was in this corner, up against the wall. Propped there, we made it."

Pons, having scrutinized the seat, now gave his attention to the floor. This seemed to me equally as futile as examination of the seat had been, for countless feet had walked there both before and after the crime and, except for dust, the floor was clear; not even so much as a shred of paper was visible. Pons, however, was not daunted; he went down on his knees and explored with narrowed eyes the area of the floor around the place where the body had been found.

At one spot he peered intently. "Let me call your attention to this portion of a footprint, Jamison."

The Inspector bent, baffled. He got cumbersomely to his knees beside Pons and stared at the spot Pons indicated, muttering, "Hundreds of footprints. What can they tell us? Nothing."

"This one is the print of a bare foot."

So saying, Pons handed the Inspector the magnifying glass he had been using.

"Why," said Jamison after but a minute's scrutiny of the small print Pons had discovered close up to the base of the seat, "that is the print of a child's foot."

"Do you say so?"

"I do. You may not know it, Pons," Jamison continued, getting heavily to his feet, "but there are still children in London who are without shoes all year long. It is to be regretted, but there is simply not enough wherewithal to take care of all the indigent in our capital. They fare better in the country, though equally bare of foot."

"A much worn, deeply callused foot," said Pons. "Could a child's be that?"

"Compared to that of the average Londoner, I may say," said Jamison pompously, "that you lead a relatively reclusive life, Pons. You have no concept of the hardships the poor endure."

"Indeed," said Pons, with a twinkle in his eyes. "Then, if this print has no meaning to you, the Yard will not object to my scraping up some of the dust from around it."

Jamison hesitated, cannily aware of Pons's intuitions. "No, I'd say it won't matter. Spilsbury hasn't seen it, of course, so, if you do find anything, we'll count on your letting us know. In any case, the car goes back into service tomorrow."

"I will measure it first."

"It isn't even a complete print," Jamison said, as if excusing his permitting Pons to disturb the scene in any way.

"The ball of the foot and toes can be seen; the heel part has been trodden upon," agreed Pons. "But there is enough here to give us the dimensions."

He took from the capacious pockets in the lining of his cape a tape measure and went about his task. From outside the guard looked curiously in. Jamison watched tolerantly. The dimensions taken and set down in the little pocket notebook with pencil attached that Pons had fallen into the habit of carrying, Pons next brought out a small envelope into which he scraped the dust outlining the print on the carriage floor.

"I fancy that will do," he said, coming to his feet.

We left the carriage and mounted to the street, where Jamison's police car waited. The Inspector, thoughtfully silent now, had us taken back to our quarters and took his leave of us there.

For some time after our return Pons busied himself with the dust scrapings he had taken from the sequestered Underground carriage, working with his chemicals. He pored intently over the infinitesimal particles, saying nothing, though from time to time a small sound of discovery or pleasure rose from his corner. I sat impatiently waiting on him to finish his analysis, unable to concentrate on the evening paper, though the *Chronicle* did carry a further paragraph on what was now being called "the Underground murder," in which the only additional information given the public was the identity of the victim and some biographical details concerning him.

But at last Pons finished, put away his microscope and chemicals, and washed his hands.

"I suppose you can now give me a description of Ruthel's murderer," I said as he came over to lean against the mantel while he stuffed his pipe with the abominable shag he smoked from time to time.

"Oh, that is elementary, Parker," he replied. "He was a man of considerably less than average height, dusky skin – perhaps yellow-brown in color, bare of foot, Indo-Chinese or Burmese. In London he lives somewhere along the Thames, in the region of the East India Docks. A fragment of hemp which very probably came from his foot suggests as much, and there is alluvial soil peculiar to an area of excavation there. Limehouse, I fancy."

"You are having me!" I cried.

"That fragmentary footprint was certainly not a child's," Pons continued. "It was too broad for its length, for one thing, and its lines were too deeply etched. Its calloused character, too, indicated age. Moreover, there was just visible in part along the ball of the foot on the left edge – you will have observed that the print was of the left foot – a scar long ago healed. No doubt you also saw that the print had been made with some force..."

"Ah, a heavy man!"

"No, no, Parker," said Pons impatiently. "He was light, slender of frame – the impression was forcefully made because he put more than his ordinary weight on it during the act of strangling his victim."

"Fantastic!" I protested. "We began this inquiry with seven women, as I recall. This does not sound like the crime of a woman."

"The murder was committed by a man, Parker."

"A hired killer, then?"

"A professional."

"A professional assassin – perhaps from Burma," I ventured. "Was not our client in Burma? Six months in Rangoon, I think he said. Would it not be instructive to learn who is the late Lionel Ruthel's heir?"

"I daresay it will turn out to be our client."

"I need hardly point out to you, Pons, that murder for gain is the strongest of all motives."

"And for the murder of the previous victims?" asked Pons. He shook his head. "I am much inclined to doubt it. Did our client seem to you the kind of fellow who would make so bold as to bait me? I think not. No, I fancy we will have to look farther afield."

He sat for a while in an attitude of deep thought, tugging at the lobe of his left ear, a habit with which I had grown familiar early in our companionable relationship, his gaze into some distance from our quarters. He rose presently and began to pace back and forth in front of the mantel, arms folded across his chest, saying nothing. Now and then he glanced at the clock, as if estimating some matter of time, though it was not yet eight and darkness had not long come to London. For perhaps ten minutes longer he paced the floor; then he came to a stop with a sudden exclamation.

"Simon Fance!" he cried. "How blind I can be!"

Then he strode across the room and vanished into his chamber, from which came the sounds of a hasty change of clothing. In a few minutes he reappeared. He was transformed. He wore the garments of a beggar, from a battered and torn bowler down to broken shoes. The pockets of his overlong coat bulged with the kind of refuse that could be found in the gutters of many London streets in the East End. He had even stained his face and, since he habitually disliked to shave, however often he did so, he had not today done so, with the result that a stubble was clearly visible along his jaws and chin. In one hand he carried a worn paper sack, evidently filled with more of the trash the kind of man he purported to be would gather.

"I am constantly amazed at your penchant for disguise," I said. "If I hadn't seen you go into that room, I would never have recognized you."

He made me a small, albeit ironic bow. "Ordinarily I do not respond to flattery, but in this case..."

"You have certainly changed," I cried.

"Touché!" he replied. Then, sobering, he said, "I am going out," and, without any further word, he took his leave.

It was past midnight when Pons came in. Through the open door of my bedroom I saw him loom over the lamp I had left burning on the table, where I had propped up a message sent in by Inspector Jamison during his absence. I called out to him to make sure he did not miss seeing it.

"I see it," he answered.

His face in the light was a study in contrast. Clearly, what he read was neither unexpected nor wholly satisfactory.

"Jamison has looked into the accounts of the previous victims," he said at last. "Bresham withdrew no funds that could not be traced. Stoner drew out ten thousand pounds. No trace of it can be found."

"That's the same sum Ruthel paid."

"I observed it," said Pons dryly. "Bresham's death would appear to have had a salutary effect on the others. It strikes me as very likely that the three were in touch with one another, and all were implicated in the matter that served as the background of the blackmail. Bresham may have got word of the demand to Stoner and Ruthel; his death certainly prompted payment of the initial sum demanded of Stoner and Ruthel. Neither would meet a second demand, so both died. We are dealing with someone utterly ruthless, and I hope to uncover him tomorrow night."

"You know him?"

"Say rather I have certain suspicions."

More than this he would not say. He put out the light and retired to his chamber.

Well after darkness had fallen next evening, Pons proceeded once more to assume his disguise of the previous night. Moreover, he laid out similar clothing for me to wear.

"We are swimming in dangerous waters tonight, Parker," he explained. "We shall be required to go armed."

"We are two against one, surely," I said.

"Would that it were so!" he answered.

"Where are we going?"

"To the East India Docks. It will not surprise you to learn that our goal is an importing office near the site of an excavation."

"Nothing any longer surprises me, Pons."

"I found the place last night after considerable searching," Pons went on. "I looked for the excavation. The fragments of soil in the dust edging the print in the carriage were not surface earth. The importing business is quite legitimate, but it also serves as a front for something other. Last night thirty-one people entered that office; twenty came out. The other eleven were unaccounted for when the place closed. The manager also failed to emerge when the lights went out. Even though it may not be manifest to the eye, there is another exit below ground."

"Ah, the excavation!"

"The excavation has nothing to do with it. It is merely incidental to my discovery of the place, no more. I suspect that it will lead to a tenable solution of this interesting problem."

"Why do you say so?" I asked.

"It is elementary that only a comparatively widespread organization could produce, on demand, a lascar or dacoit to serve as a professional assassin. There is only one such in London, to my knowledge. It is part of a worldwide organization, headed, I am informed, by an ageless Chinese doctor of far more than average intelligence – a legendary figure not only throughout the underworld but also the political world. Perhaps you have never heard of the Si-Fan?"

"If I have, it has long been forgotten."

"The doctor's audacity is unbounded. His organization gives its name to that of the addressee to whom the late Lionel Ruth was directed to send his money. 'Simon Fance' – it was no credit to my powers of observation that I failed to see it at once. The doctor's fine hand is surely in this. Though he has been reported at various times in Hanoi, Rangoon, Beirut, Cairo, Peking, New York, Rome and elsewhere, Interpol now puts him in London. His minions, however, are everywhere, and if he is not directly involved in this triple murder, he may very well know which organization is behind it. It is imperative that I find him."

We found ourselves presently in Limehouse, concealed in the shadows from a vantage point in which we could watch the entrance to an old building that carried a poorly-lit sign announcing it as *Sam Lee Ltd., Importers.*

It was nine o'clock when we reached Limehouse. For the next forty-five minutes we observed visitors going into the importing office, and coming out again; but never quite as many emerged as entered. It was possible to see a man at a desk; he was approached by every visitor. Sometimes he unfolded brochures before callers, sometimes there appeared to be only curt, brief discussion. Now and then a visitor armed with brochures left the building; but just as frequently visitors repaired to the rear of the office, disappeared from sight, and were not seen again.

There was obviously some kind of exit at the rear of the room, perhaps leading into an inner chamber.

Before ten o'clock, a shutter was closed over the wide window facing the street and the light went out in the importing office. As Pons had seen the previous night, the manager did not emerge. The street was wanly lit, but the glow of the streetlamp was sufficient to have disclosed anyone coming from the building, which rose but two storeys above the ground level. No light appeared anywhere else in the structure; nor had any shown earlier, suggesting that the upper floor was untenanted.

Pons made no move to leave our place of concealment even after the building had been darkened, and when I leaned toward him to speak, exerted a gentle pressure on my shoulder as if to bid me be silent. So we waited on time to pass. The night deepened; the activity along the street diminished and fell away to nothing but the occasional appearance of a bobby on his round.

It was after midnight before Pons stirred. Then he led the way, drifting noiselessly across the street into the shadows beside the building we had been watching. Well back from the street, a side window invited his attention. He paused, dug down into the bulging pockets of the threadbare coat he wore, and produced, from under the nondescript items he had assembled to carry with him, a small tool.

"Lend me your back, Parker," he whispered.

I bent down.

From above I heard the rasping sound of glass being cut – then, after an interval, of the window being raised.

Pons climbed into the building. He leaned out to give me a hand up.

Once we were both inside, Pons produced a torch, the light of which revealed that we were in a room behind the front office – evidently only a waiting-room of some kind. A few chairs, a lounge, a full-length mirror could be seen. Disappointingly, though the room patently ran the width of the building, there was no door to be seen but that leading to the front office.

"It must be the mirror," murmured Pons.

He strode over to it. He ran his fingers along its edge, examining, probing, until he found what he sought; then the mirror slid noiselessly to one side, disclosing steps leading down into a passageway dark save for one dim light above the foot of the stairs.

Without hesitation, Pons plunged noiselessly down the steps, his torch lighting the way. Less than fifty feet from the stairs, we found ourselves confronted by a honeycomb of passages, all of which showed evidence of frequent use. Pons dropped to his knees to scrutinize the stone flooring laid there, judging by its appearance, decades ago, for any clue to persistent use along one passage more than any other; but this proved non-rewarding. Nor was it necessary to lead us into the most used passage. Pons stood upright, flashing his torch around. He lifted his head and inhaled deeply.

"Do you smell it, Parker?" he asked in a whisper.

"The musk of the Thames," I said.

"Try again."

I took a deep breath "Yes, I smell it now. Incense. Sandalwood."

"This way," said Pons, as he pressed on along a passage that led sharply right down a further trio of steps deeper beneath the surface.

It was presently evident that we were approaching occupied quarters, for there were occasional sounds ahead of us. Pons proceeded with greater caution, turning off his torch ever and anon, lest our progress be marked. The scent of sandalwood had grown much stronger; it now seemed to pervade the entire passage, as well as lesser passages which now and then led away from what was clearly the central corridor.

Doors began to show in the walls. At each of them Pons paused to listen. I too pressed an ear to three such doors, and heard the even susurrus of breathing behind it.

"Someone sleeping," I whispered.

Pons tried each door until at last he found one that was not locked. He opened it noiselessly, at first but enough to assure him that all was dark within; then he widened the aperture and flashed his torch inside.

The light swept over a small bed-chamber, and fell finally upon a sleeping woman, lingering only long enough to show that she was Caucasian, not Oriental, however much the appointments of the room and our general surroundings were Oriental, and that she was perhaps younger than her worn appearance suggested. Then Pons turned off his torch and withdrew.

Not far down the passage another unlocked door opened upon a similar chamber. In this room, too, a woman of indeterminate age slept. Something of Pons's excitement communicated itself to me. Could these be two of the women he sought? But indeed, I did not know precisely what he was searching for. Withdrawing from the second room, he stood briefly in an attitude of deep thought.

Ahead of us, dimly visible in the wan light of the passage, loomed a door covered with what looked like green baize with a satin sheen. To this Pons now moved with cat-like caution. Manifestly, this door led to some central place in these elaborate underground quarters.

He pressed one ear to it. He sought in vain for any knob; it had none. Its mechanism was hidden. Pons explored its frame.

From somewhere behind it came the faint sound of distant bells – a tintinnabulation reminiscent of temple bells that evoked the Orient even more effectively than the scent of incense, which was now almost overpowering and apparently emanated from the room behind the door. Then all was still once more, save for what seemed to be the sound of a generator, which had pulsed steadily throughout the time we had spent in these subterranean passages.

Pons continued to probe the green baize door with his slender fingers – and once again the tinkling of bells sounded behind it

Pons withdrew his fingers abruptly.

"I may have set off an alarm," he whispered.

Suddenly that instinct – primitive in every man – of being observed, welled up in me. I turned – to come almost face to face with a dark-skinned, half-naked Oriental, lithe and muscular – and saw others behind him, coming in from both sides of the corridor. I had time but to cry out, to reach in vain for the gun Pons had given me to carry, when they were upon us. I saw Pons go down. I felt simultaneously a leather thong descend over my head and begin to tighten on my neck.

Just before consciousness slipped away, I saw the green baize door sink inward and slide to one side, and heard a sibilant voice issue a sharp command in Chinese. Then I heard and saw no more.

I came to with Pons bending over me, chafing my wrists.

"Ah, Parker, thank heaven you're not hurt!" he cried. "I would never have forgiven myself if anything had happened to you."

I looked around dazedly. My neck burned from the friction of the thong that had come close to snuffing out my life. I saw that Pons's neck bore an angry red bruise to show that he too had almost been strangled, and had no doubt that I too carried such a bruise.

We were in a sumptuously appointed room of considerable size. Handsome Oriental rugs covered the floor; draperies of brilliant red, purple and blue hung down the walls. I was lying on a divan; an impression beside me indicated that Pons must have been lying there too until he recovered consciousness. On a teakwood table nearby stood two glasses filled with liquid.

As Pons helped me to my feet, a sibilant, almost hissing voice arrested us; it came into the room evidently from a speaking tube behind one of the drapes.

"You will find something refreshing on the table, Gentlemen. I am happy that I recognized you, Mr. Solar Pons, in time to save your life – in spite of that somewhat outré disguise you have effected."

"Doctor..." began Pons. Our host's voice stopped him. "We are nameless here, Mr. Pons. Pray refresh yourselves. I assure you it is the best obtainable Scotch. It contains none of those diabolical poisons which have been credited to my use." Pons drank, and I followed suit, knowing as well as Pons that had our deaths been desired the speaker need only have kept from interfering when his dacoits were garrotting us.

"What or whom do you seek here?"

"Elena," answered Pons.

There was a sharp hiss of indrawn breath. Then, "I am not unfamiliar with your reputation, Mr. Pons."

"Nor I with yours. 'Simon Fance' indeed. Was that not unworthy of you, Doctor?"

"That was not my hand. Some day, Mr. Pons, our paths may cross."

"I am here," said Pons.

"But not now. There are certain social considerations in this affair no English gentleman could ignore." There was, I thought, not only suppressed laughter in his voice, but more than a hint of scorn, if not contempt. "Evidence would be too difficult to bring out. I need hardly tell you that. You know little; you suspect much."

"Why only seven women, Doctor?"

"There were only that number in Marrakesch. There were others in Mexico, still others in the Middle East. Certain Amencan, French, and German men have paid. It has been and no doubt will continue to be, a profitable undertaking. Of course, the victims of these gentlemen will be reimbursed, but it is only honest to say that an organization like mine is constantly in need of funds. You are well aware, Mr. Pons, that your national system of justice leaves very much to be desired, though the British sense of fair play frequently effects a balance. Disclosure would fall most heavily upon the unfortunate young women who were the victims of such men as Ruthel, Bresham, and Stoner, but they, apart from lending me their means without their knowledge, are completely innocent of my campaign on their behalf, and were set free from their brutal service and brought here on my direction."

"A campaign even more in your interests," said Pons.

"True," said our hidden host imperturbably. "I do not think, Mr. Pons, that this fact will in sum trouble you overmuch. You are a private agent, not responsible to the police. I too am a private agent, responsible to no one but myself – as you know. I am not a philanthropist, I am too old – far older than you can believe – to subscribe to the quaint idealism of the Caucasians, and I am imbued with the philosophy of the East, which does not hold to the same veneration for life that saturates your effete civilization."

"What will happen to the women you – rescued?"

"They will be returned to the world – perhaps not the world from which they were lured, unless they wish it. They will go free to choose their own courses, and with adequate funds to live on comfortably for a while. I am not philanthropic, Mr. Pons, but I am not without compassion, despite my known ruthlessness, more compassion than British justice would afford them – merciless exposure, sympathy, but little coin of the realm."

"Eventually the Yard will reach you, Doctor."

"I think not. Tomorrow the importing office will be abandoned; the passage is even now being closed, filled in and sealed. Do not discount my thoroughness."

"I would not forgive myself for underrating an opponent," said Pons.

"Do not mistake me. We are not yet that. Had I thought we were, you would be dead. I am more familiar with your nature and your character than you can imagine, Mr. Pons." There was now a pause, during which our host's sibilant voice could be heard issuing orders in his native language to someone at his side. "Attend me now," he resumed. "You will presently fall asleep. Do not be alarmed. Do not struggle against it; that would be needlessly futile. You will be transported from here by another exit, and you will wake in familiar surroundings far from Limehouse. Farewell, Gentlemen. Until we meet again."

Even as he spoke, I became aware of a cloying perfume, fragrant as the exhalation of heliotrope or mimosa, masking the scent of a powerful sedative pouring into the room from behind the drapes. I could not identify it, but suspected it to be Asiatic in origin.

"We're being drugged," I said.

Pons made a gesture of calm assurance, as if submitting unafraid to whatever ordeal lay ahead. "We have no alternative but to take the Doctor at his word." He sat quietly, his eyes closed, waiting.

I felt myself growing drowsy. Though I fought against yielding, I knew I could not remain awake. As I fell asleep, I felt Pons's body settling against mine.

I woke to familiar surroundings indeed. We were back in our own quarters at 7B, Praed Street. Pons was just emerging from his chamber, already clad in his mouse-colored dressing-gown, and not in the least lacking in his customary alertness, though I felt groggy and dazed.

"Ah, Parker," he said, "you are uncommonly sensitive to the Doctor's sedative. I have been up and about for some time."

"How came we here?"

"We were obviously brought. The Doctor leaves nothing to chance. It would not serve his purpose to have us discovered in a state of torpor in a public park. A remarkable man! A pity that his life is given to crime and intrigue – and worse, to a megalomaniacal desire for world power!"

Struggling to shake myself free of the sluggishness that held me, I said, "I must admit I understand little of this."

"You will, Parker. I hear our client's step on the stairs even now. I sent for him."

"At this hour! Why, it is almost four in the morning!"

"Any hour will do, Parker. If we are to move, we must move quickly."

"'If?'"

Pons regarded me soberly for a silent moment. "I said 'if' advisedly. I submit there are other considerations but those of simple justice."

Norris Ruthel's knock fell upon the door.

Pons crossed the room and threw the door wide. "Come in, Mr. Ruthel, come in. Pray forgive me for bringing you out at this hour, but events have come to a head. Sit down, sir. I need your advice."

Our client, who had walked across and seated himself, looked at Pons with an air of surprised inquiry. "*My* advice?" he asked in an uncertain voice, as if he had not heard aright.

"I did not misspeak, Mr. Ruthel," Pons assured him. "I have uncovered certain facts. Before proceeding in the matter of your brother's murder I felt it incumbent upon me to consult you."

"Me, sir?" asked our client in unfeigned astonishment.

"You, indeed. As my client, you must be informed before anyone else. Specifically now, I must know whether to proceed or whether to lay such facts – I stress *facts* as I know them, other than what I surmise – before Scotland Yard for them to carry on."

Ruthel's pale blue eyes widened.

"Your late brother," continued Pons, "was, with his partners, engaged in an enterprise other than the importing of art objects. It was a kind of exporting venture, if I may put it so crudely. My esteemed companion has suggested that there could hardly be a stronger motive for blackmail than murder; I submit that there are stronger motives, and one in particular that carries a deadly social obloquy that affects all the parties to it."

Our client's bewilderment was almost painfully evident, but he interjected no question.

"To put it bluntly – your brother, with Henry Bresham and George Stoner, was engaged in supplying young girls for the purpose of enforced prostitution – the young women were lured from the country, very probably to Paris, and were abducted from there to be put into the brothels of Africa and the Middle East."

Ruthel paled. "Lionel in the white slave traffic!" he cried in a strangled voice.

"I fear there can be no doubt of it, Mr. Ruthel."

Pons waited for our client to compose himself.

"Go on, sir," said Ruthel presently.

"Seven of these unfortunate women were discovered in a brothel in Marrakesch by the agents of a sinister Oriental who heads a worldwide organization dedicated to the sinister eventual domination of the world – a fantastic dream, the dream of a megalomaniac. From these young women he learned how they came to be there. He conceived the idea of blackmailing the men responsible for this hideous traffic – not only in England, but elsewhere on the Continent and in

America. His agents rescued the girls who stood for the seven stars of the signature on your brother's levying letters – the seven for whose impressment into prostitution your brother and his partners were responsible – and proceeded to levy his blackmailing demands upon them. The name attached to the letters – 'Simon Fance' – was in fact false, but it stood for the name of the organization, 'the Si-Fan' – which, when I recognized it, led me to him.

"Faced with the threat of exposure, your brother paid the first demand made upon him. He balked at the second. Only a very powerful fear of disgrace – which would certainly have resulted from the exposure of his former activities – could have overcome his natural parsimoniousness, which you pointed out to us. But by the time the second demand was levied upon him, he had begun to recover the assurance he had lost when the first demand came to him out of a past he had thought buried in foreign brothels far from England. Your brother's death – as well as others – was brought about through the agency of men in the Doctor's service – devoted lascars and dacoits especially trained in murder."

"Monstrous!" cried Ruthel.

"It is indeed," agreed Pons.

"Can he and his men be taken?"

"Possibly. It has been tried before this," answered Pons. "Are you sure you wish it done?"

Ruthel looked his surprise. "Ought not justice to be served, Mr. Pons?"

"I submit there are some who would say that justice has been served, Mr. Ruthel."

"It must be done, sir!"

"Gently, gently, Mr. Ruthel. Pray reflect on this. I am little concerned for your late brother's reputation – but there are the young women to consider. If this matter is disclosed, they too will be discovered, their lives revealed, and their sordid evidence given to all the world. The press knows no mercy, as surely you are aware. Their lives, already badly scarred, will unquestionably be ruined. I do not condone murder – but justice, Mr. Ruthel, has more than one face. The young women are at present in London, and they will shortly be set free – with funds collected from your brother and others – to begin their lives again where and how they wish. If we proceed in this matter, they will hardly be able to do so after the spate of publicity, with their pictures in the papers that must inevitably result. The choice is yours, Mr. Ruthel."

Our client bounded to his feet and began to pace the floor in agitation. "I see your point, Mr. Pons," he muttered, passing in one direction. "It will not bring Lionel back to life" – on his return. "I suppose it could not be done without involving them," – passing again. "No, no, hardly," he answered himself, returning. It was as if the demand for traditional justice vied visibly with his sense of fair play. "The whole issue is the demand for Judaeo-Christian justice, in sum," he went on. "But what justice does that ultimately leave these unfortunate women?"

"Precisely," agreed Pons.

Our client came abruptly to a stand before Pons, planted his handsome cane hard upon the floor, and cried out, "We have had enough of it. If you will send me an accounting, I will send you a cheque, Mr. Pons. You must do as you see fit. I wash my hands of it."

After he had gone, I protested. "Pons, you cannot do it."

"Tut, tut – I can do as I like. Tomorrow I will place the essential facts before Jamison – the scientific knowledge gleaned from an examination of the dust in the Underground carriage, for example – and I will give him enough of what I surmised to put him on the track of the Doctor. But if I know our friend from the Yard, he will laugh at me, and nothing will come of it."

And so it turned out.

IX

THE ADVENTURE OF THE BISHOP'S COMPANION

"An elderly woman," said Solar Pons, raising his head from his chemical problem at the first sound from the foot of the stairs to our quarters at 7B, Praed Street one May morning in 1932.

"At this hour?" I cried. "Why it is scarcely eight – the day has but begun."

"Ah, Parker, *your* day, perhaps, but not hers."

The steps mounted slowly to the landing and ended with a timid knock. Pons strode across the room and threw the door wide.

"Why, it is Mrs. Parton, is it not?" he cried.

"I am surprised you remember me, Mr. Pons."

An old woman, wearing an absurd hat of black straw from which a daisy stuck up and wilted downward, with a shawl about her rounded shoulders, and an ankle-length dress in brown to complete her costume, walked diffidently into the room.

"Parker, you will surely remember Mrs. Parton, who was of some little help to us in that affair of the Gentle Entomologists," continued Pons. "Pray sit down, Mrs. Parton." He thrust forward a chair.

Ten years ago! I would hardly have recognized her, so much had change and time altered her appearance. She had lost weight – shrunk together, as it were – and was now an old woman who had been then a buxom lady on the fading edge of middle age. She nodded and smiled at me, gave me her hand, and sat down.

"Seeing as how I was in London, Mr. Pons, I thought I'd just step around and tell you about my trouble – if you'd not take it amiss," she said with the air of one who did not expect Pons to object.

"By all means, Mrs. Parton," said Pons, with that unfailing courtesy that always struck me as in such contrast to his views of women and wedded bliss. "Let us hear about your trouble. And with whom is it?"

"The Bishop!" she said with spirit, her dark eyes snapping. "Bishop Lamson. That's who."

"Lamson: of Norwich," mused Pons. "But he has been retired for seven years."

"Indeed, he has. And lives in my village, Mr. Pons. Retired and shut up, you might say. But I'm not the one to talk about him or anybody, Mr. Pons, I am not. But why did he now, after baptizing my grandson Peter half a year gone, set about and send me a bill? Think of it! Did we not make a freewill offering? Indeed we did. But he sent me a bill, and I went round and told him right off I would pay no such bill. Five pounds for a baptism! Mr. Pons, it's an outrage, it's a – a libel on the Church of England."

Pons's eyes began to twinkle. "Is it possible to libel the Church of England? I wonder. Five pounds, you say. Has he performed any other little services of similar nature for you, Mrs. Parton, since he came to Wilder's Weald?"

"Many a one, Mr. Pons."

"And sent you a bill?"

"Never!"

"Perhaps he is in his dotage," ventured Pons.

"He did not seem so to me," replied Mrs. Parton with asperity. "A bit muddled, perhaps, and still shaken up over the loss of his companion three months ago. But no more."

"His curate?"

Mrs. Parton shook her head. "Another old fellow come down from London to live with him on his retirement. Kept to himself. He sickened a while back and next thing we knew he was dead. Pneumonia. The two never suspected it – the Bishop nor he – but the Bishop kept a-nursing him till he was almost gone, and then he sent after Dr. Prendle, and that was an end of Mr. George Moulton. Buried and all, these months since. But it may have been," said Mrs. Parton with a momentary hesitation in her voice, "what was done to Mr. Moulton's stone in the church cemetery. Knocked about and markings scratched on – vandals' work, Mr. Pons. It may have been that upset him – but hardly to the point of quarreling with me. Now, Mr. Pons, what am I to do? Pay for his service – and I should think not – or refuse him?"

She fixed Pons with bright expectant eyes.

"You have remonstrated with His Lordship?"

"I tried."

"Ah, he would not see you?"

"Oh, 'twas not that. He saw me, but he would not talk of it. He had a bad cold and was forever coughing. Truth to tell, he had the look of a sick man. And what good would it have done? He's that absent-minded he'd have forgotten the freewill offering even if it were made but two days ago."

"Ah, well, Mrs. Parton, perhaps that is the solution of the matter – he simply forgot that he had been paid for his service."

"It wasn't, you see, Mr. Pons, that he had to baptize Peter. He needn't have done it. Mister Newell could've taken care of it, only my son had a fancy to have the Bishop do it, so I spoke to him and he did it."

Mrs. Parton punctuated her lines with little nods, so that the daisy on her hat was forever dancing and swaying.

"Ah, Mrs. Parton, I am sure this little disagreement will iron itself out," said Pons placatingly. "When the Bishop has recovered from his cold, you go around to see him and explain that the service was paid for – just jog his memory a bit."

"I tried," said Mrs. Parton indignantly. "He wouldn't hear of it. Just kept coughing and waving me off."

"And if he insists upon being paid," continued Pons, "do let me know and I will look into the matter for you."

Mrs. Parton got to her feet, her plain face showing her gratification.

The door had hardly closed upon her when I burst into laughter. "What must they think of you, Pons! Last week it was Mrs. Johnson's friend who wanted you to find her stray cat – a fortnight past that boy whose sack of marbles had been stolen – now it has come to collecting bills!"

"I fancy it is not precisely that, Parker. Rather the other way around." The twinkle had vanished from Pons' eyes, which now wore that thoughtful, pensive expression with which I was all too familiar.

"Pons, you could not have meant it seriously when you promised to take up the matter?"

"It did not seem to you to have some points of interest?" asked Pons in his most annoying manner.

"None," I replied firmly.

"It does not occur to you to wonder whether there might not be some connection between the desecration of Mr. Moulton's gravestone and Mrs. Parton's being sent an unwarranted bill?"

"What possible connection could there be?"

"Ah, that is precisely the problem that intrigues me."

"Why, we read constantly of such vandalism. It is primarily the work of adolescents bent upon mischief."

"True," agreed Pons. "But this is another of those coincidences that may have more significance than we dream of. I think we may safely assume that Mrs. Parton is one of those individuals who are forever looking about to see how much they can get for nothing – a group to which most of mankind appears to belong; so in that she is certainly not in any way out of the ordinary. We may conclude that she has been in the habit of calling upon Bishop Lamson for various services for which she would have to pay the vicar. It is quite possible that His Lordship rebelled at last, and has sought to put a stop to the practise by imposing a heavy fee."

"I don't blame him. But he ought to have done it at the time of the baptism," I said. "I have my own idea of the size of that 'freewill offering'."

"And I," agreed Pons.

"Particularly," I could not help adding, "since I noticed she made none to you."

"Mrs. Parton made no mention of the cemetery's being vandalized, however," Pons went on. "Only Moulton's stone. Is that not singular?"

"A coincidence."

"Of a kind I find suspect."

So saying, he took from its place a copy of the *Railway Guide*, and began to page through it.

"Pons, you cannot mean it seriously!"

"Nothing presses me at the moment, Parker. I have a fancy to run down to Sussex and pay Bishop Lamson a visit."

I held back the words I could have said, but I had no doubt Pons read them in my face, for he smiled impishly.

"Ah, here we are. We have ample time to make the next train at Victoria. Are you free?"

"I am always free for any adventure of yours," I said, somewhat stiffly, I fear, "though I should hate to see you come a cropper."

"A pity I cannot adequately reward your loyalty, Parker!"

Wilder's Weald was little more than a hamlet not far from the border of Surrey. It consisted of two score houses and a few shops, all on the one side of the railroad station, across from which flowed a little brook through a swale now bright with kingcups and fritillaries in blossom. Its small but old church rose on the far edge of the village, with the vicar's home on the one side, and the cemetery on the other. And beyond the cemetery, as Pons ascertained from the agent at the railroad station, was the home of Bishop Lamson.

Pons did not elect to call on His Lordship immediately, however. He went around to the cemetery, where we found the defaced stone that marked George Moulton's grave, and there we stood looking at it, while the wind carried through the cemetery the fragrance of the fields, and a lark sang overhead against the background music of a dog's voice rising at a distance. The stone had clearly been scarred, for someone had slashed the lettering.

"That was done with iron or steel," I said.

"Elementary," said Pons. "And, if I am not mistaken, in anger. Further, I submit it was not an act of adolescent vandalism. Adolescents are far more given to upsetting stones than to defacing them in this manner."

"There are always exceptions."

"True. But not, I fancy, in this case. Have you seen any evidence of other vandalism?"

"Let me just look about," I said.

I moved through the cemetery, from one gravestone to another. There were moss-encrusted stones dating back more than two centuries, weather-worn stones, plots overgrown with lilies-of-the-valley, stones almost hidden by rosebushes; there were generations of Cutlers, Swintons, Norrises, and even a Parker or two. But there was no other stone that bore any mark of desecration.

"None," ventured Pons at my return.

"None," I agreed. "Someone must not have liked Moulton."

"We might discuss the matter with the vicar," said Pons, "for if I am not mistaken, that is he coming toward the cemetery from behind the church."

I turned to look. A spare gentleman of less than medium height was hastening in our direction. He had a ruddy face, two whitening tufts for eyebrows, and closely-clipped greying hair. His gaze was unmistakably bent upon us and the expression he wore was one of enquiry.

"Can I do anything for you, gentlemen?" he asked, as he came up to us.

"Mister Newell, I presume?" said Pons, and introduced himself.

"I have read a thing or two of you, Mr. Pons," said the vicar with some manifest reservation.

"I have, unfortunately, no control over what is printed in the country's press," said Pons. Then, stepping aside a little, he pointed to the Moulton stone. "Pray tell me, sir, when was that vandalism done?"

"This past week – perhaps eight days ago. Or nights," said the vicar.

"Was this man so disliked?"

"Did you know him?" countered the vicar.

"No. But, since he was the Bishop's companion, I take it you did."

"Though it is not generally known, he was the Bishop's half-brother, Mr. Pons. Forgive me for bearing witness against my neighbor, but I had the impression from my conversations with the Bishop before Moulton came that Moulton was a wastrel and now a derelict come to live out his misspent life with the Bishop. He came here from somewhere in Spain. And since he's been here, he went nowhere except now and then up to London. But he troubled no one, did the gardening and such, and kept to himself. Disliked?" he went on, returning to Pons's question. "I should hardly have thought anyone knew him well enough to dislike him."

"And you did not?"

"No, sir. I've had a word or two with him now and then when had occasion to visit Bishop Lamson. And that wasn't often, for, you see, the Bishop is retired, and he is not *my* Bishop. If I passed Moulton in the garden, I gave him the time of day or made some comment on the flowers, hardly more."

"A big man?"

"Oh, no, Mr. Pons. A small, wiry fellow. One would hardly have thought he'd go so quick, but perhaps living on his half-brother's largesse was disheartening. He was a good man, though, surely, for he spent many hours in the church, where more than once I found him meditating at the foot of the altar, on his knees, too. Whatever his sins might have been, he certainly repented. And the Bishop has missed him grievously; he has hardly been out of the house since his death. But then, he is old, and he was never much given to going about. If he so much as attended a garden party, he would have a score of invitations thrust upon him; rather than establish a precedent, he accepted none. He prefers to spend his time with his books."

Pons looked thoughtfully again at the vandalized gravestone. Then he turned once more to the vicar. "Wilder's Weald would seem to be a small living, Mister Newell."

"Very small." The vicar sighed.

"So that a stranger would be observed. Have you seen any such about?"

The vicar paused and visibly cast his thoughts backward. "Ah, there are always those who come to look at the village – in search of the quaint. And those who take down inscriptions and epitaphs on the stones," he said reflectively.

"Within the past fortnight?"

The vicar nodded. "I seem to recall two ladies two Sundays past. And a single man after that."

"Dark?"

Newell started. "It is odd that you should say so, Mr. Pons. Uncommonly dark – but not coloured, definitely not coloured."

"Thank you. I daresay we might call on the Bishop."

The vicar looked dubious. "It might do no harm to try. He doesn't always answer a knock."

"We shall chance it."

Bidding the vicar good-day, we walked out of the cemetery and over to the Bishop's house, which was surrounded by a hedge of yew, and much embowered by trees, though there was a cleared space for a flower garden. The house itself was of brick, and, though it was not a new house, it wore an air of neatness and self-sufficience, for it hugged the ground, and the door at the front stood under an arch of ivy, its leaves now agleam in the afternoon sun.

Pons strode up to the door and sounded the knocker. Silence answered.

He knocked again, more peremptorily.

This time we could hear someone shuffling toward the door inside, and presently the door opened only far enough to reveal that it was on a latch, for the chain was plainly visible.

A venerably bearded face looked out at us, dark eyes inquiring over spectacles. In his dark clothing and gaiters, the Bishop was scarcely visible, though his pectoral cross reflected the light. "Bishop Lamson?" asked Pons.

"I am he," said the Bishop gravely. "What can I do for you?"

"We have come about the matter of the vandalism done to Mr. Moulton's gravestone."

I could not be sure, but I thought the Bishop looked momentarily startled. Then he murmured, "Oh, to be sure, gentlemen. Come in." He unlatched the door and swung it open, closed it behind us, and then shuffled ahead of us, asking us to "Please come this way." He added, "I was not aware that Constable Cowles had sent for outside help."

He led us into what must certainly have been his study, for it was a room literally overwhelmed with books. Indeed, I saw now that the Bishop carried a book open in one hand, with a thumb in it to keep his place. He tumbled a little pile of books from a chair he passed, and then went on to the chair he must have left to answer our knock.

Facing us from his chair, he invited us to sit down, fixing inquiring eyes upon us – clear, brown, alert eyes that shone from under his beetling brows.

"My name is Solar Pons," said Pons, and introduced me.

Though Bishop Lamson made no sign to indicate that he had ever heard of Pons, I thought I detected a slight quickening of interest in his eyes.

"It is hardly worth the trouble to investigate, Mr. Pons," said the Bishop. "A boy's prank. I shall have the stone replaced."

"We understand that Mr. Moulton was your half-brother."

"Yes, that is true. I fear George was always a trifle wayward. When he came back to England at last, all the family were gone except myself. So he naturally came here. He was a faithful companion, Mr. Pons, and he was quite content to rusticate here."

"Where had he been?"

"Oh, somewhere on the Continent," said the Bishop vaguely. "He did tell me, but I am so absent-minded I have already forgotten."

"Spain?" asked Pons.

"Spain," repeated the Bishop, his eyes narrowing. "Dear me, you must have been making inquiries. Did Cowles send for you?"

"No, My Lord. A lady sent for us."

"Touching of her to be so concerned, whoever she was," murmured the Bishop.

If His Lordship were hinting that he would like to know our client's identity, Pons was not about to gratify him. Instead, he drew from an inner pocket a little black leather case, opened it and handed it to the Bishop.

"Does this photograph in any way resemble your late half-brother when he was a young man?" he asked.

Bishop Lamson took the case wonderingly and studied the photograph. Then he shook his head. "Nothing at all like George, Mr. Pons. Nothing. I cannot think where you obtained this or why you should have thought it might have resembled George."

He handed the leather case back to Pons, who restored it to his pocket, then rose to his feet.

"I am sorry to have troubled My Lord," said Pons crisply.

"You've been no trouble, Mr. Pons, I assure you," replied the Bishop. But he did not rise to see us out. "I trust you can find the way."

"Indeed we can."

Pons thanked the Bishop and we withdrew.

Once outside, I could not forebear asking to see the photograph Pons had shown the Bishop.

"You would be all too familiar with it, Parker," Pons chuckled. "I found it in our quarters. It is an old one of you."

"Of me!" I cried.

"Yes, yes – any photograph would have done. You have such typically British features, Parker, that your photograph was ideal for my purpose." He paused to consult his watch. "The day is growing old, and we have one or two little matters yet to attend to. I see a stationer's shop over yonder. I want to send a note to Scotland Yard, and while I am about it, do be a good fellow and go around to the stationmaster to inquire whether he saw any stranger in the village – possibly getting off the train – in the course of the past fortnight or so. If I might venture to guess – a dark-skinned man."

"A Jamaican?"

"I have not said so," he answered testily.

I did as Pons asked.

The stationmaster, who was the same man who had directed us to Bishop Lamson's home, was a middle-aged man who had his wits about him. Directly I asked my question, he had the answer for me.

"You must mean the foreign gentleman who asked for Bishop Lamson. He came in on the train a week ago or thereabouts."

"You've seen him since? When did he leave?"

"He didn't leave by train. But he could have walked away or gone by motorcar."

Pons waited for me on my return. He listened to what I had to report, but did not comment. When I had finished he said only, "If you have no objection, Parker, we'll just engage a room at the Bell Inn over yonder, and spend the night. I have one or two little enquiries yet to make before we go round to call on Bishop Lamson once more."

"I have no urgent case," I assured him.

But once in the room Pons engaged, I could hold off my questions no longer. Pons was clearly on the track of something, which, as far as I could determine, was extremely nebulous. What was it?

"I put it to you, Parker," he replied, "that it is not just coincidence that a visitor inquiring for Bishop Lamson should arrive in Wilder's Weald at the same time that George Moulton's gravestone is desecrated."

"I confess I do not see any connection between those events."

"I submit that the visitor to Wilder's Weald was in search of George Moulton, not the Bishop, but asked for the Bishop because he had learned that Moulton lived with his half-brother."

"And, on learning from the Bishop that Moulton was dead, he was so disappointed that he went over to Moulton's grave and vandalized the stone," I finished. "I could hardly conceive of a more pointless act."

Pons smiled enigmatically. "All things are possible," he retorted.

"I know your scant respect for some members of the clergy," I went on. "Surely you do not suspect Bishop Lamson to be guilty of some skullduggery?"

"Did he impress you as the sort of man who, having served his church faithfully for all his life, would turn to something unethical in his retirement years?" asked Pons. "Come, Parker, say not so! Heaven forbid I should have infected you with some of that dubiety that comes so naturally to me!"

"By no means!"

"Splendid."

"But what is the problem?"

"I submit it is as plain as a pikestaff. The undeserved bill sent to Mrs. Parton. The defacing of George Moulton's stone. And," he added darkly, "I fear the Bishop is in it up over his head!"

"Incredible!" I cried.

"Is it not!" he replied, rubbing his hands energetically together. "But let us sleep on it."

In the morning we walked through the dew-fresh air, ringing with lark and chaffinch song, to the home of Bishop Lamson. The village was astir, but not yet the Bishop, for there was no response to our knock. Pons knocked yet louder. Still there was no response.

He set off around the house, pausing to notice that a side window was open and knocked at the rear door, which stood slightly ajar. Still there was no answer.

Pons ventured to push the door back. A sharp cry of dismay escaped his lips as he pressed forward.

The door opened directly upon a kitchen – but a kitchen in complete shambles – crockery, knives, forks, dishes, cups, towels – everything had been thrown from the cupboards, some to lie broken on the floor.

"I fear we are too late," said Pons grimly.

He made his way through the shambles into the adjacent room. Here, too, everything was torn apart and strewn about. The open window we had observed led into this room. Pons stepped over to it, made but a brief scrutiny, and said, "Forced!"

"Bishop Lamson?"

Pons made no reply. He pushed into the study, where many of the books had been thrown to the floor from the shelves, and then at last came to the Bishop's bedchamber.

Though this room too was torn apart, with the bureau drawers emptied and the closet door ajar, showing how the clothing inside had been pulled apart, it was the bed that drew my eyes as Pons stood aside for me to precede him. For it was literally drenched in blood – the Bishop's blood – sheets, blanket, spread – blood spattered the bedstead, the adjacent wall, the carpet – and what had been Bishop Lamson lay in the middle of it, asprawl on his back on the bed, his arms flung wide, his throat cut, and repeated stab-wounds in his chest and abdomen, so that his pajamas were soaked in blood.

I brushed past Pons and bent to examine the body, while Pons waited impatiently.

"Dead?" he asked finally.

"Since between midnight and two o'clock," I replied.

Thereupon Pons sprang into action like a hound on the scent. He examined the dead man's hands and discovered flesh clawed in under his fingernails. "So he had a few moments to attempt fighting off his assailant," he concluded. He uncovered part of a bloodstained footprint on the floor off the carpet, and measured it carefully. "We shall want a small man. He was barefooted here. He undoubtedly surprised his victim, but he came to kill him, and he did so. Whatever he sought was looked for after the murder. See," pointed Pons, "here and there clothing lies over the bloodstains. But did he find what he sought?"

Careful to disturb nothing, Pons now went from room to room, until he came to a small bedroom under the gable upstairs. This room had been only partially torn apart; the searcher had got down only to the second drawer of the small bureau, and there he had stopped. Some folded clothing had evidently been pulled out of this drawer, but a layer still remained undisturbed. Pons felt it delicately with the tips of his lean fingers.

"Some uneven object was hidden here," he deduced. "I should not be surprised to find that it was a pouch containing precious stones. Whatever it was, it appears to have been the goal of the thief's search."

He turned. "Come, Parker. We are finished here. Let us notify Constable Cowles. Then I must send a wire to the Yard asking them to cover all ports for a small, dark-skinned man, very probably a Spaniard, with at least two scratches down one side of his face, and in possession of a pouch of jewels.

"One little aspect of the matter," said Pons, as we came out of the telegraph office, "that continues to intrigue me, is the late George Moulton's devotion. Did he have the sound of a churchgoing man to you, Parker?"

"He did not."

"Yet the vicar told us he had spent many hours in church – at the foot of the altar, I believe he said."

"Those were his words."

"I have a fancy to view the spot."

I knew better than to challenge him when he bent his steps toward the church.

St. Christopher's proved to be a church built by an architect in love with the Gothic, and decorated under the direction of a High Church clergyman, for, though the well of the church was severe and spare, the altar was ablaze with ornaments, even to idolatrous statues and a large jeweled crucifix.

Pons made his way to the foot of the altar and stood for a few moments looking about him. The dim light entering through the coloured glass of the windows was caught on the jeweled ornaments of the crucifix and the altar. Pons moved closer to examine them.

"Glass?" I asked.

Pons chuckled. "I am no expert, but I fancy these are real. There is some evidence of recent workmanship."

"However could so small a parish afford them?"

"I submit they are not here by the will or even the knowledge of the parish – and that the stones that were here are even now being carried across England in whatever it was that was taken from the gable room bureau in Bishop Lamson's house."

So saying, he turned adding, "Come, let us go back to the Inn."

Once back in our quarters at the Inn, we found a wire from Scotland Yard waiting for us. Pons read it eagerly, nodded with satisfaction, and handed it to me.

> GEORGE MOULTON THUMB AND FOUR FINGERS
> RIGHT HAND. PETTY THIEF SOMEWHERE ON CONTINENT. Jamison.

I looked up into Pons's quizzical eyes.

"Do you see it now, Parker?"

"Let me guess," I said. "George Moulton was a thief."

"Capital! Go on."

"He carried out his thefts – of jewels – somewhere in Spain, ran off with the loot, and hid himself with his half-brother, Bishop Lamson. His partner, done out of his share, patiently tracked him down, only to find that he had died – in his anger, he desecrated Moulton's stone. Then he began to search for the jewels. A pity Bishop Lamson had to suffer!"

"Spare your grief, Parker. His Lordship did not suffer. He died of pneumonia and lies under Moulton's stone by Moulton's design. Apart from that little detail, you have substantially accounted for what mystery there is. I take it that the Spaniard recognized Moulton in Lamson's guise when he called during the night and lost no time taking vengeance. I fancy the half-brothers were not so unlike in stature and general appearance as to arouse suspicion in anyone but one long close to Moulton.

"If Moulton, having assumed his half-brother's role – in which he could live on the Bishop's income, perhaps without the necessity of running up to London from time to time to sell a stone or two – had not been so greedy as to send Mrs. Parton a bill, we might never have had this sanguinary matter called to our attention. It was the curious coincidence of death in the Bishop's house, the Bishop's suddenly doing something out of character, and the desecration of the gravestone all together that suggested something more than senile deterioration. Now let us be off for London."

Three days later a note from Inspector Jamison sent around to our quarters confirmed all Pons' deductions. Pedro Ramirez had been taken at Dover, a pouch of worthless glass in his possession, together with the murder weapon. He and George Moulton had been robbing churches in Spain until Moulton ran off with the loot.

"Taken from church and returned to church," chuckled Pons. "There is some equity in that. Give Jamison a ring, my dear fellow, and send him to St. Christopher's after the real jewels, where George Moulton hid them in plain sight while the vicar thought he was at his prayers. What better place to conceal church jewelry than in a church!"

X

THE ADVENTURE OF THE UNIQUE DICKENSIANS

"This Christmas season," said Solar Pons from his place at the windows of our quarters at 7B, Praed Street, "holds the promise of being a merry one, after the quiet week just past. Flakes of snow are dancing in the air and what I see below enchants me. Just step over here, Parker, and have a look."

I turned down the book I was reading and went over to stand beside him.

Outside, the snowflakes were large and soft, shrouding the streetlight which had come on early in the winter dusk, and enclosing, like a vision from the past, the scene at the kerb – a hansom cab, no less, drawn by a horse that looked almost as ancient as the vehicle, for it stood with a dejected air while its master got out of the cab, leaning on his stick.

"It has been years since I have seen a hansom cab," I said. "Ten, at least – if not more. And that must surely be its owner." The man getting out of the cab could be seen but dimly, but he wore a coat of ankle length, fitting his thin frame almost like an outer skin, and an old beaver hat that added its height to his, and when he turned to look up at the number above our outer entrance, I saw that he wore a grizzled beard and square spectacles.

"Could he have the wrong address?" I wondered.

"I fervently hope not," said Pons. "The wrong century, perhaps, but not, I pray, the wrong address."

"No, he is coming in."

"Capital, capital!" cried Pons, rubbing his hands together and turning from the window to look expectantly toward the door.

We listened in silence as he applied below to Mrs. Johnson, our landlady, and then to his climbing the stairs, a little wheezily, but withal more like a young man than an old.

"But he clutches the rail," said Pons, as if he had read my thoughts. "Listen to his nails scrape the wall."

At the first touch of the old fellow's stick on the door, Pons strode forward to throw it open.

"Mr. Solar Pons?" asked our visitor in a thin, rather querulous voice.

"Pray come in, sir," said Pons.

"Before I do, I'll want to know how much it will cost," said our client.

"It costs nothing to come in," said Pons, his eyes dancing.

"Everything is so dear these days," complained the old fellow as he entered our quarters. "And money isn't easily come by. And too readily spent, sir, too readily spent."

I offered him a seat, and took his hat.

He wore, I saw now, the kind of black half-gloves customarily worn by clerks, that came over his wrists to his knuckles. Seeing me as for the first time, he pointed his cane at me and asked of Pons, "Who's he?"

"Dr. Parker is my companion."

He looked me up and down suspiciously, pushing his thin lips out and sucking them in, his eyes narrowed. His skin was the color of parchment, and his clothes, like his hat, were green with age.

"But you have the advantage of us, sir," said Pons.

"My name is Ebenezer Snawley." Then he turned to me and stuck out an arm. "They're Pip's," he said, referring to the clerical cuffs, which I saw now they were. "No need for him to wear 'em. He's inside, and I'm out, and it would be a shameful waste to spend good money on gloves for the few times I go out in such weather." His eyes narrowed a trifle more. "Are you a medical man?"

I assured him that I was.

"Have a look at that, Doctor," he said, indicating a small growth on one finger.

I examined it and pronounced it the beginning of a wart.

"Ah, then it's of no danger to my health. I thank you. As you're not in your office, no doubt there'll be no fee."

"Doctor Parker is a poor man," said Pons.

"So am I, sir. So am I," said Snawley. "But I had to come to you," he added in an aggrieved voice. "The police only laugh at me. I applied to them to have the nuisance stopped."

"What is the nature of the nuisance?" asked Pons.

"Aha! you've not told me your fee for consultation," said Snawley.

"I am accustomed to setting my fee in accordance with the amount of work I must do," said Pons. "In some cases there is no fee at all."

"No fee? No fee at all?"

"We do on occasion manifest the spirit of Christmas," continued Pons.

"Christmas! Humbug!" protested our client.

"Do not say so," said Pons.

"Christmas is a time for well-meaning fools to go about bestowing useless gifts on other fools," our client went on testily.

"But you did not come to discuss the season," said Pons gently.

"You are right, sir. I thank you for reminding me. I came because of late I have been much troubled by some fellow who marches up and down before my house bawling street songs."

"Are they offensive songs?"

Our visitor shook his head irritably. "Any song is offensive if I do not wish to hear it."

"Scurrilous?"

"Street songs."

"Do you know their words?"

"Indeed, and I do, Mr. Pons. And I should. 'Crack 'em and try 'em, before you buy 'em eight a-penny. All new walnuts. Crack 'em and try 'em, before you buy 'em. A shilling a-hundred. All new walnuts.'" he said in mimicry. "And such as 'Rope mat! Door mat! You really must buy one to save the mud and dust; think of the dirt brought from the street for the want of a mat to wipe your feet!' Indeed I do know them. They are old London street cries."

Pons's eyes now fairly glowed with pleasure. "Ah, he sells walnuts and rope mats."

"A ragbag of a fellow. Sometimes it is hats – three, four at a time on his head. Sometimes it is cress. Sometimes flowers. And ever and anon walnuts. I could not chew 'em even if I bought 'em – and there's small likelihood of that. Catch me wasting good money like that! Not likely."

"He has a right to the street," observed Pons.

"But Mr. Pons, sir, he limits himself to the street along my property. My house is on the corner, set back a trifle, with a bit of land around it – I like my privacy. He goes no farther than the edge of my property on the one side, then back around the corner to the line of my property on the other. It is all done to annoy me – or for some other reason – perhaps to get into the house and lay hands on my valuables."

"He could scarcely effect an entrance more noisily," said Pons, reflectively. "Perhaps he is only observing the Christmas season and wishes to favor you with its compliments."

"Humbug!" said Snawley in a loud voice, and with such a grimace that it seemed to me he could not have made it more effectively had he practiced it in front of a mirror.

"Is he young?"

"If any young fellow had a voice so cracked, I'd send him to a doctor." He shook his head vigorously. "He can't be less than middle-aged. No, sir. Not with a voice like that. He could sour the apples in a barrel with such a voice."

"How often does he come?"

"Why, sir, it is just about every night. I am plagued by his voice, by his very presence, and now he has taken to adding Christmas songs to his small repertoire, it is all the more trying, But chiefly I am plagued – I will confess it – by my curiosity about the reason for this attention he bestows upon me. I sent Pip – Pip is my clerk, retired, now, like myself, with his wife dead and his children all out in the world, even the youngest, who finally recovered his health – I sent Pip, I say, out to tell him to be off, and he but laughed at him, and gave him a walnut or two for himself, and sent one along for me! The impudence of the fellow!" His chin whiskers literally trembled with his indignation.

Pons had folded his arms across his chest, clasping his elbows with his lean fingers, holding in his mirth, which danced around his mouth and in his eyes. "But," he said, visibly controlling himself, "if you are a poor man, you can scarcely be in possession of valuables someone else might covet."

Plainly now our client was torn between the desire to maintain the face he had put upon himself, and to lift a little of it for us to see him a trifle more clearly; for he sat in dour silence. "Unless," pursued Pons, "you have valuables of a more intangible nature. I suspect you are a collector."

Our visitor started violently. "Why do you say so?"

"I submit that coat you are wearing cannot be newer than 1890, the waistcoat likewise. Your cane is gold-headed; I have not seen such a cane about since 1910. Heavy, too. I suspect it is loaded. And what you have left outside is a period piece – obviously your own, since you drove it yourself. No one who had worn your clothing steadily since it was made could present it still in such good condition."

"You are as sharp as they say you are," said our client grudgingly. "It's true I'm a collector."

"Of books," said Pons.

"Books and such," assented Snawley. "Though how you can tell it I don't pretend to know."

"The smell of ink and paper make a special kind of mustiness, Mr. Snawley. You carry it. And, I take it, you are particularly fond of Dickens."

Snawley's jaw dropped; his mouth hung momentarily agape. "You amaze me," he said.

"Dr. Parker charges me with amazing him for the past year and a half, since he took up residence here," said Pons. "It will do you no harm. It has done him none."

"How, Mr. Pons, do you make out Dickens?"

"Those street songs you know so well are those of Dickens' day. Since you made a point of saying you should know them, it is certainly not far wide of the mark to suggest that you are a Dickensian."

A wintry smile briefly touched our client's lips, but he suppressed it quickly. "I see I have made no mistake in coming to you. It is really the obligation of the police, but they are forever about getting out of their obligations. It is the way of the new world, I fear. But I had heard of you, and I turned it over in mind several days, and I concluded that it would be less dear to call on you than to ask you to call on me. So I came forthwith."

"Nevertheless," said Pons, his eyes twinkling, "I fancy we shall have to have a look at that fellow who, you say, is making such a nuisance of himself."

Our client made a rapid calculation, as was evident by the concentration in his face. "Then you had better come back with me now," he said, "for if you come at any other time, the price of the conveyance will surely be added to the bill."

"That is surely agreeable with me," said Pons. "If it will do for Parker."

Snawley bridled with apprehension. "Does he come, too?"

"Indeed, he does."

"Will he be added to the fee?"

"No, Mr. Snawley."

"Well, then, I will just go below and wait for you to come down," said our client, coming to his feet and seizing his hat from the mantel where I had put it next to Pons's unanswered letters, unfolded and affixed to the mantel by a dagger, a souvenir of one of his adventures.

Our client had hardly taken himself off before Pons's laughter burst forth.

When he relieved himself, he turned to me, "What do you make of that fellow, Parker?"

"I have never seen the like," I replied. "Parsimonious, suspicious, and, I suspect, not nearly as poor as he would have us believe."

"Capital! Capital! It is all too human for the rich to affect poverty, and the poor to affect wealth. We may take it that Mr. Snawley is not poor. If he has a corner house and room enough for someone to walk from one end of the property, around the corner, to the other, we may assume that Mr. Snawley's 'bit of land,' as he puts it, is appreciably more than what the average individual would take for a 'bit'."

He was getting into his greatcoat as he spoke, and I got into mine. As I reached for my bowler, he clapped his deerstalker to his head and we were off down the stairs to where our equipage waited at the kerb.

Snawley ushered me into the cab.

Behind me, Pons paused briefly to ask, "How long does this fellow stay on his beat?"

"Two, three hours a night. Rain, fog, or shine. And now, with Christmas almost upon us, he has brought along some bells to ring. It is maddening, sir, maddening," said our client explosively.

Pons got in, Snawley closed the door and mounted to the box. and we were off toward Edgware Road, and from there to Lambeth and Brixton and Dulwich, seeing always before us, from every clear vantage point, the dome of the Crystal Palace, and at every hand the color and gayety of the season. Yellow light streamed from the shops into the falling snow, tinsel and glass globes aglow with red and green and other colors shone bright, decorations framed the shop windows, holly and mistletoe hung in sprays and bunches here and there. Coster's barrows offered fruit and vegetables, Christmas trees, fish and meat, books, cheap china, carpets. Street-sellers stood here and there with trays hung from their necks, shouting their wares – Christmas novelties, balloons, tricks, bonbons, comic-papers, and praising the virtues of *Old Moore's Almanack*. At the poultry shops turkeys, geese, and game hung to entice the late shoppers, for it was the day before Christmas Eve, only a trifle more than two years after the ending of the great conflict, and all London celebrated its freedom from the austerities of wartime. The dancing snowflakes reflected the colors of the shops – sometimes red, sometimes yellow or pink or blue or even pale green – and made great halos around the streetlamps.

Snawley avoided crowded thoroughfares as much as possible, and drove with considerable skill; but wherever we went, people turned on the street to look at the hansom cab as it went by – whether they were children or strollers, policemen on their rounds or shoppers with fowl or puddings in their baskets – startled at sight of this apparition from the past.

II

Our destination proved to be Upper Norwood.

Ebenezer Snawley's home was an asymmetric Jacobean pile, dominated by a small tower, and with Elizabethan bay windows that faced the street. It rose in the midst of a small park that occupied the corner of a block and spread over a considerable portion of that block. A dim glow shone through the sidelights at the door; there was no other light inside. The entire neighborhood had an air of decayed gentility, but the falling snow and the gathering darkness sufficiently diminished the glow of the streetlamp so that it was not until we had descended from the cab, which had driven in along one side of the property, bound for a small coach house at the rear corner – directly opposite the street-corner – and walked to the door of the house that it became evident how much the house, too, had decayed for want of adequate care, though it was of mid-Victorian origin, and not, therefore, an ancient building – little more than half a century old.

Leaving his steed to stand in the driveway, where the patient animal stood with its head lowered in resignation born of long experience, our client forged ahead of us to the entrance to his home, and there raised his cane and made such a clatter on the door as might have awakened the neighborhood, had it slept, at the same time raising his voice petulantly to shout, "Pip! Pip! Pip Scratch! Up and about!"

There was a scurrying beyond the door, the sound of a bar being lifted, a key in the lock, and the door swung open, to reveal there holding aloft a bracket of three candles a man of medium height, clad in tight broadcloth black breeches and black stockings, and a sort of green-black jacket from the sleeves of which lace cuffs depended. He wore buckled shoes on his feet. He was stooped and wore on his thin face an expression of dubiety and resignation that had been there for long enough to have become engraved upon his features. His watery blue eyes looked anxiously out, until he recognized his master; then he stepped aside with alacrity, and held the candles higher still, so as to light our way into the shadowed hall.

"No songs yet, Pip? Eh? Speak up."

"None, sir."

"Well, he will come, he will come," promised our client, striding past his man. "Lay a fire in the study, and we will sit by it and watch. Come along, gentlemen, come along. We shall have a fire by and by, to warm our bones – and perhaps a wee drop of sherry."

Pip Scratch stepped forward with a springy gait and thrust the light of the candles ahead, making the shadows dance in the study whither our client led us. He put the bracket of candles up on the wall, and backed away before Snawley's command.

"Light up, Pip, light up." And to us, "Sit down, gentlemen."

And to Pip Scratch's retreating back, "And a few drops of sherry. Bring – yes, yes, bring the Amontillado. It is as much as I can do for my guests."

The servant had now vanished into the darkness outside the study. I was now accustomed to the light, and saw that it was lined with books from floor to ceiling on three walls, excepting only that facing the street along which we had just come, for this wall consisted of the two Elizabethan bay windows we had seen from outside, each of them flanking the fireplace. Most of the shelves of books were encased; their glass doors reflected the flickering candles.

"He will be back in a moment or two," our client assured us.

Hard upon his words came Pip Scratch, carrying a seven-branched candelabrum and a salver on which was a bottle of Amontillado with scarcely enough sherry in it to more than half fill the three glasses beside it. He bore these things to an elegant table and put them down, then scurried to the bracket on the wall for a candle with which to light those in the candelabrum, and, having accomplished this in the dour silence with which his master now regarded him, poured the sherry, which, true to my estimate, came only to halfway in each of the three glasses – but this, clearly, was approved by Mr. Snawley, for his expression softened a trifle. This done, Pip Scratch hurried from the room.

"Drink up, gentlemen," said our client, with an air rather of regret at seeing his good wine vanish. "Let us drink to our success!"

"Whatever that may be," said Pons enigmatically, raising his glass.

Down went the sherry, a swallow at a time, rolled on the tongue – and a fine sherry it proved to be, for all that there was so little of it, and while we drank, Pip Scratch came in again and laid the fire and scurried out once more, and soon the dark study looked quite cheerful, with the flames growing and leaping higher and higher, and showing row after row of books, and a locked case with folders and envelopes and boxes in it, a light bright enough so that many of the titles of the books could be seen – and most of them were by Dickens – various editions, first and later, English and foreign, and associational items.

"And these are your valuables, I take it, Mr. Snawley," said Pons.

"I own the finest collection of Dickens in London," said our client. After another sip of wine, he added, "In all England." And after two more sips, "If I may say so, I believe it to be the best in the world." Then his smile faded abruptly, his face darkened, and he added, "There is another collector who claims to have a better – but it is a lie, sir, a dastardly lie, for he cannot substantiate his claim."

"You have seen his collection?" asked Pons.

"Not I. Nor he mine."

"Do you know him?"

"No, nor wish to. He wrote me three times in as little as ten days. I have one of his letters here."

He pulled open a drawer in the table, reached in, and took out a sheet of plain paper with a few lines scrawled upon it. He handed it to Pons, and I leaned over to read it, too.

> Mr. Ebenezer Snawley
> Dear Sir,
> I take my pen in hand for the third time to ask the liberty of viewing your collection of Dickens which, I am told, may be equal to my own. Pray set a date, and I will be happy to accommodate myself to it. I am sir, gratefully yours,
>
> Micah Auber

"Dated two months ago, I see," said Pons.

"I have not answered him. I doubt I would have done so had he sent a stamp and envelope for that purpose. In his case, stamps are too dear."

He drank the last of his sherry, and at that moment Pip Scratch came in again, and stood there wordlessly pointing to the street.

"Aha!" cried our client. "The fellow is back. A pox on him! Pip, remove the light for the nonce. There is too much of it – it reflects on the panes. We shall have as good a look at him as we can."

Out went the light, leaving the study lit only by the flames on the hearth, which threw the glow away from the bay windows, toward which our client was now walking, Pons at his heels, and I behind.

"There he is!" cried Snawley. "The rascal! The scoundrel!"

We could hear him now, jingling his bells, and singing in a lusty voice which was not, indeed, very musical – quite the opposite. Singing was not what I would have called it; he was, rather, bawling lustily.

"Walnuts again!" cried our client in disgust.

We could see the fellow now – a short man, stout, who, when he came under the streetlamp, revealed himself to be as much of an individualist as Snawley, for he wore buskins and short trousers, and a coat that reached scarcely to his waist, and his head was crowned with an absurd hat on which a considerable amount of snow had already collected. He carried a basket, presumably for his walnuts.

Past the light he went, bawling about his walnuts, and around the corner.

"Now, you will see, gentlemen, he goes only to the line of my property, and then back. So it is for my benefit that he is about this buffoonery."

"Or his," said Pons.

"How do you say that?" asked Snawley, bending toward Pons so that his slightly curved hawk-like nose almost touched my companion.

"In all seriousness," said Pons. "It does not come from the sherry."

"It cannot be to his benefit," answered our client, "for I have not bought so much as a walnut. Nor shall I!"

Pons stood deep in thought, watching the street-singer, fingering the lobe of his left ear, as was his custom when preoccupied.

Now that all of us were silent, the voice came clear despite the muffling snow.

"He will keep that up for hours," cried our host, his dark face ruddy in the glow of the fire. "Am I to have no peace? The police will do nothing. Nothing! Do we not pay their salaries? Of course, we do. Am I to tolerate this botheration and sit helpless by while that fellow out there bawls his wares?"

"You saw how he was dressed?" inquired Pons.

"He is not in the fashion," replied Snawley, with a great deal of sniffing.

I suppressed my laughter, for the man in the street was no more out of the fashion than our client.

"I have seen enough of him for the time being," said Pons.

Snawley immediately turned and called out. "Pip! Pip! Bring the lights!"

And Pip Scratch, as if he had been waiting in the wings, immediately came hurrying into the room with the candelabrum he had taken out at his employer's command, set it down once more on the table, and departed.

"Mr. Snawley," said Pons as we sat down again near the table, Pons half turned so that he could still look out on occasion through the bay windows toward the streetlamp, "I take it you are constantly adding to your collection?"

"Very cautiously, sir – very cautiously. I have so much now I scarcely know where to house it. There is very little – very little I do not have. Why, I doubt that I add two or three items a year."

"What was your last acquisition, Mr. Snawley?"

Once again our client's eyes narrowed suspiciously. "Why do you ask that, Mr. Pons?"

"Because I wish to know."

Snawley bent toward Pons and said in a voice that was unusually soft for him, almost as with affection, "It is the most precious of all the items in my collection. It is a manuscript in Dickens's hand!"

"May I see it?"

Our client got up, pulled out of his pocket a keyring, and walked toward the locked cabinet I had previously noticed. He unlocked it and took from it a box that appeared to be of ebony, inlaid with ivory, and brought it back to the table. He unlocked this, in turn, and took from it the manuscript in a folder. He laid it before Pons almost with reverence, and stood back to watch Pons with the particular pride of possession that invariably animates the collector.

Pons turned back the cover.

The manuscript was yellowed, as with age, but the paper was obviously of good quality. *Master Humphrey's Clock* was written at the top, and the signature of Charles Dickens meticulously below it, and below that, in the same script, began the text of the manuscript, which consisted of at least a dozen pages.

"Ah, it is a portion of *The Old Curiosity Shop* not used in the published versions of that book," said Pons.

"You know it, sir!" cried our client with evident delight.

"Indeed, I do. And I recognize the script."

"You do?" Snawley rubbed his hands together in his pleasure

"Where did you acquire it?"

Snawley blinked at him. "It was offered to me by a gentleman who had fallen on evil days and needed the money – a trifle over a month and a half ago."

"Indeed," said Pons. "So you got it at a bargain?"

"I did, I did. The circumstances made it possible. He was desperate. He wanted five hundred pounds – a ridiculous figure."

"I see. You beat him down?"

"Business is business, Mr. Pons. I bought it at two hundred pounds."

Pons took one of the sheets and held it up against the candles. "Take care, sir! Take care!" said our client nervously.

Pons lowered the sheet. "You have had it authenticated?"

"Authenticated? Sir, I am an authority on Dickens. Why should I pay some 'expert' a fee to disclose what I already know? This is Dickens's handwriting. I have letters of Dickens by which to authenticate it. Not an *i* is dotted otherwise but as Dickens dotted his *i's*, not a *t* is crossed otherwise. This is Dickens' script, word for word, letter for letter."

Offended, our client almost rudely picked up his treasure and restored it to box and cabinet. As he came back to his chair, he reminded Pons, "But you did not come here to see my collection. There is that fellow outside. How will you deal with him?"

"Ah, I propose to invite him to dinner," answered Pons. "No later than tomorrow night – Christmas Eve. Or rather, shall we put it that you will invite him here for dinner at that time?"

Our client's jaw dropped. "You are surely joking," he said in a strangled voice.

"It is Christmas, Mr. Snawley. We shall show him some of the spirit of the season."

"I don't make merry myself at Christmas and I can't afford to make idle people merry," replied Snawley sourly. "Least of all that fellow out there. It is an ill-conceived and ill-timed jest."

"It is no jest, Mr. Snawley."

Pons's eyes danced in the candlelight.

"I will have none of it," said our client, coming to his feet as if to dismiss us.

"It is either that," said Pons inexorably, "or my fee."

"Name it, then! Name it – for I shall certainly not lay a board for that infernal rogue," cried our client, raising his voice.

"Five hundred pounds," said Pons coldly.

"Five hundred pounds!" screamed Snawley.

Pons nodded, folded his arms across his chest, and looked as adamant as a rock.

Our client leaned and caught hold of the table as if he were about to fall. "Five hundred pounds!" he whispered. "It is robbery! Five hundred pounds!" He stood for a minute so, Pons unmoved the while, and presently a crafty expression came into his narrowed eyes. He began to work his lips out and in, as was his habit, and he turned his head to look directly at Pons. "You say," he said, still in a whisper, "it is either five hundred pounds or – a dinner ...."

"For four. The three of us and that lusty bawler out there," said Pons.

"It *would* be less expensive," agreed our client, licking his lips.

"Considerably. Particularly since I myself will supply the goose," said Pons with the utmost *savoir faire*.

"Done!" cried Snawley at once, as if he had suddenly got much the better of a bad bargain. "Done!" He drew back. "But since I have retained you, I leave it to you to invite him – for I will not!"

"Dinner at seven, Mr. Snawley?"

Our client nodded briskly. "As you like."

"I will send around the goose in the morning."

"There is no other fee, Mr. Pons? I have heard you a-right? And you will dispose of that fellow out there?" He inclined his head toward the street.

"I daresay he will not trouble you after tomorrow night," said Pons.

"Then, since there is no further fee, you will not take it amiss if I do not drive you back? There is an underground nearby."

"We will take it, Mr. Snawley."

Snawley saw us to the door, the bracket of candles in his hand. At the threshold Pons paused.

"There must be nothing spared at dinner, Mr. Snawley," he said. "We'll want potatoes, dressing, vegetables, fruit, green salad, plum pudding – and a trifle more of that Amontillado."

Our client sighed with resignation. "It will be done, though I may rue it."

"Rue it you may," said Pons cheerfully. "Good night, sir. And the appropriate greetings of the season to you."

"Humbug! All humbug!" muttered our client, retreating into his house.

We went down the walk through the now much thinned snowfall, and stood at its juncture with the street until the object of our client's ire came around again. He was a stocky man with a good paunch on him, cherry-red cheeks and a nose of darker red, and merry little eyes that looked out of two rolls of fat, as it were. Coming close, he affected not to see us, until Pons strode out into his path, silencing his bawling of walnuts.

"Good evening, Mr. Auber."

He started back, peering at Pons. "I don't know ye, sir," he said.

"But it *is* Mr. Auber, isn't it? Mr. Micah Auber?" Auber nodded hesitantly.

"Mr. Ebenezer Snawley would like your company at dinner tomorrow night at seven."

For a long moment, mouth agape, Auber stared at him. "God bless my soul!" he said, finding his voice. "Did he know me, then?"

"No," said Pons, "But who else would be walking here affecting to be a hawker of such wares if not Micah Auber, on hand in case anything turned up?"

"God bless my soul!" said Auber again, fervently.

"You will meet us at the door, Mr. Auber, and go in with us," said Pons. "Good evening, sir."

"I will be there," said Auber.

"And leave off this bawling," said Pons over his shoulder.

We passed on down the street, and Auber, I saw, looking back, went scuttling off in the other direction, in silence.

We hurried on through the snow. The evening was mellow enough so that much of it underfoot had melted, and the falling flakes dissolved on our clothing. But Pons set the pace, and it was not until we were in the underground on the way back to our quarters, that I had opportunity to speak.

"How did you know that fellow was Micah Auber?" I asked.

"Why, that is as elementary a deduction as it seems to me possible to make," replied Pons. "Consider – Snawley's valuables consist of his collection, which is primarily of Dickensiana. Our client acquired his most recent treasure a trifle over six weeks ago. Within a fortnight thereafter Micah Auber writes, asking to see his collection. Having had no reply, and assessing our client's character correctly by inquiry or observation – perhaps both – Auber has adopted this novel method of attracting his attention. His object is clearly to get inside that house and have a look at our client's collection."

"But surely this is all very roundabout," I cried.

"I fancy Snawley himself is rather roundabout – though not so roundabout as Auber. They are two of a kind. You know my opinion of collectors. They are all a trifle mad, some more so than others. This pair is surely unique, even to the dress of the period!"

"How could Auber know that Snawley had acquired that manuscript?"

"I fancy it is for the reason that Snawley has laid claim to possession of the largest Dickens collection in London..."

"In the world," I put in.

"And because the manuscript was undoubtedly stolen from Auber's collection," finished Pons. "Hence Auber's persistence. We shall have a delightful dinner tomorrow evening, I fancy."

III

Pons spent some time next day looking through references and making a telephone call or two, but he was not long occupied at this, and went about looking forward to dinner that evening, and from time to time throughout the day hummed a few bars of a tune, something to which he was not much given, and which testified to the warmth of his anticipation.

We set out early, and reached Ebenezer Snawley's home at a quarter to seven, but Micah Auber had preceded us to the vicinity; for we had no sooner posted ourselves before Snawley's door than Auber made his appearance, bearing in upon us from among a little group of yew trees off to one side of the driveway, where he had undoubtedly been standing to wait upon our coming. He approached with a skip and a hop, and came up to us a little short of breath. Though he was dressed for dinner, it was possible to see by the light of the moon, which lacked but one day of being full, that his clothing was as ancient as our client's.

"Ah, good evening, Mr. Auber," Pons greeted him. "I am happy to observe that you are in time for what I trust will be a good dinner."

"I don't know as to how good it will be. Old Snawley's tight, mighty tight," said Auber.

Pons chuckled.

"But, I don't believe, sir, we've been properly introduced."

"We have not," said Pons. "My companion is Dr. Lyndon Parker, and I am Solar Pons."

Auber acknowledged both introductions with a sweeping bow, then brought himself up short. "Solar Pons, did ye say?" He savored the name, cocked an eye at Pons, and added, "I have a knowledge of London ye might say is extensive and peculiar. I've heard the name. Give me a moment – it'll come to me. Ah, yes, the detective. Well, well, we are well met, sir. I have a need for your services, indeed I do. I've had stolen from me a val'able manuscript – and I have reason to believe our host has it. A prize, sir, a prize. A rare prize."

"We shall see, Mr. Auber, we shall see," said Pons.

"I will pay a reasonable sum, sir, for its recovery – a reasonable sum."

Pons seized hold of the knocker and rapped it sharply against the door. Almost at once our client's voice rose.

"Pip! Pip! The door! The gentlemen are here."

We could hear Pip Scratch coming down the hall, and then the door was thrown open. The only concession Pip had made to the occasion was a bracket of seven candles instead of three.

"A Merry Christmas to you, Pip," said Pons.

"Thank you, sir. And to you, gentlemen," said Pip in a scarcely audible whisper, as if he feared his master might hear him say it.

"Come in! Come in! Let us have done with it," called our client from the study.

The table was laid in the study, and the wine-glasses were filled to the brim. Snawley stood at its head, frock-coated, and wearing a broad black tie with a pin in it at the neck, though he was as grizzled as ever, and his eyes seemed to be even more narrowed as he looked past Pons toward Auber with no attempt to conceal his distaste.

"Mr. Snawley," said Pons with a wave of his hand toward Auber, "let me introduce our lusty-voiced friend."

"A voice not meant for singing," put in our client.

"Mr. Auber," finished Pons.

Snawley started back as if he had been struck. "Micah Auber?" he cried.

"The same," said Auber, bowing, his bald head gleaming in the candlelight, and all in the same movement producing a monocle on a thin black cord, which he raised to one eye and looked through at our client, who was still so thunderstruck that he was incapable of speech. "ye do me the honor to ask me to dine."

All Snawley could think to say in this contretemps was, "To save five hundred pounds!"

"As good a reason as any," said Auber urbanely.

At this juncture Pip Scratch made his appearance, bearing a large platter on which rested the goose Pons had had sent over that morning, all steaming and brown and done to a turn. He lowered it to the table and set about at once to carve it, while our host, recovering himself, though with as sour an expression as he could put upon his face, waved us to our seats.

Pons seized his glass of Amontillado and raised it aloft. "Let us drink to the success of your various enterprises!"

"Done," said Auber.

"And to a Merry Christmas!" continued Pons.

"Humbug!" cried Snawley.

"I would not say so, Mr. Snawley," said Auber. "Christmas is a very useful occasion."

"Useful?" echoed our client. "And for whom, pray?"

"Why, for us all," answered Auber with spirit. "It is a season of forbearance, perseverance, and usefulness."

"Humbug!" said Snawley again. "If I had my way, I should have every Christmas merrymaker boiled in his own pudding!"

"Ye need a bit more sherry, Mr. Snawley. Come, man, this dinner cannot have cost ye that much!"

So it went through that Christmas Eve dinner, with the two collectors exchanging hard words, and then less hard words, and then softer words, mellowed by the wine for which Pons kept calling. The goose was disposed of in large part, and the dressing, and the potatoes, the carrots, the fruit, the green salad – all in good time, and slowly, – and finally came the plum pudding, brought flaming to the table; while the hours went by, eight o'clock struck, then nine – and it was ten before we sat there at coffee and brandy, and by this time both Snawley and Auber were mellow, and Pip Scratch, who had cleared the table of all but the coffee cups and liqueur glasses, had come in to sit down away a little from the table, but yet a party to what went on there.

And it was then that Auber, calculating that the time was right for it, turned to our client and said, "And now, if ye've no mind, I'd like a look at your collection of Dickens, Mr. Snawley."

"I daresay you would," said Snawley. "I have the largest such in the world."

"It is you who says it."

"I wait to hear you say it, too!"

Auber smiled and half closed his eyes. "If it is all that matters to ye, I will agree to it."

"Hear! Hear!" cried Snawley, and got a little unsteadily to his feet, and went over to his shelves, followed like a shadow by the faithful Pip, and with Auber's eyes on him as if he feared that Snawley and his collection might escape him after all.

Snawley unlocked his cabinet and handed Pip a book or two, and carried another himself. They brought them to the table, and Snawley took one after the other of them and laid them down lovingly. They were inscribed copies of *David Copperfield*, *Edwin Drood*, and *The Pickwick Papers*. After Auber had fittingly admired and exclaimed over them, our client went back for more, and returned this time with copies of *The Monthly Magazine* containing *Sketches by Boz*, with interlineations in Dickens's hand.

Pip kept the fire going on the hearth, and between this task and dancing attendance upon his master, he was continually occupied, going back and forth, to and fro, with the firelight flickering on his bony face and hands, and the candle flames leaping up and dying away to fill the room with grotesque shadows, as the four of us bent over one treasure after another, and the clock crept around from ten to eleven, and moved upon midnight. A parade of books and papers moved from the cabinet to the table and back to the cabinet again – letters in Dickens's hand, letters to Dickens from his publishers, old drawings by Cruikshank and 'Phiz' of Dicken's characters – Oliver Twist, Fagin, Jonas Chuzzlewit, Mr. Bumble, Little Amy Dorrit, Uriah Heep, Caroline Jellyby, Seth Pecksniff, Sam Weller, Samuel Pickwick, and many another – so that it was late when at last Snawley came to his recently acquired treasure, and brought this too to the table.

"And this, Mr. Auber, is the crown jewel, you might say, of my collection," he said.

He made to turn back the cover, but Auber suddenly put forth a hand and held the cover down. Snawley started back a little, but did not take his own hands from his prized manuscript.

"Let me tell ye what it is, Mr. Snawley," said Auber. "It is a manuscript in Dickens's hand – a part of that greater work known as *Master Humphrey's Clock*, and specifically that portion of it which became *The Old Curiosity Shop*. But this portion of it was deleted from the book. It is a manuscript of fourteen and a half pages, with Dickens's signature beneath the title on the first page."

Snawley regarded him with wide, alarmed eyes. "How can you know this, Mr. Auber?"

"Because it was stolen from me two months ago."

A cry of rage escaped Snawley. He pulled the precious manuscript away from Auber's restraining hand.

"It is mine!" he cried. "I bought it!"

"For how much?"

"Two hundred pounds."

"The precise sum I paid for it a year ago."

"You shall not have it," cried Snawley.

"I mean to have it," said Auber, springing up.

Pons, too, came to his feet. "Pray, gentlemen, one moment. You will allow, I think, that I should have a few words in this matter. Permit me to have that manuscript for a few minutes, Mr. Snawley."

"On condition it comes back to my hand, sir!"

"That is a condition easy for me to grant, but one the fulfilment of which you may not so readily demand."

"This fellow speaks in riddles," said Snawley testily, as he handed the manuscript to Pons.

Pons took it, opened the cover, and picked up the first page of the manuscript, that with the signature of Dickens on it. He handed it back to Snawley.

"Pray hold it up to the light and describe the watermark, Mr. Snawley."

Our client held it before the candles. After studying it for a few moments he said hesitantly, "Why, I believe it is a rose on a stem, sir."

"Is that all, Mr. Snawley?"

"No, no, I see now there are three letters, very small, at the base of the stem – *KTC*."

Pons held out his hand for the page, and took up another. This one he handed to Auber. "Examine it, Mr. Auber."

Auber in turn held it up to the candles. "Yes, ye've made no mistake, Mr. Snawley. It is a rose, delicately done – a fine rose. And the letters are clear – *KTC*, all run together."

"That is the watermark of Kennaway, Teape & Company, in Aldgate," said Pons.

"I know of them," said Snawley. "A highly reputable firm."

"They were established in 1871," continued Pons. "Mr. Dickens died on June 8, 1870."

For a moment of frozen horror for the collectors there was not a sound.

"It cannot be!" cried our client then.

"Ye cannot mean it!" echoed Auber.

"The watermark cannot lie, gentlemen," said Pons dryly, "but alas! the script can."

"I bought it in good faith," said Auber, aghast.

"And had it stolen in good faith," said Pons, chuckling.

"I bought it from a reputable dealer," said Auber.

"From the shop of Jason Brompton, in Edgware Road," said Pons. "But not from him – rather from his assistant."

Auber gazed at Pons in astonishment. "How did ye know?"

"Because there is only one forger in London with the skill and patience to have wrought this manuscript," said Pons. "His name is Dennis Golders."

"I will charge him!" cried Auber.

"Ah, I fear that cannot be done. Mr. Golders left Brompton's last January, and is now in His Majesty's service. I shall see, nevertheless, what I can do in the matter, but do not count on my success."

Snawley fell back into his chair.

Auber did likewise.

Pip Scratch came quietly forward and poured them both a little sherry.

Midnight struck.

"It is Christmas day, gentlemen," said Pons. "It is time to leave you. Now you have had a sad blow in common, perhaps you may find something to give you mutual pleasure in all these shelves! Even collectors must take the fraudulent with the genuine."

Snawley raised his head. "You are right, Mr. Pons. Pip! Pip!" he shouted, as if Pip Scratch were not standing behind him. "Put on your coat and bring out the cab. Drive the gentlemen home!"

Our client and his visitor accompanied us to the door and saw us into the hansom cab Pip Scratch had brought down the driveway from the coach house.

"Merry Christmas, gentlemen!" cried Pons, leaning out.

"It burns my lips," said Snawley with a wry smile. "But I will say it."

He wished us both a Merry Christmas, and then, arm in arm, the two collectors turned and went a trifle unsteadily back into the house.

"This has been a rare Christmas, Parker, a rare Christmas, indeed," mused Pons, as we rode toward our quarters through the dark London streets in our client's hansom cab.

"I doubt we'll ever see its like again," I agreed.

"Do not deny us hope, Parker," replied Pons. He cocked his head in my direction and looked at me quizzically. "Did I not see you eyeing the clock with some apprehension in the course of the past half hour?"

"You did, indeed," I admitted. "I feared – I had the conviction, indeed I did – that the three of them would vanish at the stroke of midnight!"

For more details and a full list of titles:
visit https://www.hachetteindia.com/home/yellowbacks

HODDER AND STOUGHTON
WELCOME BACK TO THE GOLDEN AGE